The
UNIVERSAL
and other
TERRORS

Tony Richards

DARK RENAISSANCE BOOKS
2013

FIRST TRADE PAPERBACK EDITION

Text © 2013 by Tony Richards

Cover art and interior illustrations
© 2012 by M. Wayne Miller

Editor & Publisher, Joe Morey

Copy editor, F.J. Bergmann

ISBN: 978-1-937128-89-0

Interior design by F.J. Bergmann
Fibitz Reality Adjustment
FIBITZ.COM

In association with Dark Regions Press

Dark Renaissance Books
Colusa, CA 95932
WWW.DARKRENAISSANCE.COM

Acknowledgements

BY A DARK CANAL first appeared in *Scheherazade* #29. Copyright © Tony Richards 2006.

THE CROWS first appeared in *Midnight Street* #12. Copyright © Tony Richards 2009.

THE IN-BETWEENERS first appeared in *The Seventh Black Book of Horror*, ed. Charles Black (Mortbury Press, 2010). Copyright © Tony Richards 2010.

MR. SMYTH first appeared in *Back from the Dead: The Legacy of the Pan Book of Horror Stories*, ed. Johnny Mains (Noose & Gibbet Publishing, 2010). Copyright © Tony Richards 2010.

SENSE first appeared in *Never Again*, eds. Allyson Bird and Joel Lane (Grayfriar Press, 2010). Copyright © Tony Richards 2010.

THE VERY EDGE OF NEW HARARE first appeared in *Alfred Hitchcock's Mystery Magazine*, January/February 2012. Copyright © Tony Richards 2012.

A TOWN CALLED YOUNGESVILLE first appeared in a slightly different formt as *Yuppieville* (Screaming Dreams Publications, 2010). Copyright © Tony Richards 2010.

THE UNIVERSAL, AEGEA, BENEATH THE SHROUD, THE VISITORS IN MARVELL WOOD, and COVERED MIRRORS are all new to this collection. Copyrights © Tony Richards 2013.

Dedication

This one is for Steve Upham and Johnny Mains.

List of Illustrations

Table of Contents

Foreword

THE SHOCK OF THE NEW

Okay … it's possible you've read a collection of mine before. You've picked up *Shadows and Other Tales* or *Going Back* or *Our Lady of the Shadows*, and found yourself delving through a pile of stories some of which are fairly new, and some of which date back as far as the early 1980s, when I first started not only writing but trying to get what I wrote published.

Only that's not the deal this time.

The oldest story here is "By a Dark Canal" from 2006, and it's the granddad of the bunch. The rest are new. Very new—2010 onwards. And five entries have never before seen publication. Yes, that's right: you're going to read them here first.

So why do I keep rattling out these shorts, thirty-five years or so after my debut one?

I have less time to do so these days, and I must admit that. Publishers like Simon & Schuster and the newer Samhain keep me busy with longer works. But when I do get the opportunity to sit down and craft a shorter piece of fiction, then I jump at the chance. Because short stories … they're important.

Novels might move and flow and shunt around, but a short tale—a good one—is like some fantastical insect trapped within a bead of amber. You are capturing stuff from your own life and your perceptions when you produce a short story. They're snapshots, not only of times and places, but of emotions, reactions, apprehensions and, yes, fears most particularly. Take something from your everyday existence and flip it over to its dark side—that is how a horror story works.

That doesn't mean that anything terrible has happened to you personally. Often, the truth is far from it. "Covered Mirrors," for instance, came out of my attendance at the wedding of two friends in the West Village section of Manhattan, and a very happy occasion it was, nothing in the least bit sinister there. My twisted mind simply worked it into a far nastier scenario once I'd arrived home.

There are, equally, three tales in this book set in my fictional south coast English town of Birchiam-on-Sea, and to read them you'd think I hated the seaside. But no, actually I don't. I love it.

Except that horror stories are about "what if?" I've described them in the past as "something happening to people that they very definitely weren't expecting when they woke up that morning." Honestly, we ask ourselves, what if our fears turn out to be true? What if those old urban legends and tales told behind the bike-shed have some real basis in fact? It's only our imagination playing tricks on us, but that's what being a writer of the dark fantastic is about … tasking the imagination to jump higher, run faster, become realer for a short while. *None* of what follows has actually happened, except in that part of the human mind that constantly, subconsciously, worries about such things.

And so this is where I've been the past few years. The countries and the cities and the towns I've visited, the things I've seen and done. But all of it reflected in a darkly glistering mirror, with the words 'what if?' smeared across it by a ghostly finger.

Let's face it, what if nothing *ever* happened? That would be the worst thing of all, wouldn't it? Horror stories make the world exciting. That is all the justification they should ever need.

Twelve new journeys into the unknown lie ahead of you right now. Read on.

Tony Richards
London, 2013

That wall had bulged outward, in the shape of another human face …

The Universal

I know now why they chose to put it there. The landscape hid it. The very soil and grass conspired to keep their secrets.

At the end of the street I had moved onto was an undeveloped, windswept hill, the foot of which marked the boundary of town. I didn't bother going there at all, my first week in Birchiam-on-Sea. It looked rather steep and desolate, and I already had plenty on my hands. Getting my belongings unpacked, trying to make my bungalow look like a proper home. Finding my bearings around this new district, the location of the shops and public transport. Getting to know my neighbors.

But by the end of that first week, I was in the mood to stretch my legs and my horizons a little.

The hill turned out to be everything that it had looked from a distance. Demanding, forlorn, and abandoned. Nobody had tried to build a home or anything else up here. Not a brick or a stick or a telephone pole. Grass about a foot long hissed around me in the salty breeze.

And the gradient was mercilessly steep, so that my legs began to ache after a while of climbing. I was fifty-seven and had taken early retirement recently. My wife and I had separated six years back. There was a spare room in my new place, for my grown-up son when he might visit.

I had lived in London my entire life up until that point. And worked—for most of the adult part of it—in the science department of a TV news show. I wasn't the fellow who appeared before the cameras—I simply researched everything that guy said.

There were no seagulls wheeling overhead, I noticed. And you tended to see them in the skies over most parts of Birchiam, so their absence was odd. But I was still fairly fit, and forced myself to keep on going till I reached the top.

And there it was below me. A building I hadn't even known existed.

It was on a craggy promontory, the gray sea churning beyond it. The waves caught the weak daylight and reflected it in such a way that the building simply looked like a black outline. Then I blinked several times, my eyes adjusting, and the thing came into focus.

Some kind of enormous bunker in three stories. There were no windows, not even slits in the concrete walls as a military construct might have. Maybe they were on the far side, facing seaward.

And it looked surrounded, on its land side, by a massive barbed wire fence. Salt grasses grew beyond the barrier, right up to the edges of the structure. And leading down into the water past it were huge jagged boulders, so profuse and tightly packed they looked impossible to cross. Whoever had built this place had wanted to keep people out.

There was an area inside the fence that looked as if it had been intended as a car park. But there were no cars there; weeds had cracked the asphalt up. There was a guard's booth by the gate, but no one in it. Nothing moved.

Off to the left, I thought I could make out a length of rusted small-gauge railway track. It came from nowhere, went nowhere, and was heavily overgrown as well.

Faintly intrigued, I started making my way down.

I was halfway down the slope when something very curious appeared to happen.

As I'd said, there were no gulls above me. I could see them cruising in the distance, off in the direction of the ruined pier. None of them were coming near this place. But then a magpie flew in from the west.

Landed on the building's roof.

And seemed to vanish.

Perhaps the angle I was looking from, the glitter of the sea, were playing tricks with my eyes?

And that was proven to be the case, a moment later. A bird of the same size came flapping away from the building, heading back inland. But it lifted from the far side of the roof I'd seen the magpie land on. And it looked, to my gaze, wholly black, no white or sapphire patches visible.

It was moving too fast to be entirely sure.

I pursed my lips, and then continued down.

As I got closer, I began to notice what a total mess the place was. The concrete walls had those blackened swathes that look as if there's been a fire, but are actually the product of the filth we've spewed into the air for decades. There were dandelions everywhere. And gathered up against the fence were crumpled plastic snack bags, candy wrappers, the silver paper and the polythene from cigarette packs, soggy sheets of old newspaper. The winds must have carried them all here, the fence trapping them like a net. My step became a little warier. This looked like the kind of place you might encounter rats.

The fence wasn't barbed wire, as it turned out. It was razor wire. I could see a signpost hanging from it.

MINISTRY OF DEFENCE. KEEP OUT.

I moved up to it, staring at the building. It was truly huge, the size of the big supermarket down the road, but taller. There really was not a single window. And no visible doorway either, just the top of a flight of steps out front, which looked as if they led downward.

What had the MoD been doing here? This whole place looked impenetrable.

Something moved on the ground in front of me, making my gaze dart abruptly down. But it was not a rat, it was a crab. I'd never seen one come this far inland, so maybe it was lost.

It was the general size and shape of the lid of a coffeepot, but its hue was a sickly mottled green. Its claws were disproportionately large for its body. It kept one curled beside its shoulder, and held the other one out like a jazzman with his saxophone. And it was moving across the grass with a steady, almost purposeful air.

It was neither lost nor purposeful, I finally decided. It was just plain stupid, and was headed nowhere.

3

I was about to look away from it, when it disappeared behind a broad-leafed dandelion and …

And nothing.

It did not emerge.

And the dandelion wasn't large enough to fully hide a creature of that size for very long.

I took my glasses off, rubbed at my eyes. And when I put them on again, there were two dandelions on the spot that I'd been staring at. No crab at all.

Maybe age was getting to my eyesight worse than I had thought.

Something else caught my attention a few moments later. And this time, it was a noise, that of a diesel engine coming up behind me. A navy blue Range Rover was approaching me along a bumpy gravel track. I thought that I could make out two men in the front seats, and could hear ferocious barking from the back.

The car stopped about a hundred yards off. The doors came swinging open and both men got out.

They were in their early thirties, topping six foot tall and powerfully built. They both sported moustaches and cropped haircuts, and were dressed as if they were going hunting—boots, blue jeans, plaid shirts and sleeveless padded jackets.

The man who had been driving was now dangling a six-pack of what looked like beer from one clenched hand. He leant against the hood. The other went to the rear of the vehicle, opened the tailgate and hauled out a pair of enormous Dobermans on thick chain leashes. And the dogs immediately started howling at me, straining angrily in my direction.

The man with the beer simply yanked loose a can, tugged at the ring-pull, took a heavy swig. Then stared across at me and called out, "You all right there, granddad?"

Who were these people with their furious animals? It was likely they were just a pair of thugs who came here for the sake of it. But whatever the case, this had become no place in which to hang around any longer. So I headed back toward my home, going as steadily but quickly as I could.

My mind was working, all the same. I'd already decided I might ask around a bit, and find out what this building had once been.

"**T**revon Point Research Facility," I was told. "I worked there from '72 till when it was closed down in '79."

Someone at the Fox and Hounds pub, on the corner of my street, had directed me to an old regular called Reggie Trunch. *That place? He can tell you all about it.*

And now Reg and I were sitting in the beer garden out back, despite the blustery weather. Reggie was a heavy smoker, and he didn't like to stop inside.

He was hunched over in a metal chair, rolling up a fresh cigarette. His overcoat looked too large for him, and his sparse gray hair kept flapping in the wind.

"What was being researched?" I asked.

"Whole variety of stuff," he told me. "Separate departments, none of them supposed to know what the other one was doing." He blinked at me with very pale and watery blue eyes. "But you'd be surprised how hard it is to keep secrets with the same people working in the same building for years. Toward the end, I knew a lot."

He pinched the loose end of his smoke and then applied a flame. I waited.

"Some of it was genetics," he went on. "One department, mind-altering drugs. Yet another one, psychology would you believe?"

"The MoD was into that?"

"Yeah." And he shrugged. "This was, to the casual observer, silly stuff. Cold War, scooby-dooby, secret squirrel stuff. But all of it approached with deadly seriousness, like the future of the entire nation might well be at stake."

"And you?"

"I was never told what the real point of it was," Reg explained. "But, during the time that I worked there, I saw several thousand subjects passing through our lab. My job was to show them cards with different symbols on them, give them tests involving blindfolds, and then record the results."

That sounded like …

"Testing for psychic ability, yeah," Reg agreed. "I figured that out in the first five minutes. I was just a humble lab tech, though, and being well paid. So I did what was required of me and kept my trap shut."

My initial astonishment had transformed to a stunned feeling. And my mind had slowed down enough that I had to hunt around for my next question.

"What do you think they were trying to achieve?"

"Personally? I think they were trying to make a better spy."

"Don't you mean 'train'?" I asked.

"No. Make."

Reg sucked in smoke, then grinned at me with yellow teeth. He was being slightly enigmatic, but I could still see his point.

"What closed it down?" I asked him.

And it turned out to be either the right question or the wrong one, because all the humor vanished from his face.

"The project leader—a Professor Marsters—disappeared one night, apparently. And that was the end of it, all at once. A bunch of suits turned up from the Ministry. A good number of them struck me as being spooks. We were shut down and turfed out of there inside three hours. They were padlocking the front doors while I was still walking to the gate."

A whole big place like that, shut down because of the disappearance of one person? That wasn't merely peculiar—it didn't make any sense.

Reggie tipped his head to one side, took another draw of smoke, then told me, "I'd say bugger-all at Trevon Point made sense."

So I pressed him about this Professor Marsters. It turned out that Reg had never spoken to the man, and had only ever seen him some dozen times in all his years at the facility.

"Completely bald and with a hugely bulbous forehead, like some alien," he said. "His lab was in the basement of the place— we called it 'The Inner Sanctum' and were never let inside. He'd sometimes spend several days at a stretch down there. The man appeared obsessed."

"With what?"

My new companion shrugged again, saying precisely nothing. He just didn't know.

"And did he live around here?"

A discolored finger pointed off in the direction I'd gone yesterday.

"A cottage, past that hill and then another half a mile along the coastline. Here's another funny thing, though. The same night Trevon Point was closed, the place burned down."

Darker clouds were gathering above us, the air growing damper. And my head was reeling slightly by this time.

"What kind of coincidence is that?" I pointed out. "Didn't you ever wonder?"

Reggie eased himself back in his chair. He'd rolled up yet another cigarette and was lighting it off the first.

"I'll give this to the MoD," he said in a quiet voice. "Their severance pay was … shall we say, impressive? We were being paid to keep quiet, that was pretty obvious. Besides, I was just a tech with no connections. There was no one left to ask."

A plume of gray smoke drifted from his mouth and was snatched away immediately by the stiffening breeze.

"Better not to anyway, if you want my opinion, mate. Best to just forget it. Cold War, super-secret, silly, silly stuff."

The following morning, I went up to the top of the hill again. Didn't attempt to go any further. Simply stood there, being ripped at by the cold wind coming off the sea. The abandoned building stood below me.

Why would they shut down an entire facility simply because one man—even the leading man—was no longer present? What had happened to him, where exactly had he gone? I was pondering over matters like that when the dark blue Range Rover appeared again. It came trundling along the same path, braked on the same spot. But this time when the Dobermans were let out, they were not on leashes. They ran to and fro at a brisk pace, the two men leaning against the hood of their car, drinking beer and watching them. I could hear the barking from up here.

And that was when it occurred to me. These guys had shown up again not long after I'd come into view. Maybe they'd been on the lookout for me. And so could they be not simply idle thugs, but there to scare people like me away?

It was either a very troubling possibility, or I was getting paranoid.

Two days later, I went back again. And crested the hill to find myself looking down at an unexpected sight. The Range Rover was already there, parked closer to the fence than usual. All five of its doors were open, but the men and dogs were nowhere to be seen.

Other people were, however, and there were different vehicles in attendance. Four saloon cars were pulled up around the Range Rover. About a dozen men, all dressed in dark suits, were moving across the landscape below me, obviously searching for something.

Beyond them, further inland, was a large black Bentley. I thought I could make out the outline of its chauffeur past the windscreen. But as to who might be sitting in the back ... it was impossible to tell from here.

The men on foot scoured the landscape around Trevon Point for another five minutes or so, their gazes pinned firmly to the ground so that they never even noticed me. Then one of them stopped and shouted, calling the rest back. They mostly headed to their cars, all except for one, who climbed into the Range Rover and started it. Where had he even gotten the keys?

And then the whole procession moved off, gradually disappearing.

But the Bentley was still sitting there. I thought that I saw one of its rear windows slide down a few inches. And stood very still at that point, feeling someone's gaze on me.

Then the Bentley drove off too.

I t was in the local paper by Friday. Three Birchiam youths, all of them known to the police, had gone missing. A fourth had been found very badly injured, although there was no mention of exactly how. And he had been found not far from Trevon Point, which caught my interest.

I'd been around journalists long enough to do some asking around of my own. I phoned the hospitals first, and managed to get a response. No one was sure how the kid had got hurt, but his injuries were so severe he had been taken to a medical facility at …

I was given the name of a nearby Air Force base.

I put the phone down, pulled my shoes and coat on, and went out and climbed the hill again.

A deserted shell like Trevon Point invariably gets visits from the local vandals. Those two louts with their Dobermans had kept them away so far. But now that they were gone … call it instinct if you will, but the boys had realized that the way was clear and seized the opportunity.

They had actually hauled a sleeper and a length of iron rail from the little stretch of railway I had noticed. And had set them against the razor wire, pushing its coils down and providing a way across.

I walked toward it carefully, keeping a sharp eye out for any more approaching vehicles.

I studied the makeshift bridge the boys had made, but decided against using it. It was awfully narrow, and my balance wasn't all that good. And the drop on the far side had to be at least eight feet.

Then something else that Reg had said came back to me. I stared off to the east. Half a mile from here was Professor Marsters' old home. It might have burned down, but it wouldn't hurt to take a look at what remained.

So I set off.

We were talking about three decades, a whole generation. But the blackened ruins of the cottage were still lying as they must have been the morning after the fire. No one had attempted to rebuild it. Nobody had even tried to clear the wreckage.

There was not a wall left, only shallow stubs of bonded brick. Every single wooden beam was black and cracked and looked like coal. The furniture had burned to ash. If Marsters had owned ornaments, they were ash too.

9

But I climbed in all the same. What was I looking for?

The debris crunched under my shoes. And I could smell something very faintly, even after all these years. Paraffin, or petrol.

What was I searching for, some clue, some kind of record? Nothing could have survived this. But I continued to hunt around for a while. And the noise that I was making must have covered her approach, because when a female voice abruptly sounded from behind me, it alarmed me enough that I jerked.

"You won't find anything in there," it was saying.

It was a very high-pitched, brittle voice, belonging—as it turned out—to a small, elderly woman in a motorized wheelchair. She had approached me down a narrow path I had not noticed until now. Her hair was pure white and her face was crumpled. She had on spectacles, and was squinting at me curiously.

I wondered who she was and where she'd come from. Then I looked past her and saw a rooftop, past a rise and closer to the sea. This had to be some kind of neighbor.

"How can you be sure I won't find anything?" I asked her.

"They came the night after the fire, with big lamps," she explained. "Did exactly what you're doing now, except they came away with several boxes full of charred stuff, everything that they could find."

"Who's they?"

"The men in black, I suppose you would call them."

Spooks, in other words.

I didn't even know this woman's name. It turned out to be Emily Prentice. She indeed lived in the house that I had spotted, and had done so all her life.

"Then you knew Professor Marsters?"

"Strange man in some ways," she nodded. "But I was the only neighbor that he had, and so we got to know each other fairly well."

"And you don't know how he came to vanish?"

"No. He simply disappeared one day."

Once again, I thought that over.

"Did he seem … bothered in any way, when you last saw him?"

"He always worked extremely long hours," Emily informed me.

10

"Sometimes didn't come back home for days. And when I did bump into him, those final months, he seemed more strained and agitated than was usual."

"Did he ever discuss what he was working on?"

Emily was studying me carefully by this stage, with a faint smile in her gaze.

"I *knew* that that was what you might be looking for." She steered her chair a little closer. "*You're* not a man in black, now are you?"

I explained to her who I was, and listening to me, she looked quietly satisfied.

"I might be able to help you, then. Please, come with me."

She maneuvered her chair around and trundled off toward her home, leaving me to follow. Gulls were wheeling in the sky beyond her rooftop. Trevon Point was still the only spot along this coastline where they were not present.

Her cottage was single-story, dimly lit and with that grandma smell, but clean. I was shown into a living room full of crystal, chintz, and Capodimonte.

"Take a seat," Emily told me.

Then she began hunting through a chest of drawers.

She finally found what she'd been looking for. Handed me a notebook with a light-blue cardboard cover.

"His?" I asked.

"The professor gave it to me the last time we met. Told me it should go to no one from the government. Someone independent instead. Someone scientific. I got the men in black asking around a few times those first years after the fire, but I told them nothing. You're the first *suitable* person who has come along."

I stared at the notebook blankly, my mind clouding like a thick, damp fog was filling it. I might be holding in my hands a genuinely important piece of science, and this woman had been holding onto it for decades.

"To be honest," she told me, "I can't make head or tail of anything it says. Maybe you can do a little better."

So I opened it, and started reading.

11

It was mostly very long, extremely complex equations. I flipped through one that lasted thirty-seven pages. And had no more idea what it genuinely meant than Emily did. My science is of the kind that knows the difference between a sulfate and a sulfide, and did not extend to stuff like this.

But there were three-dimensional sketches in some places, of what I was unsure. And even some lines of handwritten script.

We are looking in the wrong place, started one of them. *We are tinkering with the edges of the subject in question, when we should be looking at its core.*

And then, among the final pages, I found more.

This is generally acknowledged to be one of the great Universal Laws. Events that are impossible are never allowed to happen inside our sphere of existence. If that were not the case, then reality would be under constant threat of breaking up in places or even collapsing entirely.

Which was fair enough, and widely accepted. Stephen Hawking had written about this very matter in a Sunday supplement article a couple of months back. But Marsters appeared to have gone on past that.

Words like 'law' and 'allowed,' however, imply intent, a will, a guiding force. A creator. And, being a purely scientific man, I cannot countenance that. But if there is no guiding hand, no actual law, then this characteristic of our everyday existence—this absolute forbidding of impossible events—has to be produced by something physical and real. Perhaps it is a special kind of energy, or matter on the sub-atomic scale, brother to the quark.

It must exist. There is no other explanation. There has to be some actual element surrounding us that binds the fabric of reality together. I call it 'The Universal.' And if I can find it, isolate it, maybe it can be altered somehow, to our greater benefit. Just think what we could manage if the plain impossible could be achieved?

I read those words through several times, feeling my temples begin to throb. What he was proposing, if I'd got this right, was … unpicking the fabric of reality. Allowing things to happen in a universe where they should not.

And *this* had been sitting in a chest of drawers all this time?

"Did you find anything interesting?" Emily was asking.

By the time that I'd returned to Trevon Point, it looked like there was going to be a storm. The light had faded badly. The clouds had thickened and were churning across the heavens. Sea and sky were two wedges of almost identical gray, both of them shifting through a wide variety of patterns. The wind was fierce, the grasses hissing loudly.

I steeled myself and made my way up the railway sleeper that the youths had put across the wire until I reached the iron railing. Once on that, I was forced to continue on all fours. The wind kept trying to unbalance me. The coils of wire creaked ominously. I was tense and sweating, but I pressed on till I reached the end, then lowered myself down.

Another crab went scuttling by. Except it had a long pink tail, like a rat's. *That* sent a chill right through me, but I pressed on. Hurried over to the stone steps leading down. There were double metal doors hanging open at the bottom, and a padlocked chain dangling from a handle, except that it had been broken.

On the wall to one side, someone had spray-painted a graffiti tag. The paint looked fresh. So, yes; the missing vandals had been here.

I went inside, going slowly so my eyesight could adjust.

At first, there was only a corridor, smelling of stale air and nothing more. There were doorways off to either side. The outlines of a few items of furniture were in the rooms beyond them.

And then another stairway took me further down. I thought I heard a noise. Was that a laugh? I wasn't sure. My heart was bumping.

I was now in a shorter corridor with a lower roof. I shouldn't have been able to see at all, not this far underground. But a very faint light seemed to be coming from some source. I turned round several times, but couldn't make out where.

At the end of this passage was a far-heavier metal door, like one of those hatches in a submarine. It was halfway open too. I could make out a faint clattering from beyond it. Then the clattering turned to grinding. Then the grinding stopped.

When I swallowed, it was painful. But I stepped around the hatch, and found myself inside the 'Inner Sanctum.'

This room was absolutely bare. Whoever had come here that last day had not left anything behind. The place had to be some forty yards long by thirty wide, and had a cavernously high ceiling.

I could hear something breathing, and it wasn't me.

A rat went past my feet, making me jerk. Except that it had half a dozen armored, pointed legs, just like the crabs I'd seen. It clattered across the bare floor, reached the nearest wall and vanished.

Only ... there was no hole for it to vanish into.

A moment later, the same strange creature re-emerged at the far side of the room, appearing from three foot up on that wall and dropping with a heavy clack. The thing began growing, swelling as I watched. It had turned into one of the Dobermans before much longer, and it started barking at me.

I drew back, getting really frightened. But the very next second, the dog changed into a silent shadow, which gradually faded away.

Something began lifting from the center of the concrete floor. It looked as if it was concrete too, but kept on growing. When it had raised itself to about six feet high, it began reassembling itself into a vaguely human shape. Its face took on distinctive features. This was one of those youths in the local paper, one of the boys who had gone missing, or else a facsimile of such.

It raised a hand in my direction. Then it burst like a bubble, vanishing as well.

Something else was happening behind me. I could sense it, and I turned.

That wall had bulged outward, in the shape of another human face, but massive. The top of its head was completely bald, and its temples were protruding.

So ... Professor Marsters?

He blinked at me. His eyes were not evenly placed. As I watched, one of them began sliding down in the direction of his chin. I was so shocked, I couldn't even speak at first. But finally, I got past my fright and bewilderment.

14

"Professor Marsters?" I yelled out. "You've got to *stop* all this! People are getting *hurt!*"

His mouth dropped open. There were the heads of tulips in it, and a starfish.

"Testing," he said. "Scooby-dooby secret squirrel. Did you find anything interesting?"

Could he see and hear outside this place? Or maybe he could see my thoughts. If impossible things were happening down here, then couldn't that be one of them? It wasn't a particularly comforting idea, and I ignored it as best I could.

"Professor, I'm not sure what's happened to you, but you've got to come *back* from there!"

"Define there?" was his garbled answer. "How do you get from there to here? If you want to get there, then I wouldn't start from here. Yes? Hah!"

The sliding eye had reached the bottom of his chin and was hanging off it, like a drop of water. Another had appeared at the center of his forehead. He swallowed the tulips, but the starfish stayed in place. The face staring out from the middle of the starfish was a caricature of his own.

"The world is the world is the world is the world," he told me.

How long had it taken him to go insane, once he had tampered with The Universal? Five years, or five minutes? It didn't really matter. No human could hang onto his mind once that reality was gone. We pin so much of our existence—don't we?—on believing that the chair we like to sit in will still be a chair tomorrow, and will be the same chair a year after that. Take that away from us, and everything else breaks down.

"Did you know," he raved, "that seventeen times the event that took Demosthenes and then there is the vertical implosion? Fact!"

Thin, rubbery arms began growing from the walls and trying to grab at me.

And that clinched it. There was obviously no way I could get through to him. Nothing more that I could do. And so I panicked. Ran.

On the way back, parts of the corridor began opening and

shutting, like fishes' mouths. I had to slow my progress and time my escape. And it wasn't just the Inner Sanctum that had been affected.

While crossing the open ground back to the fence, blades of grass grew to several times their length and kept trying to snare my ankles.

I finally reached the iron rail. Jumped up, grabbing hold of it and hauling myself up. And was sliding down its gradient, then running once again.

I must have only got a couple dozen yards before I stumbled, fell. I lay there on my face, my breath like fire in my chest and my pulse galloping.

There was a soft metallic *tuck* nearby, and I managed to lift my gaze slightly.

The Bentley was back.

One of its rear doors had come open. A pair of expensive and well-polished shoes was making its way in my direction. There were pale gray trouser legs above them with immaculate creases. I didn't have enough strength left to raise my head and make out more of this approaching man, not at the moment anyway.

But he stopped directly in front of me. Both his narrow hands came into view. And with the thumb and forefinger of each, he pinched his trousers at the knees and lifted the fabric slightly before squatting down.

He was a thin but healthy looking man in his late sixties. His eyes were a granite gray. His silver hair had been combed very neatly into place and was resisting the wind. Everything about him looked manicured and polished.

His expression was quietly patient. He had on a handmade shirt, a club tie, and a navy blue blazer with golden buttons. This was no spook. He was most probably a 'mandarin,' someone from the very lofty apex of the Civil Service.

"Are you all right?" he asked me.

I came back with, "Who're you?"

One of his eyebrows lifted, and his mouth formed itself into a tight, humorless smirk. I had just asked a stupid question—stupid in the sense that it had not the slightest chance of being answered.

"Do you know what's going *on* back there?" I gasped, pushing myself up onto my elbows.

The raised eyebrow remained in place. Why else would he be here?

"You need to blow that place to smithereens!"

"And scatter its dust to the four winds?" The man shook his head slowly. "Who knows what effect *that* might have?"

"But the unreality's begun to spread," I pressed on, getting angry. "That's what you really need to understand. It's not just in the Inner Sanctum anymore. That's very likely how you lost your two dog-walking thugs—they got too close."

He crooked the index finger of his right hand, pressed it to his chin, and spent the next half-minute in reflective thought.

"If I were you, Mr. Sayers," he said finally, "I'd go away from here. I'd go away and not come back."

An hour later I had a suitcase packed and was waiting for a train back into London.

But I wasn't even sure if that was going to be far enough.

Then she seemed to feel his gaze on her, and her head turned.

Aegea

His first thought when he saw their bodies lying on the shore was 'seals.' The darkness of their skin, the way that they were evenly spaced out, the way that all their heads were pointed in the same direction. Did they even *have* seals in the Aegean?

But then he removed his sunglasses, cupped a hand above his eyes and took a closer look. And could see that they were people, each of them apparently young, and half of them women. Maybe this was what he had been looking for.

Matt Souther lowered himself back into the seat of the little rented car that he was driving, and let the vehicle roll forward till its tires were crunching on the granulated golden sand.

It had been settled on in January, back in Chicago. And had sounded extremely appealing in the Windy City's winter months. Come summer, they were going to treat themselves to a whistle-stop tour of Mediterranean cities, with a rest break at the end. Madrid and Barcelona, Cannes and Rome and Florence, Athens, and then finally the ferry ride which would bring them here to Xanakos. Back when the vacation had been in the planning stage, he'd fully been expecting Margie to accompany him. They'd been going out for two years, and so that seemed right.

But simply going out had not turned out to be enough for her. She'd wanted to move in with him. She'd pointed that out in February. And when—by April—she could see that he was still thinking it over, she had left him.

He'd adored Margie on some levels. So what exactly did he want?

The vacation had already been paid for, though. No refunds. July came. And Matt decided he would do it on his own.

He slipped his loafers off before he got out—he was wearing no socks. The sand was the color of expensive gold, but felt harsh and gritty in between his toes. Coarse and crude. Which told him this might be an untamed place, and he liked the idea of that.

Matt was in his early thirties, not badly off and not bad-looking. And he'd had a few encounters with new women during his tour of the cities. But what he had been waiting for, what he *really* wanted, was to meet somebody special during this part of the trip. A beachside romance. He'd never had one, and the whole idea appealed to him in ways the more sensible parts of his mind couldn't begin to understand.

But he had gone down to the shore, his first morning at the resort hotel. And it had all been families and couples, not an unattached woman close to his age anywhere he looked.

That was when he'd hired the small car, and begun his search for something better.

None of these guys were lying together. And that was pretty damned unusual, he thought. Even at the lakeside beaches in the city he had come from, you could find loads of people lying side-by-side or intertwined when the weather was good.

But the people in this hidden cove … there was a five-yard gap between the closest of them. What that meant, he wasn't sure. They were lying perfectly still, mostly on their fronts. And not so much as a single head came up when he approached them.

His first impression from a distance had been right. They were mostly around his age or younger. Their bodies were smooth. Their flesh was tanned a deep, dark gold. And they appeared to be wearing, to the last, exactly the same bathing costume: a pair of navy-blue briefs that wrapped itself, skin-tight, around each pelvis.

That was when it struck him that the women were all topless.

20

Matt felt his pulse starting to tick over, but was not quite sure how to approach this. He had brought a beach-bag along with him, and so he chose a spot some thirty feet from anybody else, then dug out a towel and spread it out. Stripped off his chinos—he had on swim trunks underneath. Took off his shirt and put it away.

There was sun cream in the bag as well, and so he started to apply it.

Xanakos was a craggy place. Like most islands in this part of the world, it was actually the peak of a low mountain that protruded from the blue Aegean. Most of the roads that he had traveled along since leaving the resort had been precipitously high ones, with a wall of dense rock on one side and a steep drop on the other. It was not what he was used to, in a car. Matt had driven carefully and sought to get to lower ground as soon as he was able.

He'd wound up on the south side of the island. There, the mountain dropped away. He found himself on very narrow, rutted lanes, weaving the open-topped renter between boulders. Kept on catching glimpses of the sea on either side of him every so often, and figured out that he had ventured onto some kind of panhandle.

After a while, he'd realized this was getting him nowhere, and he'd started thinking about heading back. But an instinct had told him to take a final right, where two paths up ahead converged. And then he'd come across this hidden cove.

You couldn't even see it from the road.

He was applying the sun cream to his legs when several of the other bathers started to take notice of him. Two, then three more heads came bobbing up. The men and women alike had short black hair and tanned oval faces. They were all wearing sunglasses of precisely the same kind, with small round lenses, jet-black and impenetrable.

They stared at him expressionlessly. Why were they all wearing the same shades?

And there was something rather odd about this beach. Normally, the sand would be flat. Whereas here, it rose and fell, dipped and curved, not unlike the waves of the surrounding blue Aegean. Maybe it was the incoming sea that made it this way—but on Greek islands, he already knew, there was barely any tide.

Maybe the wind? But he could feel none.

The terrain had the effect, when he sat down, of rendering the people around him only partially visible. They had ceased their study of him by this juncture, their heads dropping back. And there were hardly any of them he could make out clearly. Mostly, he could only see divided segments of their bodies—an arm, a leg, part of a face. The breadth of a back or the curve of a shoulder. Each of them was darkened to the same deep gold. And none of them was moving any longer.

Then something else struck him. He had seen no towels or inflatable beds. These people were lying directly on the gritty sand—and why was that? Their skin was glossy, so they'd obviously oiled up. It was curious behavior, but he still believed he might get lucky here, so he lay back.

Matt couldn't help wondering, all the same, where he had found himself. Everyone here had on the same type of bathing costume and sunglass design? It was as though he'd wandered inadvertently onto a fashion shoot. Or perhaps they were some kind of club, some group?

The sun beat down on him more fiercely the longer he lay there. The air around him wavered. Perspiration sprang up on his body. He heard someone grunt and lifted his head to see who it was, but there was no way of telling.

Then his gaze went to the right, and he caught sight of someone who he'd not noticed when he had first arrived. Maybe forty feet from him was a statuesque woman. She was lying down like all the others, only he could tell that she was taller than the rest. She had on the same briefs and shades as they, but her short dark hair had a distinctive reddish tinge. Matt immediately felt fascinated by her.

She'd been supine, but had raised herself onto her elbows, with her full figure in view. And what a figure. He tried not to stare, but it was difficult.

She was peering out in the direction of the water. Then she seemed to feel his gaze on her, and her head turned.

An oval face, exactly like the rest. Expressionless until … had her lips moved? Matt's pulse quickened again and he found himself holding his breath.

The next moment, though, she eased herself back down and rolled away from him, leaving just her delicately muscled back to look at.

How could he approach these women? He wasn't entirely sure. Back at the hotel, there'd been a bar, a café, volleyball, the pool. Whereas here, there was no point of contact. He could make out no other beach bags either, so where were their clothes?

It occurred to Matt that he might have stumbled across a type of resort where clothing was not overly required, and whose guests had come out from their rooms with just their lower swimwear on. He rolled onto his stomach, raising his face and peering inland. But the only things that he could see were rocks, no buildings.

His gaze went back to the tall woman with the red-tinged hair. She hadn't moved a muscle. Her skin was so slick it reflected the sunlight in wide yellow bands. As he watched, a dragonfly alighted on her shoulder, but she didn't even twitch.

What was it with these people? Normal vacationers on a beach, they moved around, played games, scrawled their names in the sand. And went swimming too. If one of the women would only do that, if one of them would only stroll down to the water's edge, then he could do the same, using that as a pretext to start talking to her.

The dragonfly lifted from the woman's shoulder in a blur of crystal wings, circling briefly and then vanishing. But that was the only movement anything was making. And the sunlight was so powerful that it was making his brow pound a little. Matt covered his temples with a forearm.

Another five minutes and he'd made his mind up. If no one here was going to swim, he needed to. Maybe his example would encourage them to do the same. Matt levered himself to his feet and brushed himself down before heading to the water.

His route took him within a dozen feet of one of the women. She was prone, the front of her body pressed against the beach. And the skin on her back appeared a little rough, in spite of the fact that it was slickly oiled. Matt tried to ignore that, making a point of stepping heavily and kicking up a little sand as he went by. But she remained perfectly motionless, not even seeming to be conscious he was walking past.

He stopped at the tideline, pale foam bubbling around his feet. The sound of the waves ought to have been soothing to him, but his nerves felt slightly ragged. When he jerked his head back quickly, nobody was looking at him.

So he decided to forget about them, striding in. The further into the sea he got, then the less it looked blue, the more it shifted to the greenish side of turquoise. The water felt cold after the basting he had taken, but by the time it was around his chest, that passed.

Matt shoved himself forward, breaking into a quick, sloppy freestyle. He kept on wondering if anyone was watching, but did not look back. Swam until he had to be some fifty yards out. When he tried to touch the bottom with his toes, it was no longer there. And so he finally turned.

The beach was empty.

He could still see his bag and his car up past it, but there were none of the sunbathers anywhere he looked. He lifted his head as high as he was able, trying to see past the dips and rises in the sand. But there was no one.

Then he noticed something even more peculiar. He could see the trail of his own footprints, leading downward to the water's edge. Except there were no others of that nature.

There appeared to be ... wide drag marks instead.

As if the other people in this cove had pulled themselves down to the tideline on their bellies, without getting up.

Something brushed against his leg.

Matt stiffened, his limbs going rigid. He began to sink, and had to force himself to tread water again. It had only been a fish or a piece of weed, he kept on telling himself. Except that it had felt much larger.

The surface in front of him suddenly bulged. And what had made it do that?

In another second, it was happening all around him. The water was being pushed continuously out of shape. He tried to squint down through its depths, desperate to find out what was going on. But the sunlight was reflected on it brightly, and the surface had become opaque.

Something broke through, about five yards off. It was there and gone so quickly that he barely saw it. But Matt was left with an impression of a deep gold color and a flash of navy blue. And in the last moment before the object disappeared, he thought he saw a pair of feet and ankles, pressed tightly together.

The sea around him kept on humping up and bulging, although it was fairly flat when he stared further out. Matt felt panic overtake him, but his instincts still remained in play, and they were screaming at him to get back to dry land.

He began to swim in that direction, trying to keep his head up so that he could keep an eye on what was going on around him. His arms and legs worked desperately, his breath hissing in his skull.

Something else came up into view, directly ahead of him. Only for a short while, but he got a better look at it this time. It was one of the male bathers, and at this close range he got a far truer impression.

The man's skin shone, though not with oil. Perhaps the slick of fresh seawater had brought it out, but Matt could now see that the fellow had a covering of tiny golden scales. He was not tanned at all.

And not genuinely a man either.

When another two of these things broke the surface, they both dived again immediately, jack-knifing at the waist, and he could make out something else. They were not wearing briefs, as he had first supposed. Their scales simply got darker and a different color around the pelvis, phasing through to navy blue the way a fish's back might.

One of them rolled just before the water closed above it, and its groin was featureless and bare.

And then another head came bobbing up, still closer. And Matt felt a fresh rush of amazement. This was one of the women. And incredibly, she was still wearing her black shades.

But then they blinked. They narrowed, vanishing entirely for an instant before reappearing.

There were no wire frames connecting them. These were not sunglasses. They were eyes.

What kind of creatures were these?

Although ... they were not hurting him. Matt forced himself to recognize that fact. They were simply gamboling and cavorting around him in the same manner as a school of dolphins.

All of them went back under. The sea became momentarily flat. But then another head arose, barely two feet in front of him.

It was that of the statuesque, red-tinted woman he'd been taking such close interest in a short whole back. But it was not hair on her head. They were darkened scales as well, their tips curling out into a softened fringe of spikes.

Those round black eyes of hers gazed back at him impassively. She lifted herself in the water, her smooth shoulders breaking clear.

Her arms remained by her sides, however. She was simply studying him.

Matt's heart was pounding like a hammer, fright and adrenalin washing through him. But he tried to hide that from her, afraid he might provoke an attack. He trod water clumsily, and kept his face as calm as he could manage.

And that seemed to work just fine until her mouth came stretching open. Wider, and then wider still.

Many teeth.

The blue Aegean held him like a glove.

Beneath the Shroud

He'd never seen a fog like this. Not one that stretched for hundreds of miles, the way that this one seemed to do. Buck had first run into it a couple of hours after he had crossed the border into Kansas. And now he was just starting to head up through Nebraska, and it was still with him. He reckoned it had to be rolling in off the Missouri River—but how far did it extend?

His old Dodge pickup creaked and rattled as he drove, the engine thrumming at a noticeably low pitch. He'd been keeping his speed down around the twenty mark for … how long now? An exhausting while, that much was certain. And he knew he ought to find somewhere to stop. But word had reached him that his Pa was really, really sick and had been asking for him, and that was up in Mitchell, South Dakota. So his conscience wouldn't let him rest. He needed to get there as quickly as he could, and so he kept on going.

Buck had traveled around a lot since leaving home. He was in his mid-twenties and had been working for the past four years as a farm laborer, picking up work in any section of the country he could find it. He had been all over the Midwest and a good deal of the South, and had even ventured into Florida and California. But it was Arkansas that he was headed from right now, outside of Springdale.

His headlights kept on trying to pierce the rolling gloom ahead of him, but they were having very limited success. Once in an occasional while, a truck would loom up, coming back the other way and going past him with a muffled roar. Apart from that, the road was empty.

He felt jumpy, rather wired, but fought against that so he didn't let his speed pick up. He'd driven in all sorts of conditions, heavy rain, and snow, and ice. And none of that stuff bothered him. But fog—he saw that as a different matter. It was like trying to drive while mostly blind, a sheet of gauze pulled down across your face. All it took was for there to be a side-road up ahead, a tractor rolling out of it, and that would be his journey's end, much sooner than he'd thought.

Buck reached the outskirts of some nameless hamlet, started passing through it, but then let his speed drop a little more. There were pedestrians to think of when you went through inhabited places. If some little kid ran out in front of him ...

But it was late by now, and no one was abroad. He could make out blurred lit windows, indistinct shapes moving within some of them. They looked very distant in this murk, despite the fact they really weren't. That was when it struck him—fog could leave you isolated in a way that nothing else quite managed.

He'd passed through the whole small town in no more than a minute. Its lights faded behind him and were lost from view entirely. When he glanced up at his rear-view mirror, there was nothing to be seen but shifting grayness once again. The hamlet had been swallowed up. Or maybe *he* was the one who'd been swallowed.

There was sweat on his chest, making his shirt sticky. His shoulder blades were aching, and his eyes were sore. And the road ahead of him—what little he could make of it—simply appeared to go on and on indefinitely.

It started to occur to Buck that he was acting crazy. He would never make this journey in a single effort. It would be difficult enough in ordinary conditions, let alone in ones like these.

Better that I make it there a little late than not at all, he told himself. So he began to scan the roadside for some sign of a motel.

And he'd been at that for several minutes, when he noticed what the fog was doing.

It was coming in through one—only one—of the three heating vents in his scuffed old dashboard; the one on the right-hand side, beyond his reach unless he stopped. And it was drifting almost purposefully through the air inside the cabin, floating over to the passenger seat and then accumulating there.

As he watched, it grew in size and density, taking on what practically looked like a cylindrical shape. And fog plain didn't do that.

His aches and pains, his worries, were forgotten in an instant. Buck sat bolt upright and yanked the pickup over to the ditch. He lashed at the fog with his right hand, and some of it dispersed. Another few swipes, and the rest had turned to swirling filaments. But what had made it do that in the first place?

He was still pondering on it when he heard the thunderously loud blast of a truck horn to his rear. He stared across his shoulder, just in time to see a Mack semi loom out of the murk behind him, swerve to avoid his parked vehicle, and then go grinding past. It had almost hit him, and the narrowness of his escape made his heart pump harder and his eyelids widen, so he became intensely aware of his new surroundings.

He was at the center of a massive cornfield, not even a small light shining anywhere he looked. The massed stalks had grown to full height and were entirely motionless. But was that a human figure he had spotted in among them? He could only very vaguely make it out. Buck finally decided that it had to be a scarecrow.

It occurred to him, after a while, that he was still a static target on this road. Another truck might come along, and the next time he might not be so lucky. He had better move.

Half an hour later, his eyes were stinging terribly. He could only have traveled partway through Nebraska, and he understood this was no use. He genuinely needed to find somewhere he could stop and rest. Except there'd been no motel signs this entire while, and not the tiniest glimpse of human life.

The fog hadn't lifted the least bit. There was something almost alien about it, he thought. It had turned the countryside around him into a quite baffling and shapeless landscape, with nothing familiar in it at all. The world became a wholly different place when it was covered up with this kind of gray shroud.

It got turned into ... a dead place. Buck chewed carefully on that particular thought. Sight was obscured, sound was muffled, every normal point of reference was lost. There were no colors he could see. Most probably, the moon and stars were out, but on a night like this there was no way of telling.

Maybe this was what the afterlife was like. So … could great fogs like this come spilling in from unseen worlds beyond our own?

That was a completely nutso notion, wasn't it? Buck shook his head, then frowned unhappily. The whole idea of an afterlife had made him anxious to get home.

Except that—damn!—it made no difference, did it? No, it didn't *matter* what he wanted. He doubted he'd so much as reach the state line in one jump, let alone getting as far as Mitchell. And he simply had to face that fact, and find someplace where he could stop.

In the end, he found an open stretch of dirt beside the road where he could pull the pickup off. Another shape loomed up ahead of him as he slowed down and braked. It was large and pale, and had a vaguely human shape, but it turned out to be only a lightning-blasted tree stump. His muscles unclenched.

Cramp and exhaustion started flooding through him, pain mingling with tiredness to act like a strong drug. Buck slumped back. His eyelids closed.

He was awoken by a movement, which he felt rather than saw. His eyes came open a wary crack, and he thought that he could make out another blurred shape beyond his windshield.

Buck jerked forward, sucking in a breath. There was a shape out there, vaguely like a woman. And he wondered who she was, and what she might be doing in the plain middle of nowhere. But once he had calmed down a touch, he figured out that this was just another trick played by the fog.

Some of it had formed into the strong resemblance of a female figure. As he watched, it filtered outward till the illusion was gone. Didn't thick fogs do that sometimes, make you convinced that you were seeing stuff that was not really there?

But then he got a sense of something else, much closer in, and turned toward the passenger seat once more. He felt the fine hairs rising on his body and he nearly yelled out loud. The shape that had been trying to form there, earlier on? It had returned.

It still had a cylindrical trunk. Two slimmer cylinders that looked like legs. Another pair that might be arms, although there were no details in the least, no hands or elbows.

A pallid oval for the head. No ears or nose or eyes or mouth.

But nonetheless, it appeared to be gazing straight ahead. Waiting for the journey to continue, maybe?

Buck didn't need telling how insane that was. This stuff was only vapor, and was doing no such thing. He almost had to steel himself to manage it, but he lunged at the cylinder and swept his hand right through it, like he'd done the last time. His palm met with no resistance, and the shape began to break apart.

Once he was satisfied the thing was gone, he reached across and shut off all three of the dashboard's heating vents. And then he tugged at the ignition key, rekindled his lights, and yanked his pickup back onto the blacktop.

It was almost midnight. He had already decided he would stop at the next town he reached. He didn't even care if there was only a bus station bench to sleep on—it would have to do. And maybe he could find a phone and call ahead to tell his family where he was, and ask how Pa was holding up.

Except there were no towns. He kept on driving down the same road, which ran straight as a needle for mile after exasperating mile, and not even a signpost came in sight.

Various other things did, however, and in ever greater numbers. There were more of those strange, human-looking shapes. Some of them were in the fields, among the lofty cornstalks. Others were just past the ditch.

Their faces seemed to follow him as he went by them. And he thought he saw one figure raise its arm. That couldn't really happen, could it? But the idea started forming in his mind again.

Could this fog have come through from another world and … brought some of its inhabitants with it?

That's purest bull, he told himself, trying to force a smile and

31

But the fog inside *his cabin—it had started taking on definable shapes once more.*

failing. *All these are just accidental forms.*

He was beginning to wish he'd stopped at the little town he had passed through a couple of hours back, but it was much too far behind him now. Everything normal seemed a long way back behind him.

He'd lost track of what hour it was by the time he started taking note of something desperately odd. The view ahead of him was getting worse, the shroud of fog becoming even thicker. Oughtn't it be starting to lift after all this while?

And then he realized he was wrong. What he'd believed that he was looking at was not the case. The fog up ahead was no denser than it had been, but it looked that way because the stuff was all around him now. It had somehow gotten back inside the car.

Buck stared down, and saw that it was pouring upward from the floor, from holes beside the pedals. It was behaving like water, and he knew it oughtn't act that way. And he was breathing the pale vapor in. He quite likely had been doing that for a good while. The long road had been holding him so mesmerized he hadn't even noticed.

It felt chilly in his lungs, unpleasant and clammy, like breathing in the moisture off the surface of some frigid lake. Buck retched gently and tried to cough it out.

But that was when he heard the voice. It wasn't coming from beyond the Dodge, or even from in it. It was inside his own head, but it was definitely not his voice.

Buck couldn't make out what it was saying. It was droning away in a flat, indecipherable monotone, with not the slightest variation to its solemn pitch. And he had to be imagining this—there wasn't any other explanation. Except he began to panic all the same.

He shook his head fiercely, and then clamped his free hand to his ear. It made no slightest difference. The voice was being joined by others, which were equally unfathomable and were growing louder in his skull.

A bend came up ahead of him, the first one that he'd seen in ages, springing suddenly out of the fog. But, panicked as he was, he

33

didn't manage to react in time. If he'd still been going twenty, then the outcome might have been a painful one, the pickup hitting a ditch and then overturning. But his feet had left the pedals by this stage and the old Dodge was slowing down.

It left the blacktop and went rolling off into a cornfield. Stalks were crushed beneath its tires with a sound like grass in flame. The rusty suspension ratcheted and groaned, the needles on the dashboard dropped, and then the engine finally stalled.

A depthless silence closed around him after that. Even the murmuring voices stopped. There was only gray around him, and Buck felt like he was drowning in a sea of that non-color. The entire world might have died and then been covered up with this dull, filmy shroud.

But the fog *inside* his cabin—it had started taking on definable shapes once more. Figures that were, again, vaguely human.

Their pale, blank faces turned to him. Despite the fact they had no eyes, he knew that they were staring at him.

And he was *sure* of it, this time. Buck just *knew* it. This fog hadn't rolled in off of any river. but had come from somewhere else entirely.

The shapes were closing in around him now. But they didn't lift a single hand to touch him. Simply merged together and then pressed up closer in one swirling mass against his face

He was breathing in their chilly vapor. It began to fill him, top to toe.

His family's home was right out on the far borders of Mitchell. Single-story, wood-built with a covered porch, a picket fence surrounding it. Except the yard had not been tended in a good long while. And the lace curtains at the front windows were all tinged with yellow, which was not the kind of thing you usually saw.

Four cars, none of them exactly new, were parked out on the driveway.

When Buck finally got there, at ten the next morning, the fog had lifted so completely that you couldn't even tell that it had ever been around. The sky was clear and blue, and the sun shining brightly. The sparse local traffic was flowing at a casual pace, and a few pedestrians were ambling around.

Someone must have noticed him arrive, because the front door came swinging wide open before he'd even reached the porch. His three sisters were standing there beyond it.

There was no need for too many words, since he could already see it on their faces. They were trying to smile, genuinely pleased that he was back for the first time since Thanksgiving. But their gazes were damp and their eyes red-rimmed.

His heart becoming very heavy, Buck stepped over and hugged each of them in turn. Ethel went a little stiff, when he did that.

And Kate gasped out, "Oh man, you're cold!"

"I've been on the road all night, so what were you expecting?" he came back at her gently. Then he looked around. "Where's Ma?"

"Trying to get some shut-eye in the back room, Buck. She's been up the whole night too."

There was a sour stink to the house's air when he walked in, and Buck thought that he recognized it from the time when his grandparents had been dying. It was the smell of far too many people all becalmed in one small space, with sickness crammed in with them too. Sweat, mingled with helplessness and desperate sadness. Oh, yes, bad emotions had their own peculiar odors.

And it got worse when he went into his parents' bedroom. There were no lights switched on, but the drapes were opened a small gap to let the daylight through.

One pale shaft revealed a figure—lying on the bed—that Buck could barely recognize. A shrunken little feller who looked decades older than the last time that they'd met. His hair had turned completely white, and there was silvery stubble covering his cheeks. The skin around his eyes was practically obscured by shadow.

And the eyes themselves seemed to be a far paler blue than Buck recalled. They widened slightly when he came in but were filled with little more than resignation. Buck found himself stopping in his tracks, that sight was such a shock. He'd never once seen Pa give up. But then he let a breath out, his whole frame relaxing.

"Can I have a while with him?" he asked.

He was the eldest child, the only son, and so his sisters nodded and withdrew.

Buck went across and sat down on the edge of the bad-smelling bed. This felt practically like visiting a sickly child, his father looked so small. The old guy's mouth started trying to come open, but Buck shook his head and then smiled wryly.

"We both know what's happening. Don't waste your strength."

A trail of vapor drifted from the corner of his mouth when he said that. His Pa's gaze darted to it, his dark pupils widening a fraction more.

"In fact," Buck was continuing, "I met some fellers on the road, last night, who all knew what was happening as well. They're from the place you're headed to, Pa. And I've brought them here with me so they can help you find your way there."

At which point, he opened his mouth fully wide. A pall of fog came rolling out. It closed around his Pa, who gasped with startlement—a faintly strangled, sucking, wheezing noise.

Buck stood calmly up, crossed over to the windowpanes and pushed one open. And when he looked back, his Pa's eyes were shut. Pa's jaw was hanging loosely, and his face was very slack. There was no hint of motion anywhere about his body.

The fog re-emerged from the old man's mouth and nostrils— slightly thicker than it had first been,—and then drifted through the window to the open air beyond, where it dispersed.

There wasn't so much as a smidgen of it left a bare few seconds later.

A bird began singing somewhere off in the far distance. A wood thrush, perhaps.

The Visitors in Marvell Wood

"**M**r. Joe?"

It was a small, lisping voice and came sneaking across the low wooden fence dividing the two backyards. It belonged to his next-door neighbors' youngest daughter, Daisy. And she always called him that, but his name wasn't really 'Mr. Joe.' It was Edward Jonas. But at only four years old, Daisy couldn't seem to get her head around that.

"Mr. Joe? Can I tell you a secret?"

It was an autumnal evening, the night closing its fist quickly around this street, around the whole town. Most of the windows near him were lit up, some of them misty with the steam from cooking pans. And a few of them were slightly open—he could hear brief snatches of the TV news.

A dog barked somewhere. Jonas smiled. He wasn't quite sure how it had happened, but Daisy had come to regard him—during this past year, at least,—as some kind of confidant. Someone she could tell things to that she did not want other people, not even her own parents, to know.

The workings of the childish mind. There was no way to understand it. Perhaps it was because he enjoyed spending so much time out in his own back garden, and they bumped into each other frequently that way. He was always finding things to do out there as soon as he got home from work.

Daisy moved closer to the fence, her face pale in the dimness and her blue eyes huge. And she honestly had an expression like, if he did not want to hear her secret, she'd burst into urgent tears.

"I'm listening," Jonas told her.

"You know what there is in Marvell Wood?"

Which terminated at the end of this very street. And so far as he knew, there were only trees there.

"There's fairies. I saw them yesterday."

"Really?" Jonas's grin grew slightly broader. What it was to be so young. "And were they pretty fairies?"

"They were very bright. They tried to talk to me."

"And what did they say?"

A deep line appeared in the skin above the bridge of the girl's nose.

"It was mad stuff, and I didn't like it."

Suddenly, the back door of the house next door flew open. Daisy's mother's head popped out, calling her inside for supper.

"I'm so sorry, Edward. Is she bothering you again?"

"Not at all."

He and Mrs. Mitchell launched into about a minute's polite conversation. How are you? How's work? How are your loved ones?

And then the little girl scampered inside, and the door clicked shut. Jonas was alone in the stillness of the evening. Darkness continued to gather over Birchiam-on-Sea. He could hear the distant rushing of the waves beyond the cliff-tops.

He glanced in the direction of the woods, but could see no brilliant points of light.

It had been remarked that, from the air, Birchiam was the same shape as a pork chop. Most of the main section of the town was just above sea level. That was where you found the shopping streets, the derelict pier and the promenade. But then, as it got narrower, the angle of the town started to rise. The promenade gave way to cliffs. That was Eastley, the part where Jonas lived. Marvell Wood clung around the edges of the district like a thick green glove.

He loved the fresh air, and he loved to walk. By day, he was the accountant for a little manufacturing firm in nearby Stegton. His office was small and had no window. So, as soon as his wage-slavery was over, he would get into the Great Outdoors: his garden or else the woods. It felt as if he was trying to save himself from suffocating.

Dried leaves crackled underneath his shoes. It was evening once again. Maybe he should buy himself a dog, except what would the poor thing do all day while he was being smothered in his office? Jonas pressed on through the trees, thinking about what Daisy had told him the previous night. A lot of the neighborhood's kids came out here, the smaller ones like her under the supervision of their elder siblings. But what exactly could have sparked off in her mind a fantasy like that? There were no such things as glow-worms or fireflies here in Marvell Wood … at least, he'd never seen one. So it simply had to be the product of a child's imagination.

A twig snapped about a dozen yards off to his left. He glanced in that direction, but the tree trunks were dense there, the twilight weaving in among them like a purplish cat's cradle.

Jonas moved along. And became aware—after another half a minute—that someone else was moving too, staying parallel with his route, getting no further away, but no closer either. Somebody appeared to be shadowing him.

He tried to peer harder through the trees. Which did him no more good than it had done the last time.

"Hello?"

He got no answer.

But the noises tracking him had only been small, so it was probably only a couple of the local kids, playing at some silly game.

There was barely any light left around him, by this stage. He turned, and headed back.

Friday. Wage-slavery's end. He was out in his garden again, scraping at some moss, when his neighbor's back door swung open and their little girl emerged again. She usually moved around with swift, excited trots, but not this evening. Everything she did seemed rather sluggish. So … had anything upset her?

She moved over to the fence.

"Hello, Daisy."

When she stared at him, her eyes looked a little smaller than they previously had been, and appeared to have some kind of strange gleam in them. Was she sick?

"Hello, Mr. Jonas."

What had happened to 'Mr. Joe'? Well, maybe this was just a consequence of growing up, a process that, according to his friends with children, happened much too fast. Jonas forced a grin.

"Seen any more fairies?"

Her mouth dropped open slackly. "What?"

"In the woods. I thought you saw … Tinkerbell and all that. *You* know."

But she didn't seem to. Daisy was peering at him like he'd gone insane. And this was growing up *ridiculously* fast. Every scrap of childish excitement and innocence had vanished from her manner. She was holding herself perfectly still, her chin slightly raised. As he watched, her eyelids narrowed. That gleam in her pupils seemed to grow a little brighter.

"Don't know what you're talking about," she said. Even her voice sounded a little deeper.

Jonas cleared his throat. "Er … been in the woods again since we last spoke?"

"How's that your business?"

At which point, Mrs. Mitchell appeared again, calling the girl inside for supper. But she made no attempt at conversation, this time.

In fact, she looked clearly worried.

The next day was one of those in late September that make you feel as if summer has returned. It would have been a sin to stay inside. Jonas walked down to the corner shop to buy a newspaper, then—rolling it up and tapping it against his thigh—he set off into Marvell Wood.

It was cooler in here than out on the street, although still pleasantly warm. The smell was like nature's version of a bakery, crisp and dry and rich. The sunlight took on the dappled hues of the leaves above him. Insects skimmed around his ears and underneath his nose until he swatted at them.

There'd usually be other people out here on a Saturday morning. Jess and Carol Maybury from three doors down, walking their pair of Labradors. Or maybe Mrs. Perez from number 20, with a basket, picking mushrooms. But today, the woods felt perfectly deserted. Jonas pressed on.

The sound of leaves around his shoes became oppressive to him after a few minutes. It was too loud in this perfect silence. Why was there nobody else out here? He started back the way he'd come, and something struck him. He'd gone no more than a couple of hundred yards from the end of the street he lived on. Was less than a quarter of a mile from his own front door.

But here in Marvell Wood, those facts had little significance. Here among the trees, there might as well be no street or houses. He could not see a single rooftop, nor hear any traffic. The normal world of bricks and asphalt, TV sets and tended gardens … it had disappeared. He might as well be a hundred miles from civilization.

And that was the basic truth of woodlands, wasn't it? If it wasn't for the watch on your wrist, the shoes on your feet and the clothes on your back, civilized society could have vanished altogether. It might never have existed.

He had started feeling quite uneasy. Which he knew was foolish, but he couldn't help it. Jonas tapped his newspaper against his thigh again.

Another crackling noise brought his head around. There was somebody else out here, except he could not see them. But he was not being stalked this time. Whoever it was out there was going past him.

They sounded like small, light footfalls, and he decided to follow them. He kept his distance. And after a while, a familiar figure came in sight.

Daisy?

He waited for her brother or her older sister to appear, but neither of them did. And her parents weren't here either. She was far too young to be alone out here, and Jonas thought of calling to her.

But something in her manner—exactly like last night—stopped

him.

She was striding along purposefully, her small arms hanging limply by her sides. And staring straight ahead where normally, in a child that small, her head would be going around.

He remembered the look on her face and the tone of her voice yesterday evening. *"How's that your business?"* It was as if Daisy had been suddenly and magically transformed into an adult.

She didn't seem to notice he was following her. Her progress was too focused and intent for anything like that. She was heading into a part of Marvell Wood he'd never been. The tree trunks were even closer together off in that direction, the canopy above so dense that barely any light got in. The place had a stench like compost, and he had always avoided it.

But Daisy went in among the tight-packed and moss-covered trunks without so much as pausing. Jonas hung back for a while, then struggled inward after her.

And could see light up ahead of him after the first few yards. A tiny spot of it, a brilliant, dazzling white.

And it was moving. Could this be her 'fairy'?

It vanished in another second. Then another one appeared, and circled around a branch, then vanished too. Jonas was mystified.

It was almost black as night in this part of the woodlands. But that didn't seem to bother little Daisy in the slightest. She was navigating through the trees as though the area were floodlit.

What was going on? He thought that he could make out other shapes ahead of him. Other children, all of them of nursery age. They were hunched facing each other on a patch of earth where the dark tree trunks were slightly thinner. He stopped moving altogether. Thought that he could make out squeaking, clicking noises coming from their lips.

Daisy joined them. There were five of them, or maybe six. They were squatting in a ring the way that he supposed Neanderthal children might have done half a million years ago. And he'd been right … they definitely *were* squeaking and clicking at each other, the pitch of it rising and falling … was it some kind of language?

42

The ones facing toward him—he could see their eyes. Or at least, he could see the same peculiar gleam he had noticed in Daisy's. And it was not a static glow. He thought that it was fluttering very slightly.

Another point of brilliant white luminescence appeared in the air above him.

That was when one of the children noticed him and pointed. All their dark heads swung around.

What happened next was so unexpected that it sent Jonas careening back, moldy leaves scattering from his shoes, his head scraping against low branches. None of the children made any further move. But the bright point of light came hurtling at him.

Rapidly, it took on shape. And Jonas's mind struggled furiously hard to take in properly what it was seeing. Lord, it *was* a fairy! Or at least, it was a tiny human form with wings. Its head was hairless and too large. Its eyes were silver and entirely round. There seemed to be no features on its body, or else it was simply moving far too fast to make them out.

It came rushing up toward his face, and Jonas was almost on the verge of yelling. When the thing abruptly disappeared, popping out of existence between one second and the next.

Another one came into being right in front of him, its wings moving so fast that they created a twinkling blur on the dark, fetid air …

Then the creature sped across.

And was inside him.

In his body. Underneath his skin. He could feel it moving there. Blind panic overtook Jonas. He thought that he'd let out a howl, but was not sure. He doubled over. Then he tried to run away. He figured out that was not possible, and doubled over again, pawing at his chest.

He could sense the creature fluttering past his heart. It did not hurt, but was an unsettling, chilly sensation, coupled with a powerful vibration. His whole body shook, and was that terror or those madly beating wings?

43

The children were still hunched together, staring over at him. The thing inside was moving up toward his neck. Jonas flailed around some more. As it started up his esophagus, he instinctively let his mouth stretch open, hoping it would fly out through it.

But the creature had no such intention. Next moment, he felt it touch his brain.

The pictures started coming.

They were of a frozen, blasted landscape. There was nothing living in view except a couple of shattered husks that might have once been trees. Boulders had been smashed asunder everywhere he looked. Icicles hung from them and dense rime, a dully glittering gray-white, had worked its way into every crevice.

Winds moaned across this frightful, barren place unstoppably, a sound like mourning whales. And then he wheeled around and could see dozens more of his kind. Tiny winged humanoids like himself, wandering the desolate terrain. Occasionally, one of them would drop down on an ice-clad boulder to lick frost off it to quench its thirst.

And the thought came to him.

Home. We hate. We hate this place.

And suddenly, the terror in him became even greater. Because the pictures—the visions—had melted away. He was back in the woods again, back in the dark. And the creature in his head was pushing. It was no longer simply touching his mind, it was trying to shove its way inside.

And he would not allow that! No, he had to stop it! He clutched at his head. That did no good. He pushed back with his thoughts. He heaved and strained and focused every last scintilla of his will on keeping that thing out of his brain. *He'd not let it in! He'd not!*

The pressure in his head abruptly vanished. Whether he had managed to achieve something or not, Jonas was not sure. But the creature was gone, the same way the other ones had vanished.

Still reeling, Jonas stared aghast at the group of hunched children for another moment.

Then he ran.

It is traditional to tell yourself you only imagined incidents like that, but Jonas couldn't. It had happened.

He could still feel a residual coldness where the creature had passed through his body. And had developed a throbbing headache, which he never usually got. Had any damage been done? He didn't think so.

The chill stayed with him for most of the day, but the headache eased off after a while, allowing him to think more clearly. He was in his living room and had his curtains drawn. He'd poured himself a whisky, and was sitting in his armchair.

His mind kept on returning to those images it had been shown. What he had been looking at … it seemed to be a different world. Maybe one not even of this universe. Some kind of disaster had befallen it. Or, worse still, it had always been like that. Whatever, it had been the grimmest, most unsettling landscape he had ever laid his eyes on. And the creature in his head had seemed to think so too.

If I was one of them, the thought came to him, *then I'd want to go elsewhere.*

Which was maybe what the things were trying to achieve. He ran it through his head again. When the creatures had been flying through the air, they'd only remained there for a few brief seconds. Perhaps they couldn't stay any longer than that. But when their sibling had been *inside* him …

He had been so panicked that he wasn't sure. But it had stopped in there for at least a minute, maybe more.

The thing had tried to make a home inside him, pushing into his mind like a cuckoo with its egg. But by sheer force of will, he had prevented that from happening.

A simpler, weaker mind, though?

He stared at the dividing wall between his own home and the Mitchells'.

Like the mind of a small child?

And then they moved as one, funneling down and plunging into him.

"**C**ome on."

It was another whisper, coming from the front yard next to his this time. He'd been sitting by his window all day, and now dusk had fallen.

"Don't you want to see the fairies?"

Jonas got to his feet, pushing back the curtain a couple more inches. Daisy was out there. Did her parents even know? She was standing by the front gate, which was open, and had three companions with her, two more girls and one boy, all her age.

The other kids had an excited air. They were beaming hugely and their eyes were very wide, every movement of their limbs electrified.

"Let's go," Daisy whispered to them.

And they started moving.

By the time that Jonas had followed them to the edge of Marvell Wood, there were other small bands coming here from every direction. He sank behind the shadow of a wall and watched. There had to be nearly forty of them, the other kids who'd been with Daisy fetching them here.

He let the entire mob disappear into the trees before he moved again. There was no need to follow them too closely, since he understood where they were going.

But when he reached the darkest section, when he saw what was already happening there … the creatures appearing in mid-air, then diving into some child's head … the child going slack and its face becoming blank … its arms dropping nervelessly down by its sides and its eyes gleaming …

He couldn't help himself. He was yelling at the top of his voice furiously, and running forward.

The first child that he reached was Daisy. He lunged down, trying to yank her away from this place.

She bared her teeth and her pupils flared. She grabbed hold of his wrist with such intense pressure it almost broke the skin. And such was the pain and disbelief that Jonas couldn't figure what was happening at first. He was no longer dealing with a child.

Other pairs of arms wrapped themselves around his shins and ankles. And then he was being dragged down on the loamy earth.

He wound up like Gulliver. On his back, pinned down, small faces around him. All their eyes were glittering unnaturally by this time.

Daisy drifted into view above his head and made an ugly, grinning face and said, "We'll take you too."

Another of the creatures popped into being, directly in front of Jonas's nose. He wailed and struggled, but he could not move.

The creature's wings blurred even faster, and it dropped, sliding into him directly through his forehead. Jonas tried to thrash, but he was being held as firmly as if by steel hawsers. He could feel that strange, chilly sensation in his skull. And then that pressure up against his brain, as the winged thing tried to invade it.

Once again, he wouldn't let it. Once again, he pushed back. *An adult's mind! Hold on to that!*

The pressure vanished. See, they'd still not gotten him.

Daisy's face appeared above his head again.

"If we let you go, you'll tell on us." She took a decent while considering that problem.

"So if we can't take your mind, then we will have to take your body."

The section of the woodlands suddenly filled up with startling white light. Perhaps a thousand of the winged creatures had suddenly arrived, great shoals of them, spinning and eddying like phosphor snowflakes. They stared down at him, passing by his face. He thought that he could see intention in those rounded eyes.

And then they moved as one, funneling down and plunging into him. He felt the fluttering coldness of their passage fill up every section of his body. His skin was vibrating to the beat of their wings. And his heartbeat was quickening, trying to match it.

And maybe it was that the children had relaxed their grips, thinking him beaten. Or maybe his urgency was such it leant him massive strength. But he pulled loose, and was on his feet an instant later. *No, he was not taking this!* He began to run again.

Except that the things, they came with him, inside him, part of him.

He had held onto his mind, for sure. Except that … his body had become different. He could feel it, sense it, almost taste it, like a tang of copper in his mouth. The way he ran was longer, lighter, than it should have been. He seemed to leave the ground for entire seconds at a time. That had to be the flying things inside of him. Maybe they were altering him on a cellular level.

He could hear breaking waves before too much longer. This section of the woods gave out to the cliff edge. Jonas kept on plowing through the trees, trying to escape from what was happening inside him.

He was filling up with an incandescent white glow. And the vibration of wings had turned into a second pulse. There was an energy growing in him that seemed to be lighting up every molecule of his body and fusing his nerves into one solid mass.

Mind and body were not separated, were they? They were the conjoined halves of every single being. Alter one, and you inevitably changed the other. And he started realizing what he was capable of doing.

When he burst out through the trees and reached the crumbled cliff edge, he just spread his arms and then continued forward. His feet left dry land and he climbed through the air, higher and higher.

He didn't want to harm anybody, but his old life was beginning to fade in his memory. His humble old life, working in that airless office, pottering around in his back garden on his own. Maybe he could find a way to save both races, the human beings that he once had been a part of and the flying creatures too? He wasn't sure how, but it felt possible.

He was not merely Edward Jonas anymore. Something more powerful than that. Extraordinary. And he stared down.

The landscape below him was shrinking. The green of the woods and the green of the ocean. The gathered evening lending everything a purple tinge.

The world like a ripe grape, waiting to be tasted.

… what exactly were they doing? What had they become?

Covered Mirrors

That morning, his dad went around the house, rummaging through drawers and cupboards for any large pieces of cloth that he could find. Jody followed him at a careful distance. This was a difficult, emotional time, he knew.

Dad was going up and down the stairs of their tall townhouse in the West Village, hanging the pieces of cloth over every mirror in the entire place.

"Why are you doing that?" Jody finally asked him.

"It's a tradition."

"A …?"

"Death is a very solemn thing. And mirrors speak to vanity, which is frivolous. So we cover them."

Jody's eyebrows shot up. "For how long?"

"Back when I was your age, a whole month or even more. But these days? I think a week'll do. No music for a whole week either. Or TV." Dad took in Jody's numb, startled expression. "Except that that rule shouldn't honestly apply to anyone who's just seven years old. But only watch it in your room, and keep the volume down. Okay?"

Later that day a large black car arrived, and they and Mom—who was much younger than Dad, his second wife—were driven to the burial grounds. A sizable crowd of people had gathered. The day was very cold, the sky pale gray, and they were huddled closely together. But a buzz was passing in between them, despite the gravity of the occasion, and Jody managed to pick up on it. Somebody called Noam Chomsky had arrived. And who was that?

All he really knew was, when the box was lowered into the

51

ground, his throat tightened up and the corner of his eyes hurt. He would never see Grandpa Isaacson again. Jody had never properly understood the word 'final' until that point.

There was another service later, back at the house. *Shivah.* The same rev who'd officiated at the grounds intoned from a prayer book. It was up to Dad to read out the last *kaddish,* and Jody felt genuinely sorry for him, since he stumbled with the Hebrew words, his voice practically breaking.

Afterward, the caterers who had been hired laid out a big table of snacks and started making coffee and tea for people. Small glasses of wine and Scotch were passed around. Jody, who hated the smell of both, hung around at the edges of the gathering, trying to figure out exactly what was going on. This was supposed to be a very sad occasion, but the truth was most people were chatting casually, and a few were even chuckling and smiling.

His Dad was nowhere to be seen. Perhaps the other people's calmness had upset him even further. Jody found him outside the house, sitting at the bottom of the concrete steps down from the sidewalk. He was wearing no coat, but seemed unaware of the cold. And tobacco smoke was emerging from his pipe for the first time in several years.

"Won't Mom be cross if she sees you doing that?"

"She'll understand," Dad mumbled

Jody believed he did.

"What was Grandpa really like," he asked, "before I came along?"

"A strong man. Not here—" Dad touched his own bicep, and then moved his fingers to his temple, "but here. He survived the camps. He had his own opinions about pretty much everything, and stuck to them through thick and thin. I never met a student of his who didn't look up to him hugely. And he really did love you, with all his heart."

Which made Jody feel strangely guilty and uncomfortable. People as old as Grandpa had been were, to his eyes, strange facsimiles of human beings, made up of worn and damaged parts. And honestly, he had had no idea that a person who was wrinkled up and bent over like that could be capable of such emotions.

"What was he like with you, when you were a little boy?" he asked.

Dad tried to smile, but his eyes were red-rimmed and his face was very pale against the darkened sky.

"He never hit me. Hardly ever raised his voice—he didn't need to. But he ... expected certain standards of me. I didn't fully understand it at the time, but the truth is that I'm grateful now."

"Do you expect those things from me?" Jody asked.

And that got him a lengthy pause.

"I'm not quite sure." His father shrugged.

When Jody went back into the house, the living room was still packed and the chatter had grown louder. So—uncomfortable with that as well—he headed upstairs to the nearest bathroom. He wanted to see if his own eyes were red-rimmed, like Dad's. It felt important to him. But the mirror had been covered up.

He thought of lifting the cloth away, merely at the edge, to take a peek. He reached out with one hand, but then faltered and drew it back.

Would he be committing a sin if he did that? Would God be angry with him, for defying one of His traditions?

When he woke up late, the next morning, the house sounded unnaturally quiet. Heading downstairs, he passed by Dad's study door and saw that it was closed. Which usually meant that Dad was either working on a new essay, or writing his column for the Literary Supplement of the *New York Times*. There were no sounds coming from beyond the door, though, no faint hammering of any keyboard. And so Jody supposed Dad might still be sad and thoughtful.

The rule remained the same, however. If the door was closed, then he did not go in.

The living room, which had been packed to overflowing yesterday, had been completely tidied up. Except that, over the wood-burning fireplace, there had been a great big mirror in a golden frame. A bath towel was now covering it. That served to make the entire room look rather odd.

He was still peering at it blankly when Mom came in behind him, grabbing his shoulders and kissing his neck, her blonde hair tickling his cheek.

"Hey, what are you staring at?"

Jody tipped his head toward the towel on the glass.

"It looks weird, doesn't it?" Mom agreed. She came from Wisconsin, and had been brought up as a Presbyterian. "But it's what your father wants, and we have to respect that. Am I right?"

When he turned around to look at her, she wasn't wearing any makeup and she'd missed a section of her hair while combing it. So he supposed the mirrors in his parents' bedroom had been covered up like all the rest. She didn't look too pleased about that.

But she fixed him breakfast in the downstairs kitchen all the same, Cheerios and freshly squeezed orange juice. There had never been any mirrors down here, so the place looked normal and he could relax. And afterward, since school was out, he had the whole day to himself.

He found himself explaining the 'tradition' to one of his best friends, Julius, on his cell phone a while later.

"Then how do you know you're still there?" Julius asked him.

His father was the CEO of a new, very successful PR firm on Madison, and Julius was the smartest, sharpest person of his age that Jody had ever known. But he could act and talk a little off-the-wall sometimes and, apparently, this was one of those occasions.

"How do you mean?" Jody came back at him, rather startled.

"If you can't see your own reflection," Julius persisted, "how do you know you're still there?"

"Vampires can't see their reflections," Jody pointed out, "and they're there."

"And are you a vampire?"

"No, I'm pretty sure I'm not."

At which point, they both started laughing.

"You coming out to play?" Julius asked him, once that they had stopped.

It was a simple enough question, but it managed to leave Jody feeling noticeably confused.

"I ... don't think so. I don't think it would be right to, with Grandpa only just passed on. Maybe tomorrow?"

"Okay, then. See ya later."

"See ya."

And they both hung up. Except the 'how do you know you're still there' part of the conversation—it remained with Jody. And he found himself wandering around his room a little desolately, wondering if he really ought to uncover a mirror and find out.

But finally, he started noticing that small reflections of his face were still around. He could make out sections of them on every shiny surface that he looked at. And a faint, dim image of his entire head stared back at him from the blank screen of his portable TV when he approached it.

He got so close to that one they were almost touching noses. And that should have satisfied him, but it did not altogether.

He was still around, for sure. But he was very much diminished.

Come dinnertime, Dad arrived at the table unshaven. Jody had never seen him that way this late in the day before—it was definitely a first. The stubble made his Dad look like a rather different person, slightly older, slightly wilder, and perhaps a little crazy.

"Stop scratching it," Mom hissed at him.

"It's driving me nuts," was Dad's response.

"Then shave. Or I'll do it for you, if you like."

Mom lifted her eyebrows, and Dad smirked.

And they disappeared upstairs as soon as they'd fetched Jody his dessert. He was pretty well used to this kind of behavior. His folks, when they got in certain kinds of playful moods, were prone to behaving as if they were kids themselves. He heard a chuckle from the stairway but ignored it, concentrating on his slice of pie instead.

The very next moment, though, he heard something that was ... different altogether. Something like a breeze, except it wasn't coming from outside the house. It sounded far closer than that, practically on top of him. And the mirror over the cabinet where the china was kept … it was covered with a dishcloth, but he thought he saw the edges of the fabric pulse a little.

Jody froze still, staring at it fixedly with his mouth hanging open. But it didn't move again and there were no more sounds. So maybe he had only been imagining it.

He tried to tell himself that, over and over. Wished that Mom and Dad would come back down. He could hear them giggling upstairs and saying stuff, except their voices sounded terribly faint and faraway.

It was like they might be sinking off into the dim recesses of this sightless house.

The next morning, both of his best friends, Julius and Enzo, turned up at the front door, with Enzo's mother in tow.

"I was thinking of taking the boys down to the beach," she told Mom.

Who beamed. "That's good to hear. Jody's been moping around the house since the funeral. Upset about his granddad."

"Sure, I understand. Some fresh air ought to do him good."

It wasn't a real beach, but if you headed right down to the end of their street and crossed West, the shore of the Hudson had been turned into a narrow park with paved walkways threading across it. People sunbathed there in the summer, cycled and roller-skated any time of year. Enzo's mom had brought a ball with her, and she let them have it and then found a bench while they played catch.

When Jody fumbled for the fourth time in a row, Enzo yelled out, "What's wrong with you, *bee-atch*?"

Which got him an angry bellow from his mother. "Get your foul-mouthed hide over here, young man!"

While their friend was being dressed down—along the lines of "Don't you understand what he's going through? What is wrong with you?"—Julius took Jody by the elbow and then led him over to the water, staring at him gravely.

"Seriously, it's not like you to fumble. What's up, bro?"

Jody peered across in the general direction of the New Jersey shoreline. The surface of the river was reflecting the tall buildings and the sky above, which was the same gray color it had been during the funeral.

"The mirrors. They're still bothering me, covered up the way they are."

Julius pulled a face and guffawed gently. "I was only kidding with you. Worried if you're still around? Of course you are. I'll demonstrate."

He punched Jody gently on the soft part of the arm to prove his point.

"No, it's not that." Jody tried to explain to him, struggling to find the correct words. "It's like … the house has changed. The place looked bigger when you could see mirrors. Now, it's like it's shrunk."

He didn't really want to mention the noises or the movement that he thought that he'd seen yesterday. That would sound completely crazy, and he knew it.

"It's called an 'optical illusion,'" Julius was telling him. "Seems like that way, but it's not. How long till the mirrors get uncovered?"

"Six more days."

"Okay, that's not so long to wait. Everything will all go back to normal when they're clear again. I promise, bro."

I n bed that night, he could hear his parents talking in their room.

"I don't get it, Paul. You're not even religious."

"But he was, deeply, his whole life. It's a mark of respect for him."

"It's so damned inconvenient."

His Dad's voice rose a little. "And that's *all* it is—a temporary inconvenience. I never ask much from you, do I? So can't you respect my wishes just this once?"

Jody thought he understood the problem. Mom was very beautiful and knew it. She nearly always wore makeup, and was very fond of buying clothes and trying them on again as soon as she got home. She could spend whole hours in front of her vanity, deciding which accessories went best with each new outfit. And now, all of that was being denied her.

"I've brunch with the girls tomorrow," he could hear her complaining. "And I'm supposed to turn up looking like a wreck?"

"Get there early. Use the mirror in the restroom. Honestly, I don't want to hear any more about this."

Their voices trailed away, and Jody fell into a doze. From which he was awoken, some while later, by another kind of noise.

There was a night-light on beside his door. It was very dim, and gave the objects closest to it merely the narrowest semblance of reality. But those included a small mirror, the only one inside his room. Except that Dad had covered it with a pillowslip.

That breeze-like sound came drifting to Jody's ears again. And then the fabric seemed to move.

Jody lay dead still, his heart pounding and sweat forming on his forehead. Was there, he wondered … was there something coming through?

But he caught on to something else, after another while. It wasn't really a sound like a low wind he was hearing. It was far more like a sucking noise. As if there were some kind of vacuum trapped behind the cloth, and it was trying to draw the oxygen beyond it inward.

As he watched, the pillowslip became a little concave at its center. But then it loosened, flattening out again

He was *sure* that he had seen it pucker, though. Jody found that he could barely sleep at all for the entire remainder of that night.

Mirrors. Their only job, their sole purpose in this world, was to reflect stuff. And since they weren't being allowed to do that anymore … what exactly were they doing? What had they become?

Jody prodded at his breakfast cereal, feeling pretty tired and rather disoriented too, like he was lost in his own home. Dad had left early for a meeting today, and Mom was in an uncharacteristically bad mood.

"Do I have a zit?" she asked him rather crossly, rubbing at her cheek.

"Er …" he mumbled, "yuh, you do."

"Do I have my finger on it?"

"No, Mom. It's a little higher up."

"This is *ridiculous*!"

And she went away to find some ointment.

Since there were going to be no grown-ups in the house for the rest of this morning and the best part of the afternoon, he wasn't being allowed to stay here. And when the doorbell rang, Julius was there again, this time with his teenaged sister, Ayesha.

"You not dressed yet? Man, it's ten o'clock already."

Jody hurried up to his room and dragged some clothes on, but then remembered that he still needed to brush his teeth. On his way to do that thing, he passed by his parents' bedroom door, which was hanging halfway open.

Mom was standing in front of the wardrobes. She had pulled one open and was staring at its reverse side. Jody knew that there was a tall mirror fastened there, but—like all the rest—it had been covered.

Mom was looking very thoughtful, as if she were contemplating something. And he believed he knew exactly what that was. Jody felt a twinge of nerves, remembering the stuff that he'd experienced last night. But he told himself that Mom was far older than him and knew a whole lot more, and so could arrive at her own decisions. So he went on past, feeling reasonably certain that she'd be okay.

When he came wandering back, sucking at the straggling bits of toothpaste lodged against his gums, the bedroom door had drifted almost shut.

Mom didn't answer when he called out 'bye' from the foot of the stairs. Either she was still in a bad mood, or she hadn't heard him.

Julius's family lived in a big penthouse apartment overlooking Washington Square itself. His room was three times the size of Jody's, and was filled with every kind of electronic gizmo that you could imagine. And there was a broad terrace beyond it that looked down onto the sidewalk. Once they were satisfied that there was no one taking any notice, the two boys put the games aside, then went out and tried blowing gobs of spit onto the heads of passers-by below.

Five o'clock had come around before they knew it. It was time to go back home. Ayesha walked him back to the West Village and then rang the doorbell for him.

She looked puzzled when there was no answer. Tried again, with no better result.

"You got a key, young man?"

"Uh-huh," Jody nodded.

The house turned out to be entirely empty when they let themselves in.

"She ever this late back from brunch?" Ayesha asked.

"I don't think so."

Ayesha looked a touch exasperated, but she stayed with him until his dad got home. Dad seemed in a very thoughtful mood, and barely took in what was happening at first.

But finally, he speed-dialed Mom's cell. Moving up closer, Jody could make out the flat, dull pitch of an automated message.

"The number that you dialed has not been recognized."

"What the—" Dad grunted, his expression hardening and his brow creasing up.

He dug out an address book from the bureau in the den and started calling Mom's friends, concentrating on the ones she'd told him she was supposed to be meeting.

"Did Carol show up at the restaurant?" And then, when the answer was obviously no, "Do you know where she went instead? Did you get any kind of message from her?"

"Ayesha?" Dad blurted, once he'd done that half-a-dozen times. "I hate to impose on you, but could you hold on here for ten more minutes?"

He went out again, and wasn't back for twenty.

"No one's seen her. I tried all our regular stores," he said when he returned. "The restaurant where they were supposed to meet is not even two blocks away, so where could she have gone?"

The police didn't register a missing person for at least twenty-four hours. But he called his editor at the *New York Times* and explained the situation. He got passed through to the metro desk, and within another forty minutes there was a plainclothes detective at their door.

"How were things between you, when you left?" the man asked casually, once he had stepped in.

"We had …" Dad was looking slightly awkward and off-balance, "a mild disagreement last night. Nothing, really. Not even a genuine argument. Honestly, nothing to cause her to …"

He stared at the floor, then explained about the covered mirrors. The detective seemed to know about the old tradition, in spite of the fact that he was Hispanic in origin.

"Not too much to get upset about," he nodded, accepting Dad's point. "Certainly not cause to leave. Who was the last to see her?"

Jody piped up, "I was."

"Okay, then. Show me where she was."

Jody led his Dad and the detective upstairs to the bedroom, and then pointed to the exact spot. The wardrobe door was still wide open, but the cloth over the mirror, it had obviously been moved. It was down at one corner, like somebody had lifted it and then allowed it to drop back, and gravity had done the rest, the fabric shifting off from true.

The detective reached out, fingering the material.

"The only thing that I can do, Mr. Isaacson," he explained, once he'd clenched his teeth and drawn some air in through them, "is file a report. I'll check with the hospitals, of course. It could be that she met with somebody she used to know, or else got otherwise distracted. There are a dozen explanations really, none of them particularly bad ones."

He and Dad both turned around and left the room, still bouncing ideas back and forth.

But Jody remained where he was.

He began looking around the bedroom, staring into every corner of it. Except that—almost as soon as he had started—a sudden rushing noise brought his gaze jerking back around. The swath of cloth had slipped completely off the mirror. It had already been hanging loosely, and the detective's rough touch must have finished off the job.

God's week wasn't up yet. Jody almost cringed as the long stretch of silvered glass came into view. He raised his hands and nearly closed his eyes.

Then stopped.

The only thing that he could make out was his own reflection. This was just an ordinary mirror, nothing more. The fact it had sat there covered hadn't altered it in any slightest way.

And he was still concerned about his mom, for sure. But relief flooded through him.

He was about to turn away from it, when he was brought to a sharp halt by yet another unexpected sound. A shallow thump, on this occasion.

There was a fresh, damp handprint on the mirror when he glanced at it again. And it wasn't his—it was too large. The fingers were long and slender, like a woman's.

It was only when he reached out, tried to touch it, that he realized the print was not on his side of the glass.

It began to fade, the thin dampness evaporating. In a few more seconds, it was gone.

Mr. Smyth

Two things happened to Alvin Baker's face when—after a while of rapping with his knuckles—the door to the apartment around the back of Covent Garden finally came open. His dark eyes narrowed sharply. And his nostrils became slightly pinched.

The cause of the latter? A smell came issuing from the ex-council flat he had encountered many times before in his years on the Force. That neglected odor, unattended dust and mustiness and long-ago fried food, underlain by a sharp tang that people usually identify as cat's pee. Alvin knew, from long experience, it wasn't always that. More commonly, it was just age-old dried-up sweat—the smell that accumulates when rooms are never aired, and the perspiration of their occupant lingers like an indelible stain on the stale atmosphere.

As for his eyes narrowing ...?

This was an old, four-story, thirties-built apartment block, tucked away discreetly behind Long Acre. Covent Garden is littered with such developments, though most people passing through the area, on their way to the Piazza, never even realize that they're there. And this gentleman? Looked as though he'd moved in when the place had first been built.

That wasn't quite the case, Baker took in when he looked a little closer. This guy wasn't *actually* in his seventies, just in his fifties-going-on-seventies. The type who most definitely did not take care of himself.

No taller than five-foot seven, though he stood with such a pronounced stoop he looked even shorter. Skinny arms and legs and neck, and yet a big paunch around his belly. Hair? Black, quite greasy, badly pattern-balded, in spite of which he wore it at the same

63

length that he must have thirty years ago.

His pallor was gray, his face full of creases. And he couldn't seem to get his pale eyes more than halfway open.

Baker recalled what Daniella Pearson had looked like, stretched out naked on the coroner's table, and wondered if he had made a mistake here.

And so, "Mr. Smyth?" he asked. "With a 'y'? Mr. Martin Edward Smyth?"

The man nodded suspiciously. Baker held out his warrant card.

"Detective Sergeant Baker. Can I have a word with you? Inside?"

There was a moment's hesitation Baker recognized immediately. That brief period of mental cog-whirring during which a person wonders whether such a thing as a black Police Detective Sergeant—here in good old London Town—is even possible. Then—having obviously decided that the warrant card was real and not some ruse employed by muggers—the man nodded.

"What's this all about?"

Baker didn't answer him immediately.

He had stepped directly into the small living room—there was no hallway. And, looking around now, everything he saw bore out that original odor.

The curtains were half-closed and looked, by the stains on the sill, as though they were always that way. The glass beyond them? Smeary. Badly so. Baker could only vaguely make out a building identical to this one directly across the narrow street.

The room hadn't been dusted in what had to be a year. The furniture was very old, its brown-and-yellow pattern badly faded. There was a plate with a bare fishbone on it sitting on the dining table.

Bookshelves, everywhere he looked. Baker peered at a few of the titles. History. Astronomy. Wildlife. Travel.

"You read a lot, Mr. Smyth," he observed.

"Anything and everything. I've always liked to read."

Baker came to a framed photograph. A younger version of Smyth, arm in arm with a plain but beaming woman.

"Your wife?" he enquired.

"Passed away eight years ago," the answer came back. "Cancer."

"I am very sorry."

Then he looked around at Mr. Smyth again, taking in a second time the way the man was dressed. Baggy, well-worn corduroys. A plaid shirt with a frayed collar. A loose, threadbare cardigan which only emphasized the man's posture and his paunch.

Daniella Pearson had been twenty years of age. Straight blonde hair that reached right down to the small of her back. A Pilates-slim figure, with high, firm breasts not even death could make droop. Evenly tanned skin. White teeth. Blue eyes.

And yet all the witnesses at the Three Greyhounds in Soho had sworn it. She had been all over this aging—no, *decaying*—man like a cheap suit.

When he peered at Smyth this time, it was almost warily. He just couldn't understand how such a thing could be.

And then … and then …?

And then there were the others.

The question 'what's this all about?' was still hanging between them, though.

So Baker did what he always resorted to when his thoughts were uncertain. He just got on with his job.

He produced a photograph from the same pocket as his warrant card.

"Do you recognize this girl?"

Smyth peered at it awkwardly. "I … think so."

"You were with her last Friday night. Got together at a pub in Soho. Went on for a meal—you used your credit card, which is how we found you. Can I ask, what happened after that?"

Smyth was looking quite concerned by now. "Is she all right?"

"She died of a fatal stroke in the early hours of Saturday morning."

"At that age?" The man shook his head, as though a mild blow had just stunned him. "That's … terrible. That's shocking."

Then Smyth realized that Baker was still waiting for an answer to his question.

"We came back here for a couple of hours."

Baker felt his eyebrows raise and simply couldn't help it. "Were you ... intimate?"

He already knew what the answer to that probably was, from the forensics results. But how the man answered the question? That, he thought, would be significant.

He was freshly surprised when Smyth nodded unabashedly.

"And then? After that?"

"She went on her way. She seemed perfectly all right. This is quite a nasty thing to hear." His pallor had grown even worse. "Is it all right if I sit down?"

The chair creaked loudly as he settled into it. A button on his cardigan rattled against the wooden frame. Even seated, the man was still badly stooped.

Baker stared down at him dubiously, quite unable to believe that he'd been capable of picking up a gorgeous twenty-year-old woman.

"Did you know Daniella previously to that night?"

Smyth's head gave a shake.

"You just ... hit on her?"

Smyth looked directly up at him, almost challengingly. "Am I being accused of anything?"

The lab had tested her blood for substances like rohypnol, GHB. Negative. One glass of wine less and Daniella Pearson could have even driven home. And so ...?

"You'll forgive me for saying this, Mr. Smyth, but there was ... quite an age difference between yourself and Ms. Pearson. And other differences as well—I understand that she was always very fashionably-dressed."

A gentle smile alighted on the man's face, at that point. "I've always had a way with the ladies, that's all. They don't care about how old I am or how I'm dressed."

He could say that again. Baker took out three more photos from his pocket, each a head-and-shoulder portrait.

"The thing is this, sir. We've managed to link you back to three more girls in the past few months. Jane Meadway. Katherine Marks. And Joanne Edwards. The oldest of them? Twenty-two. All beautiful. All dead."

Smyth studied the pictures and then nodded, realizing, perhaps, that there was not much else that he could do.

"I knew them too. How did they die?"

"Heart attacks in two cases. A cerebral hemorrhage in the third."

"All natural deaths, then?"

"That's right."

"No suspicious circumstances?"

"Apart from the fact that they were linked with you."

Smyth's pale slits of eyes met with his own a second time, and stayed there.

"I hate to repeat myself, Sergeant, but am I being accused of anything?"

He was right. Baker was forced to admit that as he walked back to the station house through the dimming London streets. This was a city at its most beautiful in the twilight hour, the ocher streetlamps starting to come on and suffuse the buildings with their glow, the glass-fronted restaurants standing ready for their first customers, the waiters polishing glasses and the tables all set out like pretty modern sculptures. Even the gait of the pedestrians around him had by now become much easier—the working day was done for the majority of them.

Mr. Smyth was *right*. They had found no toxins, no intoxicants, no drugs. The cerebral hemorrhage just might have been caused by a blow, and yet the coroner had looked extremely hard and found no signs of violence, nor even of restraint.

Which wasn't the end of the story. All four girls so young, and with no previous history of ill health. It just *couldn't* be the end of the matter. He knew it. So, he suspected, did Mr. Martin Edward Smyth.

He could only hope that his bosses agreed.

Baker kept on turning over in his head the astonished statements of the witnesses in each case, all of them pretty much amounting to the same general statement.

"She was beautiful! This really amazing, trendy, fantastically pretty girl! And she was all over this—what?—elderly geezer! Really dodgy-looking! Scruffy too! But she was treating him as though he were Brad Pitt!"

'A way with the ladies', the man had told him by casual way of explanation. That was the understatement of all time, now wasn't it?

Baker arrived back at his headquarters, talked it over with his D.I. and the Chief, and got the necessary approval.

In the building across from Smyth's, a number of flats were still owned by the council. And a couple of those currently were standing vacant. He'd have liked one directly opposite. As it was, he had to settle for one a story higher up than Smyth's apartment. That reduced the chances of his being spotted, he supposed. And he still had a reasonably clear line of sight into both Smyth's living room and his equally squalid-looking bedroom.

He tried to imagine Daniella Pearson, Jane Meadway, Katherine Marks and Joanne Edwards disporting themselves in there. Simply could not.

Mr. Smyth, it quickly turned out, never left the flat to go to work. Baker recalled the deceased wife. And—had there been insurance?

The man spent most of the day reading, only switching on the TV to catch up with the news. When he ventured out at all, it was to fetch in groceries, or collect a take-out meal that he had phoned ahead to order. Several times as well, he went up to the second-hand bookstores on Charing Cross Road, and returned with a pile of aged hardbacks clutched under his arm. Baker already knew how besotted with the printed word the man was, and so found nothing suspicious in any of that.

On Thursday, though—the third day after Baker had moved in—Mr. Smyth took a rather longer trip. The whole way up Charing Cross Road, across the junction at Tottenham Court Road tube station, down toward Goodge Street, then left. Baker only realized where they were both going in the last couple of minutes. The Middlesex Hospital on Mortimer Street. Which perhaps explained why Smyth was walking a little differently than he had before. Slightly more upright. Stiffer. As though apprehensive.

Baker trailed him the whole way to a door marked 'Cancer

Department, Outpatients', before figuring he could not sensibly follow the man in there. He'd be spotted in an instant.

Smyth emerged a half hour later, a tight smile on his creased face now and his manner more relaxed. He'd most probably just go home again, so Baker finally went inside.

There was a nurse in her late twenties sitting behind the reception desk. Pretty—though a bit too old for Smyth—with short, spiky-cut red hair and brilliant green eyes. They had a cynical and disappointed hardness to them, though, which Baker recognized immediately. This, experience assured him, was a woman who'd endured some serious man-trouble in her past.

Her gaze softened and she even began smiling, however, when he stood over her and identified himself. Again, he was familiar with this. She was the kind who very much liked the idea of a tall black man in his fit, lean early thirties, in a position of power and responsibility. Her body language became actually flirtatious as she started to answer his questions.

This despite the fact that she was answering him mostly in the negative.

Yes, Martin Smyth was a patient here.

But no, she could not tell him why. Or for how long. Confidentiality, you see.

He told her that the deaths of four young women might well be involved, hoping for some show of female solidarity. And it almost worked—she'd love to help. But she'd lose her job for certain. She was really sorry. Why didn't he get a warrant?

In view of the fact that no committed crime could even be proven, Baker thought that doubtful, though he didn't tell her that.

He ended up leaving the hospital with just her phone number—scribbled on the back of a prescription form and pressed into his hand—for his efforts.

It was all starting to add up in his mind, though. Smyth's prematurely aged appearance. The way the man had a noticeable paunch despite being skinny otherwise—bloating, rather than fat?

And Smyth's wife had died of cancer, hadn't she? How long had that taken? How long had the man been forced to watch?

That evening, Smyth did not follow his usual routine of reading and catching news broadcasts in his living room. He went into the bedroom instead. Switched on just the little bedside lamp, so that the room was simply limned with a dim yellow glow and remained filled with shadow. Then he knelt down by the bed.

Baker was standing at his window watching by this juncture, confident he'd not be spotted.

It turned out there was a drawer in the base of the bed. Smyth opened it, rummaged around inside, and then stood up holding a tome the size and thickness of several *Britannicas* pressed together. It had to weigh God knew how much, and he only handled it with difficulty. Nonetheless, he sat down on the edge of the bed, placed it on his knees. Opened it, apparently to a marker. And then appeared to start either reading from it out loud or else talking to himself, his entire upper body rocking back and forward as he did so.

It was the former. He was reading. That became apparent when he turned a page.

After a long while of this, something happened which made Baker stiffen.

The farthest corner of the room across from the foot of the bed? It was entirely lost in darkness, the lamp-light not even touching it.

And yet … something seemed to move, inside it. Somebody was there.

Which was, to Baker's mind, impossible. All access to Smyth's building was external. There were flights of railed-in concrete stairs out at the front, then open-air walkways which took you to the ranked front doors of the apartments. Smyth's was in clear view.

And he'd seen no one enter or leave the development for the whole past hour.

There was no other way in or out. So how were there now two people in Mr. Smyth's bedroom?

Were his eyes playing tricks on him? No, he was certain there was someone there, though he could not even make out a distinct shape. He thought he saw an arm move at one point, but might have been wrong about that.

Smyth just kept rocking and jabbering for what seemed another age.

And then he closed the book, replaced it in its drawer. And went back into the living room, switching off the lamp as he went out.

The bedroom window was a rectangle of perfect blackness now. Baker, though, gazed at it for a good while longer, quite uneasily. Could there be someone staring back?

The daylight hours of Friday passed entirely uneventfully. Reading. Watching TV. The normal routine. Smyth went to McDonalds for his lunch.

By early evening, though, he had started to become a touch more agitated than was usual.

Set aside his books and his remote. And started pacing the living room, his head bowed even lower than ever. Appeared to be talking to himself again, but turning things over now rather than reciting from a page.

By eight o'clock, he had taken off his cardigan—he even slept in the damned thing—and replaced it with a battered-looking jacket. He counted out some money from another drawer and stuffed it in the pocket of his corduroys. Then went out.

Up Long Acre and past Leicester Square and then the Cambridge Theatre, into Soho, Old Compton Street. He disappeared into the Three Greyhounds, the same pub where he had picked up Daniella Pearson.

It was a small establishment. Baker, again, could not follow him inside there without being seen. Fortunately, there was a larger, very trendy looking bar with seating by the windows just across the way. Baker settled down in there, ordering a half pint of dry cider—he had never taken to beer—and watched through the glass as the scene unfolded.

There were three girls standing chattering in a corner of the Greyhounds, all of them barely out of their teens. Mr. Smyth just walked across and singled out the most attractive of them—a

71

Just as the witnesses had described, she was all over him immediately.

shapely brunette with faintly olive skin that spoke of something Mediterranean in her ancestry. When he began talking to her, she appeared to forget all about her friends and they, likewise, seemed to forget her.

Just as the witnesses had described, she was all over him immediately. Standing right inside his personal zone, staring deep into his eyes. Laughing, or else vigorously nodding, at every sentence that dropped from his mouth. Within a minute, she was taking every opportunity she could to brush a hand against his jacket. It was startling to watch.

After half an hour of this, they went to a nearby trattoria, shared a meal. Once again, Baker found he could watch them from a bar nearby.

They didn't bother with dessert or coffee. Finally headed off for Covent Garden.

By the time that Baker got back to the window of his apartment, they were both inside Smyth's bedroom. The girl was just undoing the top button of her blouse when the hunched man pulled the curtains shut.

Baker pulled a chair up to the window and then slumped down in it, his head rocking gently. Unbelievable! Quite literally so.

It was forty minutes later when the girl reappeared, fully dressed, at the front door.

Smyth, apparently, was no gentleman, since he wasn't even there to show her out. The girl seemed quite unbothered, though. She simply headed off along the walkway as though nothing unusual had happened, and went tripping down the stairs.

She paused, however, as she reached the bottom. Her head gave a brisk shake. And—a look of surprise seemed to cross her features, as though she had just awoken from a dream.

She appeared a little startled, now. Her whole bearing was stiffer. And when she walked off from the building, it was quicker than she'd walked before.

Baker decided to follow her and ask exactly what had happened. *Why* it had happened. That was the real issue, wasn't it? She was moving at such a pace, though, that he only caught up with her again at bustling Cambridge Circus. There she was just a few dozen yards ahead, her back to him, waiting for the lights to change. Perhaps she was headed for the tube.

The lights went red before he could reach her, and she started to step across. The whole place was thronged by this time on a Friday evening. Baker called out to her nonetheless.

"Miss?"

Had she heard him? Certainly, her pace had suddenly faltered.

He was almost running to catch up with her by this time. "Miss? Please, wait a minute!"

She reached the far curb and then ... stopped. Put one hand to the side of her head, just as though she had an earache. Wobbled for a moment.

Then collapsed, right there in front of Baker's quite astonished gaze.

When he reached her, she was lying with both slim legs folded underneath her and her pretty, olive-tinged face turned toward the sky. Her eyes were wide open, but she was obviously seeing nothing.

There was a thin stream of blood leaking from the ear she'd clutched.

Breathing heavily and fighting to stay calm, Baker tried to find her pulse. Could not.

He considered using CPR. But what use would that be? She had died—surely—of yet another cerebral hemorrhage.

And if she was any older then twenty-one, then he would eat his warrant card, laminate and all.

Smyth had apparently gone to bed by the time he finally returned to the building—all the lights in the apartment were off. When the man at last answered the door, after an age of banging, he was in heavily creased and stained pajamas, with that cardigan slung over them.

He looked annoyed. His mouth came open as though to ask something. Baker just shoved past him and went straight into the bedroom. Knelt down by the bed and yanked open the drawer there.

It was *full* of books. All bound in black leather, with gold lettering on them. Latin titles. Pentagram inscriptions. Pages edged ink-black, or blood red. He flicked through a couple of the volumes. There was aged, tight-packed script, and illustrations, some of them obscene.

Presumably, he had got these from the same sources as his other books. Baker found the massive tome he'd seen Smyth reading just last night. Its title? *Modus Diabolici.*

When he looked up again, Mr. Smyth was standing over him, but passively, somewhat defeatedly, his thin arms by his sides. All the same, Baker could feel his own breath wheezing in his tightened chest. He could scarcely even take this in.

"You've got cancer?" he asked the man.

And that got a nod.

"Just like your wife?"

Smyth nodded again, but then thought to add quietly, as though explaining something, "She took well over a year to die. And in such terrible pain."

"And you knew the same was going to happen to you. The doctors couldn't help. So you called up something? Something dark?"

Smyth looked as though he was going to deny it, at first. And then he seemed to realize, in that same small moment, that this whole matter would never go—could never go—any further than this room. What exactly could the sergeant do about it? Who would even believe …?

And so, rather hesitantly now, he nodded for a third time.

"You still go to the hospital, though."

"It's still there, a distinct shadow on the X-ray. But it hasn't grown, it hasn't spread. It doesn't cause me any pain. But it's still there, perhaps always will be. It's how He keeps a grip on me."

"The girls? The way that you seduce them? That's a power granted to you, isn't it?"

The next nod was a somewhat shame-faced one.

"What happens after that?"

Smyth turned his face away as he answered. Just a little, though. Not enough to stop Baker from seeing that his lips were trembling

75

slightly, and his pale eyes had filled up with tears.

"It's not just that they're beautiful, you see?" His voice had developed a croak by this stage. "That's important, but it's not the total picture. I always choose a girl—I seem to have developed an instinct for it—with a lovely personality as well. Kindly. Friendly. Chatty. Really nice. Someone I could fall in love with easily. Someone who I usually *have* fallen in love with by the time we get back here. A man my age, after all?"

He stopped and cleared his throat before continuing.

"There has to be a sacrifice, you see. A genuine loss. The giving up of something that has real significance to you. Someone you care about."

He faltered again, and his tone became even quieter.

"After that, when she's gone off home, it's just a matter of saying three words. That's all. That simple."

"They being?" Baker asked him, very softly and intently.

Smyth's face turned completely away for a few extended seconds. Then he seemed to gather up the strength to look directly down at the policeman.

There was anguish written on his features, shame, and self-disgust. But there was something else in his eyes, deep below the tears. Defiance.

That flinty, unfaltering defiance which is born out of our deepest instinct. Survival. Self-preservation.

He even looked faintly pleased with his own cleverness when he told Baker what the three words were.

"'Take her instead'."

The Crows

"**I**'ve always disliked them intensely," Marjorie said. "They're bullies and they're thieves, and even murderers."

The crow, as if aware that it was being talked about, shuffled sideways a few inches on the garden fence, the friction of its claws producing a sharp, brittle rattling.

"They mob other birds and steal their food, and they'll kill anything smaller than themselves, no matter what it is. But that's not the worst thing about them, no. It's the way they look at you. As though ... they're waiting for you to make a mistake."

Howard Danwell looked up from his paper at the object of his wife's distaste, and felt himself shrug inwardly, although he didn't let it show.

"It's just a bird, dear," he murmured. "It doesn't think about what it does—it just follows its nature."

Heaven alone knew—as well—there were enough representatives of the genus *Corvus* in this part of England. You could see them almost anywhere you looked. Most trees had a couple perched in them. Why had Marjorie agreed to move out here in the first place, if she felt that way about a simple bird?

A faint air of bemusement hanging around him, he returned his attention to the newspaper. The Gulf Stream had begun slowing down, he was informed in the smaller print. The major glaciers were melting. All very bad news, apparently. He turned the page.

Events were spiraling out of control throughout the Middle East.

He was about to flip through to the sports' section and find out what was happening in the world of golf, when a banging sound brought his attention up again.

Marjorie had risen from her sun-lounger. Had picked up a stone, and actually thrown it at the bird, hitting the fence instead.

The crow, obviously, was no longer there. It was now sailing toward the half-bare branches of a massive oak tree in the field behind their house, to join its numerous friends.

Or were they family? Or both? He wasn't sure.

It was late autumn, but still fairly mild. Marjorie and Howard had only moved here, to the outskirts of Little Baddew, four and a half months ago. They had spent most of their adult lives in London. For convenience's sake, for work. But on reaching the age of fifty-five, they'd opted for early retirement and lived out the private little dream they'd always harbored. They had sold their suburban flat and bought a property in the green expanse of the Hertfordshire countryside, fifty miles north of the capital. They had a three-bed bungalow now, which gave them plenty of room when the children visited, and there'd never been that before. There were massive gardens front and back. They had fresh, clean air and a lovely view—the village was on one of the area's tallest hills. They had peace and quiet, in short, and everything they reasonably needed.

Looking south from their back garden, they could still see the outskirts of London, although the city was vastly diminished now. It had been turned into no more than a faint, hazy gray blur that sat like a strip of mercury on the far horizon.

That was the way Howard preferred it really, being distant from the place. Since he had never really liked it there.

The only downside to their new existence was the close proximity of the M1 motorway. It was less than half a mile from them, and on most days didn't bother them at all. But when the wind was blowing in the wrong direction, you could hear the snarling, jammed-up traffic. You could smell the exhaust fumes. It was, they supposed, a minor inconvenience. The plain fact of the matter? It was practically impossible, almost anywhere these days, to escape the sounds of traffic.

The afternoon wore on to early evening. The heat left the air, and an insistent breeze blew up, strongly enough to make their fences rattle. They both went inside and watched the evening news. There was more about global warming—big rivers in India were starting to run dry. And the next item was a fuller report from the Middle East. The senior anchorman, Jon Snow, talked to an 'expert.'

"And if the conflict does expand," he asked, "and Turkey and Saudi Arabia became involved …?"

Howard wasn't sure what that was all about, but it didn't sound exactly promising.

A massive thunderstorm broke out that night, that went on for hours and kept them both awake. He couldn't remember a time when there had been so much intensely violent weather. So perhaps the TV and the papers were right, and the climate really was changing.

The crow, or one of its friends-slash-brothers, was back on the fence the next morning, when he went out to do a spot of weeding. *Don't let Marjorie catch you,* bird, he thought with a small smirk. *She might not miss this time.*

But as he knelt down and set to work, he saw that—during her diatribe yesterday—she'd got one thing right. There *was* something unsettling about the way they tipped their little heads and peered at you. They were descended from dinosaurs, he reminded himself. All birds were. Little wonder, then, that they dispensed a slight air of unease around them. They were the heirs of monsters, after all, and had been in this world considerably longer than mankind.

The wind changed direction. The rumbling from the M1 reached the garden, and the bird flew away. It was off toward the oak tree again, which had lost more of its leaves. There were at least a dozen other crows perched in it. More of them were flapping through the gray-blue, dullish sky. There seemed to be so many around this neck of the woods. Were there more crows than there'd ever been?

If that was so, then it was rather odd. Because there seemed to be *less* of most things in the natural world these days. Fewer butterflies twirling on the air. Fewer frogs in ponds. Even fewer sparrows in the hedgerows, and there'd always been plenty of those when he'd been a child.

Far more crows, though? Was that possible?

He watched as a couple more alighted in the branches of the oak.

Howard was gazing at them, starting to get lost in a strange moment of reflection … when a squeal of tires and then a low thump, from the lane outside their bungalow, brought his attention sharply around.

He hurried out front, praying no one had been hurt. It turned out to be only a dog, from one of the neighboring houses. Mitzi, he believed her name was—a cocker-spaniel bitch, about three years old. She had escaped from her backyard and run across the street, straight into the path of a brand-new Chrysler Crossfire. The man who had been driving it didn't look apologetic. He was in a smart, dark suit, had a briefcase on his passenger seat, and was apparently on his way to a business meeting somewhere. And now, he was having to explain to Mrs. York why her pet was lying sprawled out on the road, its entrails showing.

"I didn't even *see* the thing!" he kept repeating angrily, as if she weren't listening to him carefully enough.

A small crowd was beginning to gather. Howard looked around.

He could still see the big oak tree from this vantage point. But it was almost empty by this time. Most of the crows had left their perches on it and had flown here instead. They were on the roofs, the fences, telephone wires, everywhere he looked. Hoping for a free meal, perhaps? He recalled that they were scavengers as well.

But they were simply waiting. Simply watching.

And the way they cocked their heads? The way they pointed with their beaks, the intense glaze in their small eyes …?

It made Howard become slightly thoughtful, all over again.

The news on the radio, next morning, contained nothing good. Saudi Arabia had, indeed, become involved in 'the conflict.' Squadrons of its fighter jets were striking at targets even now. And a hurricane, springing up out of nowhere, had destroyed half of Bermuda.

Things got even worse, however, when he went outside. Iris Colville, one of their next-door neighbors, came up to the garden fence with tears in the corners of her eyes and asked him, "Jack and Betty Willows' boy, Daniel? Have you heard?"

The young man, he already knew, was something of a local hero. A strapping, handsome, clean-cut sort of chap—he'd met him one time on the high street—Daniel was a lieutenant in the Royal Marine Commandos, and was currently serving overseas.

Iris explained the rest. He'd been in a helicopter near the Pakistani border, going on a mission with his men, when a missile of some kind had brought it down. There'd been no survivors. Jack and Betty had received the news at the crack of dawn, and word of it had been spreading through the village ever since then.

"I suppose there'll be a funeral," she sniffed, touching gently at her lips. "I don't know when. How long do you suppose it'll take them to bring him home?"

He couldn't even guess. But how absolutely awful. Such a fine young man.

Howard tried to put it out of his mind and get on with mowing the lawn, when a sudden shower drove him back indoors again. The rain, where it had touched him, felt curiously warm.

He turned around, once safely through the patio doors, and looked back. And could see the raindrops were leaving dirty streaks over everything they fell upon. They actually appeared to be full of dust.

And shouldn't rain … shouldn't it leave things cleaner?

The crows ignored it, continuing to flap and wheel against a sky the color of pale slate.

The funeral was on Friday. The days between were eventful enough—at least, according to the media, since nothing much actually happened here in Little Baddew.

A second hurricane had hit Bermuda, just as it was recovering from the first, and then moved on to the Carolinas. The Greenland glacier turned out to be melting at an even faster rate than previously supposed. Crops in Northern India were failing for lack of irrigation—famine alerts had been put out, whatever that entailed.

Bombs had gone off in Riyadh, Istanbul, Tunis, and Milan. Saudi Arabia had sent armored divisions into 'the conflict.' Turkey had only narrowly been persuaded not to join in, but was now having problems with militants of its own.

It all seemed so very complicated. Although, thankfully, it was all a good long way distant from here.

Almost the entire village turned out for the ceremony, so that the tiny parish church could barely hold them. There were outsiders in attendance too, Daniel's commanders and colleagues. Howard had never seen so many uniforms up close.

When they filed outside to watch the burial, he saw that some of them had picked up rifles. Betty Willows began sobbing uncontrollably. Her husband tried to comfort her.

The Commandos lined up to fire a six-gun salute.

Howard looked around, beyond the mass of silent people. The churchyard was full of trees, elms mostly, a few maples. And in their branches, on the steeple of the church itself ...

Dozens of black crows were huddled, staring fixedly down. They weren't after pickings this time. Couldn't possibly be. They couldn't know what was inside the coffin. And so, what had drawn them here?

Attending death? Howard wondered momentarily. *Is* that *what they're doing?*

But no, it was a ridiculous idea. They were only birds. They merely ... what was the phrase he had used?

Followed their nature.

He expected them to fly up when the first salvo of shots rang out. But they didn't do that. Didn't so much as rustle their wings or jerk their heads. Just sat there, perfectly motionless, as the rituals that marked the end of life were acted out below them. And that genuinely surprised him. He'd never seen any bird react that way— or rather, fail to react—to a loud and sudden noise before.

When they got back home, both of them hushed and rather

morose, it was still nagging at him. Marjorie went off into the living room and switched on one of her daytime soaps. And he took the opportunity to head back to the box room, where the computer was kept. Out of interest, he Googled "crows+mythology."

There were plenty of sites around the subject, as it turned out. A whole plethora of information.

Crows showed up a lot in Celtic and in Native American myth. They had been the 'eyes' of Odin. A certain Hindu goddess often took that form. The Babylonians and Ancient Greeks had legends concerning them too.

A sentence from one website caught his attention in particular. 'In many societies they are associated with death, since they show up in great numbers in the aftermath of battles.'

And was that why he saw so many of the large black shapes these days? Because there seemed to be, in these times, so much death around?

No, he told himself again, *you're being stupid.* He was just rather depressed today, and it was little wonder.

Later in the afternoon, he went on his own to do a major shopping trip. Which, when you lived in Little Baddew, involved driving to the supermarket on the outskirts of Pendlington. Which meant crossing the M1.

The traffic was stalled on the road bridge. The motorway swept beneath him like some huge gray roaring river. It was moving freely in the northbound lanes, but the southbound ones had stopped completely. Looking off to his right, Howard could see why. There'd been an accident. A truck was lying on its side. Several smaller vehicles were smashed up too, and there were police in attendance. He supposed that people had been hurt—how could it be otherwise?—but the ambulances were already gone.

Then he noticed something else. The spindly roadside trees, their leaves discolored from years of pollution, were filled up to brimming with small—from this distance—black shapes. Just as the churchyard trees had been.

The news got worse and worse as the days passed, till he could barely stand to read it, listen to it anymore. More disasters. And more battles. Further bombs, including one in Melbourne. The Turkish government was on the brink of being overthrown. He wasn't sure what that would mean or how it might affect him—all he wanted was a nice peaceful retirement.

The weather was bizarre as well. Howling storms came up out of nowhere, blasting through the night sky. Winds blew up— parched-seeming winds—so powerful they blew most of the garden fence down. It took him hours to repair the damage. And there was frequently an odor on the air like … electricity, or something on the verge of burning. It didn't smell clean to him anymore. No longer the kind of air he had expected in the countryside.

The next Tuesday, he saw that he was getting low on gas, and drove to the supermarket again to fill up in its plaza. He hated the stench of petroleum, and held the pump away from him as the little dials spun around. He'd read somewhere that the tiniest amount of benzene in the lungs could cause a tumor.

There was no wind at all today, for the first time in ages. Howard gazed in the direction of the motorway. He could not see the thing— it was below him, down a steep embankment—but could hear it very clearly. A pall of fumes hung over it, like some ethereal shroud.

Returning to his car from paying at the booth, he noticed something else. Something rather odd. About a dozen crows were circling, quite low in the air, above a white Mercedes transit van that was parked at the far end of the pumps. He stepped a little closer to it, wondering what was attracting them.

There was a driver inside, partly hidden by the reflective sheen on the windshield. Standing beside the vehicle were two young men in their late-twenties or early-thirties. They were either Indian or Pakistani. But cleanly-shaven and with fashionable haircuts, quite unlike those damned 'fanatics' people talked about so much. They were dressed in crisp, new-looking short-sleeved shirts and stonewashed jeans, and were both grinning broadly. They looked happy and excited. Maybe they were from the North, and going on a trip to London?

One of them took a mobile phone out of his pocket, punched in a number, spoke a quick few words. And then—to Howard's mild surprise—switched the phone off and dropped it into a nearby waste-bin.

Why had he done that? Was it broken? But it hadn't been a few seconds ago.

They both climbed in and the van headed off. The crows continued to wheel above it as it swung right on the roundabout toward the southbound section of the motorway.

Howard watched it vanish, wondering what that had been about.

The big white speck and the smaller black ones all receded into the distance.

More weeding needed doing when he got back. It always needed doing, the one thing in the world you could be certain of. A lot of men complained about this job, he knew—it was boring, played hell with their backs and knees. But he'd always been lucky when it came to his joints, and got a quiet feeling of satisfaction when he saw the end result. Keeping his surroundings neat and tidy was something that he'd always taken pleasure from.

Marjorie was in the lounge, watching more of her daytime soaps. The patio door was open—he could hear the actors talking to each other.

About twenty minutes passed before the feeling of unease began to gnaw at him again. His head came up. He peered across the fence. The oak tree was almost *full* of crows, as many of them as acorns. And beyond it?

The air, as well, was replete with them. They were perched or flying everywhere he looked. They were on most of the nearby rooftops, and clinging to pylons and lampposts.

He got up to his feet, a tightness spreading through his chest. So *very many* of them, today. And whose death might they be attending this time?

A sudden shout from Marjorie captured his attention. It sounded like she'd hurt herself, so he hurried inside.

85

More were coming the entire time, soaring inward from the north.

She hadn't. She was still in her chair in front of the TV, but sitting up rigidly. Howard's gaze went to the screen.

CHANNEL 4 NEWSFLASH, a banner at the top read.

And Jon Snow was back on, much earlier than usual, looking visibly pale and shaken.

"… two suspects were shot in the confrontation, one of them fatally, but a third managed to escape. Police are now looking urgently for a white Mercedes transit van, license number …"

When he read it out, Howard realized it was the one he'd seen on the forecourt.

"Officials are trying to avoid a general panic," Snow continued, "but an unnamed source from within Downing Street has told Channel 4 this."

His focus dropped from the autocue to a sheet of paper on his desk.

"'There is every indication that the planned attack this time is not conventional, but will take a biological, or even nuclear, form.'"

Even the seasoned newscaster had a noticeable quaver to his voice when he read that. He looked back at the camera rather glazedly, as if he was wondering what else to say.

"We'll … let you know more as soon as we have it."

Howard and Marjorie exchanged horrified glances. What kind of madness was this? What kind of frightful world, exactly, were they living in these days?

The light ebbed slightly at the windows of the living room. Which was odd, because it was only—Howard glanced at his watch—half past four.

That was when the clattering noises reached them. They fell across the house suddenly, growing ever louder, ever closer. Until they were coming from directly above the bungalow.

The couple went outside, as cautiously as if they'd both been caught up in the strangest dream. And stood there on the lawn with their heads tipped back, their mouths hanging open, tiny fluttering black shapes—great masses of the things—reflected in the cold gloss that had formed across their eyes.

The crows he'd seen before had lifted from the trees and rooftops.

87

And been joined by countless others. There seemed to be ... *thousands* of them, perhaps even *tens* of thousands. They were passing over the whole village, all of them flying in the same direction, their wings setting up a continuous busy racket. More were coming the entire time, soaring inward from the north. Yes, tens of thousands. Maybe even more than that.

Howard felt his pulse thump rapidly, his mouth becoming hot and dry. Of all the bizarre, unnerving things he'd ever seen! And what was even causing it?

"They're flying south," Marjorie pointed out, folding her arms around herself and shivering. "But it's ridiculous—crows *never* migrate all at once like this!"

He could see what it was the moment that she'd said it. His heart tried to freeze up in his chest. The inside of his body felt like ice.

But he turned around on the spot all the same, until he was facing the hazy gray blur that had sat on the horizon the past four and a half months.

And, gazing helplessly at the distant city, he knew that he was right about this.

"No, they're not migrating," he managed to get out, although his lungs could barely move in the slightest. "No ... they're heading for London."

By a Dark Canal

"God? God is just a bogeyman made up to scare children. Life after death? Wishful thinking. All religion, gentlemen, is simply superstition in much fancier dress."

The three new arrivals at the table stared aghast at the foppish-looking young man who'd just spoken, their cheeks coloring and their eyes becoming very wide. All their host, Peter Toorijen did, however, was to break into a smile.

"Gentlemen," he chuckled, "let me introduce you to Abraham Van Helsing, the most promising medical student in all of Amsterdam. Also the worst scoundrel, and the most opinionated fellow you will ever meet."

The man he had just described gave them an unaffected nod, showing no false modesty or embarrassment at all. If he was aware just how closely the three new pairs of eyes were studying him, then he displayed no awareness of that either.

He was in his early twenties and strikingly handsome. Broad-shouldered, very obviously muscular and fit. And yet his pallor betrayed a disdain for outdoor pursuits. His gaze was blue and very piercing. Long, unruly hair tumbled down almost to his shoulders, and by the flush on his cheeks he'd obviously been sitting drinking here for quite a while.

They were in the Heeren Van Amstel tavern just off Rembrandtsplein, and it was busy. Since it was late in October, a log fire was blazing in the grate. Serving wenches bustled past at regular intervals, all but the most homely of them drawing the prospective doctor's gaze. The atmosphere was thick with pipe smoke, and off in the corner of the room, several of Van Hesling's contemporaries were

89

engaged in an arm-wrestling contest.

"But …" one of the newcomers managed to come out with, "what you're saying is blasphemy, surely?"

"Your blasphemy, sir. My truth."

"Come on, now," the second put in. "If there is no God, what are we left with?"

"Ourselves and each other, sir. And scientific fact. That which we can test and measure. That which we can prove."

"We become God, in other words?" the third asked, very thoughtfully.

"That would be one way of putting it. Yes, perhaps."

"Have you ever read, Mr. Van Helsing, *Frankenstein,* by Mary Shelley?"

And those piercing blue eyes twinkled. He could see what his interrogator was now driving at.

"I have."

"And is that story not a dire warning against what you suggest?"

"I disagree. It simply points out, in a fairly robust fashion, that the possibilities before us are endless, and that being so, not all of them are good ones. It's the simple truth, but we should not be cowed by that. We should march bravely into the future, certain in the knowledge we are right and everything that came before us—religion, myth, superstition—was utterly wrong!"

It was an impressive speech, but this young Van Helsing seemed to forget all about it in the very next instant. Grabbed hold of the sleeve of a tall, red-headed serving girl who was just passing, pulled her toward him and asked her: "Matti, would you not spend the night with the most brilliant student in all this city?"

She smiled at him coyly, just a little malice dancing in those deep green eyes of hers.

"I already did."

"You *did*?" Van Helsing looked astonished.

"Just last month. You were drunk as a lord." Her coy smile flowered into something darker, though not truly cruel. "I spent a whole half hour under you, and I got nothing but a cramp."

The whole table burst into laughter. Van Helsing let go of her, a chastened grin alighting on his own eye-catching features. But he did not look humiliated, as most men of his age would have done.

"Well!" he remarked. "You find out something new about yourself every day."

Then, without further preamble, he stood upright, snatching up the cane that had been propped against his chair.

"Gentlemen," he announced, "it has been enjoyable talking with you, but I must be on my way. I believe it to be scientific fact that, if a grown man should retain his health and sanity, then he must go through the motions of breeding at least once a week. And if Matti will not oblige, then I must find another subject for my biological destiny."

The astonished guffaws that rang in his ears as he walked away? They pleased him, if the truth be told.

They proved, if nothing else, that he had made an impact.

A wind tugged at Van Helsing as he emerged onto the lamplit street. If he'd had owned a coat, he would have pulled its collar up—but he'd been forced to pawn it just last week to settle a debt with a vintner.

People went by constantly, either on foot or in carriages, all of them dressed more warmly than himself. He drew himself up straight, would simply brave it out.

The truth was, he was growing very tired of being a student and he yearned to graduate. Not just to earn a living, though that would be very nice. What he wanted most, he supposed, was … respect. To have people listen to him not just because he was being loud, outrageous, but because they thought what he said was worth listening to. Authority. Gravitas. These descriptions were beyond his reach thus far, and yet they sounded like music to the young man's ears.

The money would be pleasant as well, he had to admit. He owed all over town, and the dandyish manner which he liked to affect grew harder to maintain with each passing academic term. These had been his best clothes. But now, the lace at his cuffs was grayish-

... as the light revealed her features he could see that she was very pale ...

yellow, the pattern on his waistcoat was half-faded, and his breeches had the look of having been laundered a few dozen too many times.

Still, he had his youth, his rude health. Better to make good use of them while he had the chance. Though the city's canals, at this time of year, lent the air a chilly dampness which made him wonder, occasionally, if he would ever survive until these impecunious times became a fond, rose-tinted memory.

Van Helsing headed down in the direction of the Rokin and then, crossing a succession of small bridges, found himself in a district by the side of a pitch-black canal where there were no carriages and no families on foot. All of the men walking here were alone. As were all the women, who were mostly standing still.

Red lights shone from the windows of several of the nearby houses, although heavy velvet drapes hid the activities within. There were comfortable furnishings in them, Abraham knew. Free alcohol and music. And women of real grace and distinction. But the plain fact was that he had barely fifteen gilders in his pocket to last him the entire week, and so he would have to make do with one of the street girls.

He wandered among them now, being careful not to overly catch any single one's eye. His own practiced one was alert for the signs of disease. Many of these sad creatures were on the verge of cirrhosis, he could see. But it was afflictions of the venereal kind that he was on the lookout for and could see evidence of aplenty.

He almost had an instinct for detecting who was sick and with what sickness. Yes, he'd make a very fine doctor, one day.

And he had almost given up on finding a girl who combined good health with genuine beauty when, a block further along, a figure stepped into a streetlamp's glow.

Merely a silhouette at first, and yet a perfect one, as though cut out of black paper by the same Greek who had sculpted the Caryatids at the Acropolis.

His pace lengthened slightly as he strode toward her. And yes; as the light revealed her features he could see that she was very pale-complexioned, and yet healthy as a newborn babe in arms. He felt a stirring in his loins.

"Good evening, dear."

"And you, sir."

Her smile was rich, delicious. He had never seen skin so pale combined with such dark eyes. He could detect no accent, and yet … might her ancestry be Eastern European, even from some corner of the Russian Empire?

"It is my genuine pleasure to meet a young lady so very beautiful," he told her.

"*Name* your pleasure, sir," she next came back at him directly, "and I'll name my price."

Her room was at the far end of a little alley which he went down with his cane held ready, though no trouble came.

When she lit her lamp and it came properly into view, he was relieved to see that it was very clean and tidy.

"I'll be with you in a moment."

She retreated to the bathroom.

Now there was what he considered the greatest thrill of all in such encounters. The one of anticipation. *Knowing* what was coming next. The exchange of funds and then the partial undressing. The freeing of the hair, the laying back, the creak of bedsprings. What real joy there was to be had in such ritual. Though he despised all religion, he could understand it now.

The bathroom door came back open. Van Helsing turned around. To see, to his utter bewilderment, that the woman was shaking, almost crying. And that she was holding, grasped in both hands, a wooden stake, perhaps eighteen inches long and whittled to a sharp tip at one end.

What kind of madness was this? What fiendish perversion?

"Sir, please!"

And the woman thrust the stake into his numb, unwilling fingers.

"Drive it through my heart, please! End this nightmare for me!"

He could only stare at her aghast, since he had obviously chosen a madwoman.

"Kill me, sir! This is the only way to do it! And, once done, cut off my head!"

Any other man would have turned tail and run, but not Van Helsing. His 'biological destiny' was wholly forgotten by now. He was engrossed by this woman's dementia. Suicidal she quite obviously was—and who would blame her, living the life that she did? But why did she wish to perish by his hand and not her own?

He managed to calm her down enough to get her to sit on the edge of her soft bed.

"You wish me to slaughter you, behead you? But you realize that is murder, and I would go to the gallows?"

"No, sir." And by this time she was weeping freely. "It is only murder when you kill a human being. And there'd be no evidence besides, since my whole corpse would turn to dust."

Slowly, gradually coaxing her, he managed to get from the beautiful young woman her insane, demented story. One, she had not been a whore last year, but a seamstress. She had fallen victim to a fellow that she called a 'dark one' at that time, and now was forced to lure victims, innocent men, to her bedchamber like this, so that she could feed. Had become weary and repulsed by her existence, and wished nothing more than for it all to end.

"Let me get this straight?" he asked her once that she was done. "'Dark one'? You're saying an African of some kind forced you to sell your body on the streets?"

"No, sir; you don't understand at all! I fell victim to a vampire!"

Van Helsing grinned broadly. Of course, he had heard of the legend—everybody in a European city had. It had its current origin in the behavior of Vlad Dracul, ruler of an Eastern province off in the Carpathians, though wordsmiths had been turning it to fiction lately, most famously in a work attributed to Byron, though the English lord denied it.

"You …? But my dear, calm down. There is no such thing."

"If not, then why do I drink the blood of my customers, yes, several times a week?"

"You … really?" He was much stronger than her, and so was not afraid. "Show me then, dear, where are your sharp fangs?"

"They are concealed, sir, like a serpent's, and they only come out when I feed. Were I to show them to you, they would be the last things that you'd see. But feel how cold my hands are!"

She closed them over his, and yes, they were certainly quite icy. A circulatory complaint? Van Helsing wondered.

"If I were to hold a crucifix toward you, might you then cringe back?"

"A cross would only cause me pain when wielded by a believer. And you do not strike me, good sir, as much of a religious man."

How had she known that? Abraham's brow furrowed. It seemed that he was not the only person in this room with well-tuned instincts.

He tried a different tack.

"If you wish to end this terrible existence, why ask me to risk the courts by doing the job for you? Why not kill yourself?"

"A vampire cannot, sir. Survival is etched too deeply into our base natures. I chose you, sir, because you struck me as extremely strong in character from the first moment I saw you. Resolute and fearless. I have a sense for such things."

He could not help but feel a little flattered, even though she was completely mad. Van Helsing held the pretty woman in his gaze for a long while, wondering what to do. Then finally came to a decision.

"Dear, there is a man I know, older and wiser than myself, who might be able to find some way of helping you that does not involve stabbing or beheading. If I were to bring him here, at the same hour tomorrow, would you give him just that chance?"

Tears dripped along her cheeks as she nodded. And to Van Helsing's delight, she even managed to force a tight, wary smile.

What, in all religious imagery, could match a beautiful young woman's smile?

"I've never seen anything like it, Andreas. The most perfectly self-justified dementia I have ever come across. Every question that I asked her? There it was, an instant answer waiting on her lips. She could not show me her fangs because of such and such. I could not harm her with a cross and so on. She has constructed her own fantasy world in which nothing can be proved *or* disproved."

He was sitting in the study of his favorite Professor the next afternoon, his feet up on the desk. And was allowed to do so, and to call the fellow by his given name, because that favoritism worked both ways when it came to Professor Andreas Vander Hoog.

Who tugged at his small beard now, adjusted his eyeglasses, and said, "It is not as uncommon as you might think, Abraham. If a merely sane mind is capable of remarkable feats of creation, then think what a deranged mind might find itself capable of. But ...?"

He smiled at his best-loved student warmly, glad to have been brought such shocking news.

"She thinks herself a true vampire, you say?"

"Absolutely. Have you ever heard anything like it?"

Andreas Vander Hoog was, among other things, one of the world's leading authorities on mental incapacity—an advocate of gentle rehabilitation and a tireless campaigner against the bedlams that were now the rage—and so was exactly the right person to ask.

"I came across a lycanthrope once." Van Helsing's look of bewilderment brought a tighter grin to his face. "A woman who believed that, at certain times of the month, she would turn into a wolf. It was my strong belief that the cause was sexual, though no one would listen to me at the time. But a blood-drinker? No, never."

"Might this also be a sexual matter?" Van Helsing knew all too well how badly shocked the faculty would be if they were ever to eavesdrop on these private conversations that they had.

"In terms of self-loathing, possibly. Think. She does take strange men to her room. She drains them both of their loose change and of their vital essence. And, if she has been forced by circumstance down such a route, and was yet a respectable woman just the last year ... all the necessary elements are present for her to escape mentally into some inner drama."

"Do you think that you can help her?" Van Helsing next asked him straight out.

"That's what I like about you, Abraham. You see no case, no patient, in mere terms of academic interest. No, you genuinely want to help, and have the skill and wit to do just that. A great many people will be glad of you, one day."

"But …?"

"I don't know if I can help her till I see her, man. It depends how far along the path of madness she has gone. Seven this evening, you say?" The Professor withdrew his watch from its pocket and inspected it. "Well, we had best get prepared for this peculiar consultation."

He opened a drawer of his desk and took out from it a silver crucifix and a small leather-bound bible. And then, reaching further in, produced two little pistols, one of which he held across in Van Helsing's appalled direction.

"Andreas? We're two grown men, and talking about a mere slip of a girl here."

"In the first place," Vander Hoog replied, "you have to understand how very, almost inhumanly strong the clinically insane can be. In the second, even you must agree that vampirism is a violent fantasy. When we step off into the unknown, my lad, we surely cannot foresee every eventuality. That is in the unknown's very nature. But that does not excuse us from taking every last precaution we possibly can."

Van Helsing looked extremely thoughtful for a moment.

Then he said, "Ah, yes. I'll do my best to remember that."

She was there as promised when they knocked on the door. A fine rain had started up, and the smell of moldering, waterlogged leaves was drifting from the dark, nearby canal. Van Helsing, as before, was coatless and a touch bedraggled-looking. The Professor, by far the neater and more stalwart looking, took his hat and cape off as he stepped into the room.

He got her seated on the bed—just as his student had done last night—and let her once again recount her entire story to him. And, when it was done, glanced at Van Helsing with his eyebrows raised. There was not the slightest flaw in her tale, and they both could see it. Not a single contradiction.

"So." He turned his attention back to her, removing the cross and the bible from his bag. "If I were to hold these out toward you, would they cause you great discomfort?"

"Once, they would have done so," she responded. They had by now established that her name was Eadie, by the way. "Once, sir, you were in possession of a solemn belief in the power of such things. That belief, however sir, has waned in recent years."

And the Professor looked astonished. Flabbergasted, almost.

"It is true. My mind has, in recent years now, taken an agnostic turn. But how …?"

"Oh, my kind? We just know."

Then she gazed at the pair, dully exasperated.

"You still don't believe me, do you? You both think me mad. What are you going to do, have me locked up? I can't countenance that."

"Just wait a moment …"

The older man had stiffened slightly, Van Helsing could see. Was trying to remain calm, but in vain. He had become taut with anticipation. And Van Helsing could understand why.

This Eadie? She seemed to be growing angrier with every passing second.

"What do I have to do?" she barked out. "How can I prove it to you?"

She was staring fiercely at Van Helsing by this juncture.

"I *asked* you to finish it all yesterday! It could be over and done with, you could be safe by now! Instead of which, you try to turn this entire matter into some kind of strange freak show. If I give you a real show, sir, will you countenance destroying me then?"

The next moment, a strange red sparkling flickered startlingly across her eyes. Her features contorted, all the tiny muscles bunching up.

Her mouth stretched wide open.

The long sharp fangs at the canines were revealed.

Van Helsing jerked back so hard that he hit the wall.

Eadie dove forward and buried her head in Vander Hoog's neck. The Professor could only let out the most stifled, the most pathetic of howls.

Was she …? Abraham could only stare aghast. Actually biting him? Actually drinking? The Professor was growing pale, seeming to deflate, before his very eyes.

Even if she *was* drinking his blood, the thought came to him, nobody could ingest it that fast. No one human, at least.

But it became apparent to him, after a few numbed seconds, that things were badly wrong here, and reality was not as it should be. The first thing to do, he somehow decided, was to drag the woman off of the Professor.

So he lunged forward himself and grabbed her by the shoulders, yanked. She would not budge. He tried far harder, actually getting one arm around her throat and then pulling with all his might.

It was as though she had been nailed in place.

Worse, she finally took notice of his efforts. And pushed him away from her as easily as though he were a child, with the fingers of just one hand.

And the next moment, without even looking around, fetched him a crack with her slim knuckles that sent him spinning across the room and slamming into a wall again, all the breath knocked out of his strong frame.

By the time that he'd sufficiently recovered to look up again, Professor Vander Hoog was lying sprawled across the carpet, quite unconscious at the very least.

And Eadie was advancing on him, her dark eyes still sparkling redly. His brain fought to think of some sane, medical explanation for that, and could not. Her fangs were still bared. And her fingernails looked sharper than they'd been before. They were now reaching toward him.

Van Helsing suddenly remembered the small pistol in his pocket, the one Vander Hoog had given him. And … thank you, good Professor! He pulled it out, cocked back the hammer. And then, when the woman still did not come to a halt, fired directly at her chest.

The lead ball left a scorched hole in her clothing that let out faint wisps of smoke. And yet there was no blood, no sign of injury at all. She did not falter, even for a second.

A lesser man's mind would have turned completely blank and helpless at that awful sight. Yet Van Helsing realized, even if he could not comprehend what was now happening, that he had better do something to save his own young skin, and do it very quickly. So his gaze darted around. And alighted on the chair by Eadie's bedside.

Lying there was the same stake she'd shown to him last night. He dived toward it. Snatched it up so quickly that he tumbled to his knees. Clasped it in both hands as she loomed over him.

And as she bent …

Lunged upward.

Abraham spent the rest of that darkest of nights sitting on the steps of a small church on Rokin, utterly motionless for hours, with his head clasped in his hands.

No, not quite utterly motionless, if truth were told. He wondered if the shivering that had taken hold of his whole body would ever quite stop.

The howls Eadie had let out when he'd plunged the stake into her heart. The way the blood had sluiced out from her, darker by far than it should have been. And when he'd brought a knife through from her kitchen and cut off her head …?

He knew it for a certain fact. There was no scientific explanation in the world for the way her entire frame had crumbled into dust.

Professor Vander Hoog, it turned out when he inspected him, was quite dead, drained of all his life essence in just a bare few seconds.

He had run away from there.

He had run mostly because he knew that … it was all his fault.

If he had not in the first place been so brash and so idealistic. So certain of his convictions. He could see it now. He had been certain, until this point, that *he* was the enlightened one. He, with his belief in only science, was the visionary, or so he had thought.

Now he understood. He'd closed his mind, dismissing beliefs that men had held down all the centuries. He'd just blinkered himself. And the man he most respected in the world had died because of that.

It was an hour before dawn when his head finally came up and he inspected his pale, trembling hands. And if the shaking never stopped? Then perhaps he deserved it.

Well, at least the thing was done. The entire awful thing was over. He could move on, build a new life for himself as best he could, though he couldn't even begin to imagine as yet what form it would take.

There were a few people about now, even at this early hour. A milkman with his horse and cart. Fellows going along the curbs with long poles, putting the streetlamps out. Vendors heading up toward the Flower Market to set out their wares.

Abraham walked slowly to the edge of the wide, glistening canal, gazed at his reflection in the darkened waters. Then, an instinct took him and his head came up again.

There were people moving on the far side too, in the direction of the district where Eadie had plied her gruesome trade. And one of them ... he only was in view for a few moments before disappearing around a corner. But ...

The little beard? The eyeglasses? The slim frame, and the hat and cape?

Had that been ...?

Abraham recalled the final part of the old vampire legend.

And he took in the truth, with an increasingly heavy heart, this whole business might not be over and done with quite yet. No, not by a long shot.

The In-Betweeners

Our main shopping street was closed to motor traffic a couple of years back. And since then, I have never felt particularly comfortable going there after dark. Don't ask me why, but there's something reassuring at night about the hum of a passing car, the fleeting glow of headlights.

Nowadays the shops close their doors at five-thirty, everybody leaves the area, and there is only silence.

Broken up, this particular evening, by my footsteps. I'd been forced to park at the edge of the zone and walk the rest of the way.

I was headed for the only pharmacy open at this hour of the night. Not that I was ill … but the single mother's little boy in the apartment next door to mine was running a fever. And understandably, she didn't want to leave him on his own. I'd offered to go out instead.

It was freezing, a biting wind coming in from the English Channel. Birchiam had only just emerged from the grip of the heavy snows that had descended on the whole of the UK. The streets might have cleared up, but the temperature had not improved a great deal. The town stretched off around me, black as anthracite to my chilled gaze. I was alone out here.

But how true was that? One moment, there was only the repeated clatter of my shoes. And the next, I thought I heard a voice. My head swiveled around.

Birchiam is a humble little seaside community. We don't get too much in the way of crime or violence here. But when we get the latter, it is usually alcohol-related. And I was just fifty yards up from the seafront, where several pubs were clustered.

103

"Don't know," came the voice again. "Could be."

My gaze darted to the right. A few streetlamps were broken, off in that direction. It was difficult to make out anything, at first. But then I noticed the small group.

They were standing in the shelter of what barely qualified as a lane. An access route to the backs of a couple of the larger stores. The only things I'd ever seen going down there were delivery trucks. And yet these kids had claimed it as their own.

None of them had even noticed me. Until, that is, I stopped and stared. At which point, instinct seemed to overtake them. Faces turned in my direction.

There were five of them, three boys and two girls. At a guess, I put them as fifteen or sixteen years old, one of the girls perhaps a little younger. Except that—typically for our burger-fed times—the boys were larger than I'd been at that age.

Maybe it was just the cold, but they were the palest-looking teenagers I'd ever seen. It was as though sunlight had never even wandered briefly across their flesh. And my immediate thought was *drug addicts*?

I felt myself tensing, for an assault that never came.

They just kept staring at me. Their eyes seemed huge in their gray-white faces. And had a glossy quality to them, made worse by the fact that none of these kids even seemed to blink. Their gazes bored into me. I almost flinched, it was so uncomfortable.

And then they turned away, seeming to forget me. They were in a circle, facing each other. And another word came drifting out, made dully echoey by the confined space that they were in.

"Suppose."

They were just a group of kids, out loitering for the evening, minding their own business. I supposed they had that right. And if a part of me wondered why anyone would hang around outdoors on an evening like this one …?

I believed I'd done some similarly stupid things when I had been that young.

I calmed down, took a shallow breath, and continued my journey to the chemist.

The little boy next door got better. And the temperature outdoors went up a few degrees. Not that it wasn't still pretty cold. There was a lot of rain. When you walked down to the seafront, which I did practically every day, the waves were high, the water a shade of gray that looked utterly lifeless and icy. Every time that the breakers crashed on the shore, a fine spray was blown across and hit you in the face.

The dead tramp was found at dawn the next Tuesday by somebody walking his dog. He was known to the police, and had been seen by most people in our town at one time or another. 'Old Henry' or 'Old Harry' … something along those lines. He was mostly seen wrapped up in plastic sheeting in one abandoned shop doorway or another, dividing his time between swigging from a can of cider, singing some vaguely obscene song, and holding out his grimy hand for money.

He hadn't drowned. He had *been* drowned, which was a big difference. The medical examination proved it. Somebody had held him down. The gulls had got to him before the walker with his dog had. It was the big story in the local news.

I went to the spot where he'd been found a couple of days later. It was about two hundred yards to the left of the old, broken-down, closed-down pier. And—despite the fact that it had been the main feature on provincial TV and in the *Birchiam Record*—there was not a sign that anything had happened. What exactly had I been expecting? Yellow tape and markers on a weather-ravaged beach?

The waves struck down upon the fine pebbles unstoppably. And a couple of gulls circled overhead, like they were still looking for scraps.

When I turned away, I saw the group of youths again.

They were on the far side of the beachfront street, and fifty yards closer to the pier than I was. Were bunched together in so tight a group they seemed to form one single body. All similarly dressed, in clothing that could have been either black or a very dark navy. Slightly shiny fabric, like they'd gotten it wet.

I couldn't see from this distance, but I imagined their unblinking gazes. We stared at each other for a few seconds, and then I got uncomfortable again and looked away.

When I turned my head back, they had moved. And in the opposite direction to mine. They had crossed the road, were on the way to the pier itself. And once they had almost reached it, they climbed over the seawall and headed down under its pilings. I had done that when I'd been a little kid, I recalled. My friends and I had pretended it was some kind of enchanted maze, down there.

But there was none of that eagerness to the way the group of youths approached the structure. They just shambled along the edge of the beach until the bulk of the old pier swallowed them up. And that was the last I saw of them, until the next occasion.

Birchiam was full of groups of kids like those ones, I began to notice. Maybe 'teens' was the wrong word to describe them. 'Tweens' would have been the better choice. Not children any longer, and so subject to harsher rules. But not adults either, so they had no purpose, and could not even invent one for themselves.

They hung around outside our town's little mall, or on random street corners, or in the car parks of pubs that they were not allowed to enter. Smoking. Drinking from cans. Swearing. Waiting to grow a couple of years older, so that they could stop being in between the rest of us, and find out what was really happening to their lives.

They were stranded, marooned. Becalmed. And because of that, they frightened people, much the same way they had frightened me that first night. So much energy and so little to do with it in a small town like our one. It was like discovering a small cluster of time bombs, with no way of knowing exactly when they were likely to go off.

It was February by now, still freezing. An old school friend who'd moved to London had come back to visit his aging parents, and had suggested that we meet up at a restaurant that night. He had no way of knowing that La Bella had been swallowed up by the pedestrian zone, and got so few patrons these days it was on the verge of closing down.

The standard of the cooking had collapsed accordingly. We both ordered lasagna that tasted as though it was coated in cheese-flavored plastic. But we tried to ignore that, laughing and joking and catching up on each other's news. London sounded like an interesting place, but I wasn't sure that I could live there.

On the way back to my car, I heard another voice. And not a a few dull, muttered syllables, this time.

"Who the fuck you staring at? What's wrong with you ... you stupid or something? How'd you like a bunch of fives?"

The group that I'd originally seen were back in that side lane. But another group, half a dozen older boys, had decided to confront them. They all had the look of being drunk, and I supposed they'd wandered up here from one of the nearby pubs. They appeared just about old enough that they could get away with being served.

The one who had been shouting lurched forward and raised a fist.

"You gonna answer me or what?"

The younger kids stared at him glassily, their expressions impassive.

"Suppose," one of the boys said.

"Suppose what?"

"Maybe."

The older youth swung at his head. Specifically, at his mouth.

Which suddenly expanded, and swallowed up the fist and half of the forearm behind it.

The rest of the drunken mob flailed back. I could only stand there, unable to take in what my eyes were seeing.

"Aahhh! Get it off me!" the attacker yelled.

Then he screamed with pain.

Somewhere between the restaurant and my car, I had to have fallen asleep. I kept trying to tell myself that. In which case, why was I still standing up? I had to be dreaming that as well, the same way I was dreaming the rest of this. It was the only explanation. This could not be real.

When the boy's arm slid out of that unnatural mouth, the fist was crushed and bleeding. He went away howling down the street, with his friends scurrying around him.

The face that had contorted had returned to normal. I was the only person out here with the group of teenagers by this stage. My mind was almost wholly blank, and there was very little strength left in my arms or legs.

They began to move toward me. Had to all be wearing rubber-soled shoes, because their tread made only a subtle smacking noise on the dampened concrete. I managed to draw back into some deeper shadow, frightened they would see me. Braced myself for what might happen next.

But they were only exiting the alley. Didn't even seem to realize I was there.

As soon as they'd reached the main street, they turned left and headed for the seafront once again.

They paused when they reached it, and took another left, in the direction of the pier. I stepped out from cover, just before they disappeared.

No human being could have noticed that. No one could have heard.

But several of their faces swung around, their gazes fixing on me.

And the only sensation I was aware of, after that, was running.

We hang onto certain rituals in our lives, the same way that our ancient ancestors used to. Getting into our car. Locking our door. Turning the ignition key. All acts of subservience to the God of Personal Safety. And then getting home and locking more doors. That had to be the most important ritual, ever since we'd left behind our caveman days.

I didn't sleep at all, that night. Every time I closed my eyes, I'd see that boy's whole forearm disappear inside those pallid features. What had I been looking at? Some kind of mutation?

It occurred to me the injured youth would have to go to the hospital. What story would he tell the doctors? He had not only been drinking. He'd been drinking underage.

There was something less than human in our town, and I was the only reliable witness to it.

The weather was still bitingly cold the next morning, with a heavy wind still blowing. When I looked out through my window, herring gulls were being spun about like scraps of paper overhead.

I made myself a light breakfast, then puked part of it up.

The idea came to me while I was washing my face with cold water. *The pier.* When I'd seen them on the move, they had been heading for the pier both times.

Spray struck me in the face again when I stopped my car and got out. It was too early in the morning for even the commuters who parked here for the train station to be in evidence, the seafront completely empty.

I went across the road beside the promenade, then clambered over the seawall. My feet hit the wet sand with a flat noise like a broken kettledrum. The light around me was as cold and dead as the sea looked, adding extra layers to the shadows underneath the pier. I could barely see anything until I went beneath it.

It had been closed down years back. No one ever goes out there. But human beings have a funny habit. If anything falls into disrepair, they don't simply leave it at that. They treat it with contempt.

Everyone had dumped their junk here. Up near the entrance, it looked like fly-tippers had been at work. Further along there were drink cans, plastic bottles, piles of cigarette butts, candy wrappers and discarded newspapers. There were even a couple of syringes and a condom.

I picked my way past society's droppings. The crashing of the breakers sounded like an earthquake, underneath this rotting wooden structure.

Then I stumbled over something that I hadn't previously noticed. I swiveled around, got my balance back, and inspected it.

The impact of my shoes had broken it up along one edge ... but it looked like, at first glance, a raised ring of concentric circles in the sand. Two feet wide, maybe eight inches high. They weren't perfectly even. Then I thought I might be looking at some kind of spiral. I was not completely sure, because the light was very dim back here.

They were like the casts left by worms that lived beneath the beach.

It couldn't have been fashioned by the motion of the sea. The tide never came up this far. So who had done this, some budding Dali, fashioning a surrealist sandcastle?

It looked wetter than the area around it.

I moved on and found another. Then a clump of them.

I had lived near the seashore my whole life, and thought I recognized the shapes. They were like the casts left by worms that lived beneath the beach.

But this size?

And there were other footprints all around me. But they could be anyone's.

I write for a living. Except I couldn't write for the rest of the day. Couldn't so much as lay the tip of one finger against an expectant key on my laptop. It would begin shaking before it got that far. What could I speculate about today ... the truth? Did such a creature actually exist in any normal sense?

Go to London, my mind kept telling me. Steel yourself, and finally make the move. To a place where the Earth itself is held in bonds of brick and concrete, nature and its vagaries kept mostly out. I had come across some kind of mutation; I was pretty sure of that.

As so often happens when you start out early in the day, the hours passed rapidly. Some rain hammered against my window at about three in the afternoon. An hour later, I could hear my next-door neighbor telling off her little boy for spilling something. But most of the rest was a shapeless blur. I barely even realized it was growing dark until I noticed that the streetlights outside had come on. The fact was, I was very badly confused, moving around my home like an automaton.

Some walkers went by on the street below.

And a few minutes after that, I heard someone mutter, "Mmm."

I thought I recognized the tone. It had a hollow, echoing quality to it. And when I had first heard it, I'd supposed it was the high walls around the lane shaping it that way. But that wasn't the case.

I had only turned one light on, in the kitchen, where I had been making coffee. So when I went back to my living room window, I was reasonably sure that I would not be seen. I eased my head around the edge.

The youths were standing there. But not just five of them.

There were about twenty. How'd they found me? They all looked similar, very pale and glassy eyed. Their faces were rather flat, with no freckles or marks that I could see. And they were still all dressed in the same manner, which was not unusual for bands of teenagers. Dark padded jackets, black or navy blue. Jeans of the same color. Heavy boots. There was something almost paramilitary about the way they looked.

I saw the nostrils of a couple of them suddenly expand, far wider than should have been possible. No words seemed to pass between them. But they all looked up, simultaneously, in my direction.

They started walking toward the double front doors of my apartment block.

Which were on an entryphone system. They could not get in without being allowed.

There was movement in the corridor outside a minute later, nonetheless. I turned off that final light and stood by the wall near my apartment door, holding my breath, wishing that my pulse would stop banging so loudly.

The wood shifted slightly in its frame. I thought that one of them was trying to prise it open. Then I saw something moving on the parquet floor.

It looked like a pale worm. No, several of them. And then dozens.

They were all attached, I could see as they came oozing in. A great gelatinous mass of some writhing pale substance formed a heap on my side of the threshold. And then began changing shape again, lifting itself into the air and taking on a figure and features.

The youngest of the girls that I had seen that first night stared at me unblinkingly. Her mouth dropped open. Her lips didn't move, but a word came belching out.

"Suppose."

It wasn't a comment. It was part of their disguise. They hung around the darker, more deserted parts of our town, mumbling the same kind of inanities that most teenagers did. Up this close, I could see her clothes were no such thing. They were part of her body, but a greatly darker shade. The glittering damp look appeared to be tiny little scales.

What were these things, some deranged experiment of nature? But they'd come from their home between the land and sea, and fitted in among us, without most of us even noticing.

There was more writhing near her feet. Several others of her kind were coming through. I knew that it was useless to lash out at them. I'd seen what had happened to the drunken kid.

And so I turned tail and ran, into the bedroom. Slamming the door. Locking it. It wouldn't be long before they got underneath that as well. I went to the window, sliding it open, the icy night air hitting me.

Tendrils were already appearing on my bedroom carpet.

This was the top story of the block, and there was no way down. No drainpipes and no balconies. Above me was the guttering alongside the roof. I grabbed for that. It groaned and shuddered slightly, but it took my weight, allowing me to pull myself the rest of the way up.

The tiles were damp. I slithered several times before I reached the ridge, and my pulse was thumping through my whole body, my breath like the panting of a hunted animal. Had my life been reduced to just a pair of simple choices—have those things kill me, or fall to my death?

Several worm-like shapes had spiraled up and attached themselves to the gutter. More were following.

Which made me scuttle along the top of the roof on all fours, my feet still skidding.

I reached the far edge. There was a sheer drop below me. When I glanced across my shoulder again, the girl and two larger boys were making their way calmly toward me, seemingly unbothered by the slippery tiles.

There had to be some way down. I looked out further, saw a tall, bare tree.

I backtracked several yards, stood upright, and ran again. And hurled myself into the air, my arms flailing desperately.

A branch slammed into my chest, tearing through my shirt and peeling flesh away. I managed to grab hold of it just as I was falling past.

It broke.

The next branch down caught me squarely in the small of my back, flipping me over. My fingertips clung onto it, but only for a second.

I didn't even get hold of the one after that. Simply dropped across it, so that it was pinned beneath my armpits for a brief while. Pain ripped through me. I hung there like a rag doll on a washing line.

And the next time that I fell, I hit the ground.

Both my legs were broken, though I only found that out much later. Consciousness left me for a while.

When I came awake, pain had become the new God of my world. It had invaded my whole frame, distorted my thoughts, and even blurred my vision. I stared through the haze above me. Vaguely, I could make out faces.

They were clustered around me, the whole group of them. Indistinct blobs of paleness and darkness. No one else had even noticed me falling. We were alone on the street.

They studied me a while. And then a mouth came open, I heard something blurting out.

"Could be."

They turned away, and melted off into the night.

I slipped into unconsciousness again.

Perhaps the drunken tramp they'd killed—down by the waterfront, near their home—had tried to attack them. After a couple of days, I came to understand why they had spared me.

The nurses in the hospital were efficient but rather quiet, the doctors businesslike in their examinations of me. And even while I was lying in traction, I was visited by someone who was obviously a psychoanalyst. I was being given medication, I was quite sure, that was intended to keep me calm.

A writer of bizarre, fantastic fiction, who was something of a recluse, had not changed his clothes or shaved in a couple of days, and who had thrown himself off the rooftop of his apartment block, only a nearby tree preventing him from taking his own life.

Who'd accept a word I told them?

Who'd believe me?

You?

But however hard he pumped his legs, he couldn't manage to run fast enough.

Sense

November, 2015

This area had changed so much. Pulling down the shutters on his tiny jewelry store late that afternoon, Frank Aaron was forced to admit it. When he'd been growing up here, this street would have been bustling, everyone preparing for the coming Sabbath. Whereas these days, it was practically deserted.

He clamped the heavy-duty padlock in place, straightened, and made his way home.

A good few of the neighboring shops had closed down, their empty windows covered up with flyers for rock concerts. Except that many of those were out of date. And had been covered, in their turn, by posters from the NBP, the Sword of St. George standing out prominently in the growing dimness.

'Nazis,' his friend Stewart called them. Frank wasn't so sure. The economy was in the toilet. The current party in office wasn't doing any more about it than the last one had. Maybe a fresh approach …?

He loved *erev Shabbat,* the evening of the Sabbath. The familiarity of it, the closeness. All the family gathered around the dining table as one bonded unit. The prayers said and the candles lit. It had been that way since he had been a little child.

At which point, Frank had an insight. He genuinely thought, the way most people in the country seemed to these days, that things needed to change. But at home, and in his personal life, he didn't like that word.

A yell brought his gaze up. On the opposite pavement, a group of half a dozen tall black boys—he thought they might be Somalis—

117

were tussling with each other. He was worried at first that it might be a gang fight. But they were only playing.

Frank watched them suspiciously. He knew that they were only teenagers, and he had been high-spirited at that age. But there was something deeply alien about them. And it wasn't the color of their skin ... he was friendly, after all, with the Olawis, two doors across from his house. Those were decent, lovely people.

These were ... what? Not at all like his little community. They cared nothing for family; doubtless their fathers were long gone. They cared nothing for education either; they could be seen out on the street during the hours when they should have been in school. And they talked constantly about 'respect,' but seemed to have not much of that, for the district, the people around them, or even themselves.

They'll integrate eventually, the way our people did, he tried to tell himself. But they seemed to have no will to do so.

He reached the corner leading to his street and turned down it, dead leaves blowing around his shoes. And was halfway along, when he heard footsteps running up behind him. When he glanced across his shoulder, the same six boys were hurrying toward him. One of them had produced a crowbar, seemingly from thin air.

He saw what they were going to do, and turned away, trying to escape.

But however hard he pumped his legs, he couldn't manage to run fast enough.

A COUPLE OF DAYS LATER

"**O**f course they're British," Ray Kingdom was saying, on the TV screen above the hospital bed.

Frank had a fractured skull.

"But why should this country be forced to import criminality? We've enough bad boys of our own, after all. We're a wicked lot, us Brits."

Most of the audience laughed.

118

"What the New Britain Party is proposing is this. Immigrants, and their children—'

"Second generation?" the interviewer broke in.

"Yes. If they're prepared to abide by the laws of this country, they're welcome to stay. But if they're not, maybe they'd be happier somewhere else. So we'd withdraw their citizenship and require them to leave."

There was a round of applause. And Frank would have nodded, but it hurt too much to move his head.

One disgruntled soul in the audience shouted, "You going to start gassing people next?"

"You're not listening to me. Anyone law-abiding is welcome to stay. Wouldn't that make for a better country?"

It certainly sounded like it made sense. The local elections were coming up. And he usually voted for some small, moderate party. Maybe he'd consider something different this time?

AUGUST, 2016

The Citizenship Act had been amended just last week to include third and fourth generation immigrants who committed crime. Frank had to admit, the area felt a whole lot safer. What had happened to him last year ... it wasn't common anymore. He felt glad of that. He still had partial memory loss, and suffered from awful migraines sometimes.

But things in general were looking up, he told himself as he walked home from the shop. Business was improving. Both his daughters had got into university. The world seemed more cheerful, and less cluttered.

A yell brought his gaze up. On the opposite pavement, a group of half a dozen white boys—each of them wearing a Sword of St. George armband—were following a woman in a burka down the street. They were keeping their distance, but were yelling at her angrily.

"What you dressed like that for, then?"

119

"You hiding something?"

"Maybe you'd be happier somewhere else?"

Frank couldn't be sure, under the long black robes that she was wearing. But the woman seemed to be teetering on the verge of trying to break into a run. The same kind of burst of speed that he had been forced to attempt last year. Dressed the way she was, though, she could never manage it.

He felt a twinge of sympathy for her, having been in a similar position once. But then he told himself, *What does she expect, dressed up like a crow like that? She's brought it on herself.*

And actually, he didn't completely trust Moslems, or like some aspects of their religion very much.

"We're talking fundamental differences," Ray Kingdom said on the TV that evening.

The General Election was coming up in a few months.

"Of course they're British, legally. But there is a direct opposition between Islamic attitudes and democratic ones. What we're proposing is this. They sign an affidavit stating that they put this country and its values first, and their religion second. Otherwise, they're not allowed to vote."

Which seemed reasonable to Frank, who had been born here and had always considered himself a patriot.

Someone set fire to the local mosque that night. Which saddened him, not least because he could still remember it when it had been a synagogue.

JANUARY, 2017

Everything had settled down at last. There had been weeks of riots when the election results were made known—a hung Parliament, with the NBP holding the balance of power. Millions of pounds worth of property had been destroyed, and three people had died.

"What's wrong with these idiots?" he'd complained to his friends. "They have to accept how the public voted."

Except his friends were getting fewer these days. A good number of the people who he'd grown up with had moved away to Canada, America, or Israel. He thought they were over-reacting. Ray Kingdom had never said a single word about their kind.

The local mosque had not been rebuilt as such and was now a Kwik-Fit car tire store. After the election, the NBP's researchers had matched the electoral roll to those people with Moslem names who had not signed the affidavit, and had used the expanded Citizenship Act to have them deported.

The area was still changing. Several eateries and stores had closed down, becoming bookmakers or off-licenses instead. It left the main street with a good deal less character, he had to admit. But was a little blandness so great a price to pay for better safety?

Mr. Olawi appeared from a parked car and stopped in front of him, looking grave and shaken.

"Luther, are you all right?" Frank tried to put a hand on his shoulder, but the big Nigerian shook him off. His eyes were bulging and seemed glassy.

"Toby was attacked last night." His eldest son. "A knife barely missed his heart. It was the same kind of thugs you people voted for."

Us people? He meant white? "How do you know?"

"They were wearing armbands."

Which proved nothing, Frank thought. But he was still mortified. He'd known little Toby almost since his birth—a fine, polite, intelligent boy.

"Which hospital is he in?"

It turned out to be the same one he'd wound up at after he'd been mugged. He visited, but Toby was sullen and uncommunicative for the first time ever. And as soon as he'd recovered, they all went back to Nigeria.

The family who moved into their house were not what he'd expected. There were five of them, a father and four teenaged sons. No mother in evidence. The father seemed to own no shirts, and went about constantly in his under vest. The sons were all crop-headed and wore armbands. They seemed to drink from cans constantly, crushing

121

them up and tossing them in the gutter. They were always out on their front porch, and continually making noise.

He went across rather nervously to ask them to tone it down a little when they disturbed the prayers on *erev Shabbat.*

The eldest boy started to get up, his eyes ice cold, his mouth puckering. His fists clenching. When suddenly, the father appeared in the doorway. Laid a hand on his son's shoulder. The boy settled back down unhappily.

"Sorry about that, mate," the man grunted. "You naff off and say your prayers, and put one in for me."

"Course he's British," one of the boys muttered when Frank turned away.

The whole group of them snorted with suppressed laughter.

June, 2018

Several coalitions had collapsed. The economy had grown inexplicably worse again. There was another election, which got no clear result. So it was held a second time the following month. People were exhausted with the whole damned thing.

"… cannot be trusted," Ray Kingdom was shouting.

It was Prime Minister's Question Time. Just yesterday afternoon, a Moslem teenager had tried to set off a bomb on a bus, and had burned himself to death instead. Several other passengers had been taken to the hospital with minor injuries, mostly caused by the panic that had ensued.

"I accept that it's not fair to some. I understand that some of them are fully integrated and accept our values. But the safety of the British public must come first."

Several MPs booed. He shouted back, "Do you want the blood of innocent Britons on your hands?"

The Citizenship Act was expanded hugely, requiring all Moslems to leave. There were more riots. And a lot more rioters killed this time, the police on huge pay rises and heavily armed. Several MPs resigned. There were bye-elections, and the NBP got a three-seat majority.

"Can you tell the difference—on a street, on a Tube train—between a Hindu and a Moslem?" Ray Kingdom yelled from the front bench. "Can you tell the difference—on the street, on a Tube train—between a Namibian Christian and a Somali fundamentalist?"

"Look at their identity cards!" someone shouted. They had recently been introduced.

"People can fake names! We can't fully trust *any* of them!"

And Frank could see that most of that made a kind of sense. Nobody was being picked upon without good reason. Nobody was being hurt. And none of what had been said applied to him or his—admittedly dwindling—community. He felt like he was on the right side of this argument.

Before they were forced to do so, most people with darker skins were leaving. Even people with olive skins, in fact. There had been an Italian restaurant on the high street Frank had eaten at since he had been a little boy. The original owner's son—Marco—had continued the business. It was gone, and so were that whole family—grandparents, toddlers, all. The windows were now bare. Posters with the Sword of St. George began to obscure them.

Later that same month, a mob of some eight hundred youths in armbands ran amok in Chinatown. The TV news broadcasts kept showing it until an emergency decree under the Security of Information Act shut them down.

Frank had never really thought about the Chinese before. They seemed to exist on the edges of your consciousness. Kept completely to themselves. But they were hardworking, he knew that. And had never caused any trouble. So why pick on them?

Later on, there was footage of Ray Kingdom condemning the attacks. But for the first time, there was something rather insincere about the way the words came out, which made Frank uneasy. He started feeling very glad that he looked just as British as any other man.

The trouble was over and done with in one night, though, and he finally decided it was not significant.

February, 2019

A lot of the abandoned shops and eateries on the high street had not re-opened. There were posters everywhere. One convenience store had turned into a games arcade, from which a constant racket of electronic pings and gunshot sounds emerged. There were boys with armbands on every corner, apparently with nothing much to occupy them. They sneered at Frank when he went quickly by.

A man about his age, but more scruffily dressed, was handing out copies of *The Briton* up ahead of him. PLENTY MORE TO ACHIEVE, SAYS KINGDOM, read the headline.

Frank reached out for the one being proffered, but the man jerked it away.

"I thought they were free?" he asked.

The man stared at him wordlessly.

It was disturbing. But there always had been, always would be, ignorant people who took a blinkered view of life. Frank walked off sadly, trying to push the incident to the back of his mind.

This area had changed *so much*. There was practically nothing that he recognized. He had hardly any friends at all left around here anymore. And he realized, perhaps for the first time, how broad and general a term 'friendship' was. The man at the corner shop where he bought his morning paper, who had always smiled at him and exchanged a few friendly words. The young couple from the dry cleaners, who had come outside and helped him one time when he had slipped over on a patch of ice—they'd waved when they had seen him through their window after that. The little Kurdish girls who used to play hopscotch on this very stretch of pavement, and wished him a good morning when he passed.

All gone. He was surrounded by unfamiliar faces, uniformly pale and grim and drawn.

And then he realized he was wrong. There was someone he definitely knew. Walking toward him was the unmistakable portly figure of Ivan Bremman, one of the regulars from his synagogue. They'd often sat together, chatting in hushed tones during the service.

Frank started raising a hand, to signal to him.

Then thought better of it.

Parked against the curb was a large, unmarked black van. Three men stepped from the shelter of it—they were plainly clothed and wore no armbands. But they confronted Ivan in the street and seemed to ask him a couple of questions, then looked at his identity card.

Frank could see the man's head shaking. What exactly was the problem? It didn't make any sense.

And then something incredible happened.

All three men were young and tall. And two of them suddenly hooked their arms around his friend's and hustled him in the direction of the van. The third pulled the back doors open. Ivan was pushed inside.

Were these police? They didn't look like it. An awful feeling of suspicion began to creep over Frank. His brow became clammy, his palms damp.

He'd been going to open up his shop, just like on any other normal day. But now he turned around, and started heading back the way he'd come. *Get back home, where you'll be safe.*

There was a shout behind him. When he glanced over his shoulder, the back doors of the van were firmly shut. One of the men was pointing at him. They began to move in his direction.

Frank reached the corner leading to his street. Went around it, just as his pursuers' pace began speeding up.

He started to run.

But however hard he pumped his legs, he couldn't manage to run fast enough.

Just bare ribs, a few ragged strips of skin. Part of the head was either caved-in or gone.

The Very Edge of New Harare

I can still remember seeing my first-ever free giraffe.

I must have been about, oh, six years old at the time, and was driving back from the town center with my father, along the Mutare Road. Do you remember that old urban wildlife area that used to be there, with the observation platform, and those woods, the Mukuvisi Woodlands, at the back of it? It's all a Zim-World Shopping City these days, of course. It was a process that was already in full swing back then, but ... Africa has become fully modernized, since I was a young child.

Anyway, we were driving past the north of it, just talking and laughing, when this ... *shape*, it didn't register as anything more than that, at first. This spindly, skinny, totally unworldly shape comes stumbling out from between the trees, and runs across the railroad tracks and then through the municipal campsite. And, almost tripping on the crash barriers, staggers out onto the road, which was already a six-lane freeway by that stage. Steps out right in front of us.

And I begin screaming my head off, you see. I was perfectly convinced that the aliens had landed. But my father? I can still conjure up, with exact clarity, the look on his face, the huge disparity between what his eyes were doing and what the rest of his features did. I'd never seen his eyes so wide, so totally astonished. But the rest had set itself into that grim, determined hardness that I certainly *had* seen a hundred times before, when a heavy job around our house needed doing, or when I came home with a less than perfect school report.

He practically leaned over sideways as he swung the wheel around. I realize now that he was going into a controlled skid, the same way we are trained in the police. And we skewed away from this apparition, almost clipping it. And wound up at a dead halt on the hard shoulder, with our car turned back-to-front.

We were still looking at the creature, therefore, through our windscreen. And I could see in an instant how far from dangerous it actually was. How pathetic, lost. I stopped screaming at that point. And asked, "What *is* it, Pappy?"

He murmured, in a voice so awed, so dream-like I can still hear it quite clearly, "It's a giraffe, Abel."

I had not been taken to the zoo, at that age. Nor to any of the few nature reserves that still remained—the nearest, Lake Chivero, had been closed for redevelopment the same year I was born. But there was a photo of a giraffe pasted to the window of my classroom. You'd never have believed that this thing and the creature in the photo were of the same breed.

This thing? The colors of its hide looked faded, as if they'd been slowly bleached away. It had mange, and even gray patches of fungus, and one of its eyes was blind. So skinny it could barely stand. Its long neck was so chronically bent that you wondered it could still lift its tiny head at all.

It was still a living thing, however. And still trying to *remain* alive.

Its good eye stared around at its surroundings. All the thousands of cars around it, all the smoke and noise. It seemed uncertain what to do. The sensible thing would have been to head back to the woods. But it had already come from that direction. Had it been hiding there for years, now? Was it trying to escape?

Nearly all the cars behind us, in our lane, had done the same thing as my father. The next lane, and the ones beyond that, though? The traffic was still moving fast, cars wobbling as they went by.

When the giraffe tried to get further across, then, the inevitable happened.

It only got three paces before an Assegai Roadster hit its front right leg, smashing it so brutally that you could see the shattered bone. The giraffe looked like it might stay up on three legs, for a few seconds. Then it toppled over like a big, unbalanced pile of twigs.

I remember it trying to lift its head from the pavement. And can still recall the miserable look in its good eye. I suppose it would have died of shock before much longer. But the next vehicle, a massive truck, went straight over its neck.

I looked away as the airbrakes shrieked.

And my father ...?

My father was ever so quiet, during the rest of the drive home. And solemn the remainder of the evening. And, even at that early age, I sensed that it was because he felt that he had ... what exactly?

Lost something. Or rather, been given something back for a few seconds, only to have it snatched away again.

That's the story. I should wind it up. Dad died three years later, his great frame devoured by cancer, leaving just my mother to finance me through school, college, and finally the Academy. And twenty-six years later on, history repeated itself back-to-front, when my wife died of the same disease, leaving me with my own small boy to bring up.

I never visit Zim-World Shopping City, which is a shame, because my neighbors tell me they have wonderful bargains there.

And that's my first—and my last—free giraffe.

There's plenty to keep a Homicide Lieutenant of the Zimbabwe State Police Division busy in today's New Harare. We have a crime rate comparable to Greater Los Angeles, which means not terrible, but it could do with some improving. And my jurisdiction covers the entire Highveldt Province, which means on top of liquor-store shootings and gangland hits, I have to deal with housewives who've done in their faithless husbands in the sticks. I was entering the details of one such into my sat-com, when Captain Maalu came walking toward my desk and asked me, "Hard at it, eh, Enetame?"

"Always," I said, without looking up at him.

He threw a thin file down beside my screen. "Something might have happened out at Binaville."

Right out by the Mvurwi Mountains. That's about as far-suburban as this city gets.

"One of those little farms out there. The owner lives alone. This morning, his neighbors notice that his door is hanging open. He's not there, but there's blood all over the hallway and the porch."

"Could he have just gotten drunk, bashed his scalp, and gone wandering off?" I suggested.

"In which case, this will be one of those all-too-rare assignments with a happy ending. Go out there and give it a look. Take Petrie with you."

Which was fine by me. Steve Petrie's a Caucafrican, which is to say, of distant European origin. There are a few of them on the force, and they're hardworking although generally unimaginative detectives. I put on my jacket, got him from his office, and we went down to the parking lot, where my brand-new toy was waiting for me.

An Impala Terrain ZF 400, semi-solar-powered, and as sleek and quiet as a well-groomed cat. Within minutes, we were on the Julius Jones Elevated Highway, speeding out toward the suburbs.

Petrie—blond, broad-shouldered, and seven years my junior—kept on calling me 'sir' until I told him to drop it. I didn't know too much about him personally, and so I asked about his home life.

He'd been married eighteen months, as it turned out. Had a baby boy, just three months old. And he grinned massively when he conveyed that information, which made me rather like him.

"You've a son too, so I hear?"

"Oh yes," I nodded, still watching the road. "Joshua. He's seven."

Petrie's whole manner became a little awkward, at that point. Everyone at the station house knew about Kissi's death.

"It must be tough, bringing him up on your own?"

I could feel my shoulders hunching up, but had got used to questions of that kind.

"It can be. But when you have no choice, you simply get on with it."

Petrie turned his attention to the windshield, and said, "I don't know. I'm not sure I could cope. I'd be completely lost without my Trish."

Which told you all everything needed to know about the fellow. Loyal, affable and decent, but not particularly driven or bright. Exactly the way I like my subordinates, in fact. It makes me feel less guilty, assigning them the dull jobs and the donkeywork.

Massive, gleaming skyscrapers whizzed by us. And then the lower buildings of the light industry zones. Then finally, an uninspiring mosaic of fast-food joints and mini-malls, car showrooms and discount superstores, and geometrically laid-out rows of houses.

It was four-thirty in the afternoon by the time that we reached Binaville. Something *might* have happened here, the Captain had informed me. But it looked to me like if anything ever did, half the inhabitants would die from the surprise of it.

We were on the very edge of New Harare. Less than two klicks in the distance was a thinly forested section of the Mvurwi Range. Most of the houses around us looked the same, single-story affairs with verandas and flower gardens and low wire fences. But there were a few small semi-urban farms here too.

It was as quiet as a church, and the sun-baked earth clunked under our footsteps. We made our way over to the house, where a few local cops and some civilians were waiting.

Nowhereville, I thought. Except that, just before we opened the gate, Petrie looked around sharply, seeming to remember something.

He piped up. "Isn't this where those two girls disappeared, about a year ago?"

And yes, I could see, he was absolutely right. My respect for him went up a notch. Yes, Bridget and Marie Makabe, eight and ten years old. They'd been out playing in the fields one evening, and had never come back home. It had been headline news for almost four months, and the search for them had been a massive one. How had I forgotten that?

No trace of them had ever been found. Well, maybe Binaville was not quite such a dull place after all.

A uniformed sergeant came over to greet me as I walked toward the porch. "Lieutenant ...?"

"Abel Enetame. Could you show me where the blood was found?"

He led me up to the doorway. I could see dark stains immediately, on the porch and the soil beyond it. And then I looked inside, and cursed silently. There was plenty of blood spattering both walls. And loads more, still partially viscid, on the tiled floor. Except several people had walked right through it. The neighbors, I supposed, going in to try and find the occupant. So the whole scene had been compromised.

Still clearly visible, however, was a large drag-mark leading out through the door. And so ... a body had been moved. Alive or dead, though?

"Who was it who lived here?"

"Simon Nkomo, 54, a bachelor. Pretty much a loner. Kept to himself, so far as we can tell. Just unassuming, quiet."

"Can I talk to the person who first found this?"

I spent the next half hour talking to bystanders. Did they hear anything? Or see anyone suspicious? All of their answers were in the negative, as they usually are. By then, a forensics team had arrived and was getting busy.

"You reckon we've got a homicide here?" Petrie asked me.

"There's about a quart of blood in there," I told him. "If Mr. Nkomo's still alive, I'd say he's starting to feel pretty light-headed right about now."

My eyes followed the drag-marks as they went across the porch's splintered edge. There was more dried blood beyond that, and much thinner scuffmarks on the hard earth for about twenty meters, till they reached an area of grassland and low brush and disappeared.

"You'd better start rounding up a search team," I told Petrie glumly. "This is looking to be a long afternoon."

And a pretty dull one. Somewhere around forty uniformed men turned up in the next hour. I stood by the gate, watching, as they formed a line, and started picking across the fields and wasteland. The descending sun beat down on me, and flies buzzed in the heat. Every so often, my attention wandered off in the direction of the mountains.

This section of range is one of the few truly wild places left in Highveldt Province. Acid rain has taken its toll on the trees. But people used to spot small antelope around its edges. And I've even heard there are a few baboons living up there. You'd think that rich people would clear the area and build some mansions there. But, fifty years ago, a seam of uranium was found in that part of the Mvurwis. It's been mined out long ago. But no one who has a choice in the matter lives where there's been radiation.

I took in the fact I'd be home late. I called my housekeeper, Mathilda, on my cell phone. Yes, Josh was already back from school. She'd be happy to stay till I returned, and did I want her to cook supper? I thanked her, but told her that there was no need.

There was a shout from the fields. My head came up. A circle of blue uniforms had gathered by the time I'd run across. Faces were screwed up. There were disgusted hisses.

I pushed my way through, then came to a frozen stop.

A Lieutenant of Homicide—in circumstances such as these—expects a body for his efforts. But whatever this shrunken and shapeless thing was, it had been left on top of an anthill. Was entirely carpeted with moving, shiny, red-brown dots. I gawped at it for a little while, then re-gathered my wits. Pulled a clump of twigs from a nearby bush and, using them as a brush, flicked away as many of the insects as I could.

There was no full-sized cadaver here. Just bare ribs, a few ragged strips of skin. Part of the head was either caved-in or gone. It could have been road-kill, except road-kill doesn't wear shoes.

I turned again to the sergeant. "Is there a medical examiner for this district?"

"No. The nearest one's in Morning Ridge—Dr. Alice Sususa."

I knew her. "Get her out here, then. Tell her that she needs to bring dry-ice."

I stared back at Mr. Nkomo, if this was him, registering that whoever had killed him had been very smart. His body hadn't been dumped here accidentally. Most forensic evidence had been chewed away.

The sun was already setting by the time Alice arrived. We greeted each other, then I left her and the local boys to the unenviable task of picking up the pieces. They were setting up floodlights as I left.

I dropped a weary-looking Petrie off at a midtown subway station, and then headed home, stopping at my local Rockin' Rooster on the way. Picked up a jumbo bucket of fried drumsticks, potato chips, and spicy coleslaw, Josh's favorite meal.

And opened my front door to … wailing police sirens, squealing tires, and gunshots. Josh was with Mathilda in the den, watching his favorite web-vee show, *Nairobi P.D.* I paid off Mathilda, giving her an extra five. And then I settled down next to my son, and we ate fried chicken with our fingers and watched Sergeant Zak Ngengi hunting down yet another vicious drugs baron.

During the final, stunt-filled shoot-out, Josh asked me, "Do you ever do that?"

"Oh yes," I smiled. "Almost every day."

But he knew that I was lying, and he punched me on the thigh.

A news update followed—Mr. Nkomo got a brief mention—and then *Summer: Cape Town High*. A bevy of cute starlets gossiped in their locker-room, then went to party on the beach.

"Which one do you like?" I asked Josh.

"That one!"

He pointed to a very dark-skinned Venus with an hourglass figure. He already had good taste, for one so young. But I still asked him, "Why?"

"She's got a nice smile," he said, very seriously.

At which I burst out laughing, and then hugged him till he got embarrassed, squirmed out of my grip.

"Bedtime now," I told him.

And he didn't argue with me. Never has, ever since those terrible first six months after Kissi died.

I could hear the faucet running upstairs when the phone started to ring. It was Alice Sususa, and she sounded pretty unhappy.

"Can you come here, Abel?"

"Now?" I glanced at my watch. "I'm with my kid."

"Yes, I'm sorry. But there's something here you ought to see. I'd rather not tell you on the phone."

I was exasperated, but she seemed entirely serious. Fortunately, my neighbors were in.

"How do you fancy spending the night with Manzi and Tessa?" I asked Josh.

"Yay!"

The highway was much quieter as I sped back down it. I arrived quickly at Morning Ridge. The mortuary was set behind a wide grass strip, and there was some movement visible on the neatly mown turf.

If you want to see Zimbabwe's remaining wildlife, outside of the reserves, the suburbs at night are the best places to find it. Small monkeys rustle through the trees. Jackals and caracals have adopted the same survival trick as Western foxes, moving into built-up areas. And we've never been able to get rid of every single snake.

The building's front door was unlocked. I went through to the examination theatre. Alice was beside one of the stainless steel tables, gazing down at the collection of bones and ripped skin on it.

"*Is* it Mr. Nkomo?"

"Dental records confirm it."

"Thank God the ants can't eat enamel," I opined.

She looked up at me, squinting unhappily. "I think something might have fed before they did."

"Meaning what?"

"Did anybody tell you? There've been several cattle mutilations in Binaville, the last couple of years."

I waited.

"There's a dairy farm about half a klick from the Nkomo place. Three times that I know of, a cow has been badly maimed. One actually had its throat torn out. No one's ever found out what did it."

"Feral dogs?" I suggested. "Even those baboons up in the mountains?"

"Baboons don't attack cattle," she grinned, amused by my city-dwelling ignorance. "But come here, look at this."

She indicated some deep gouges on an exposed clavicle. "What would you say these were?"

They didn't look like knife, or even chisel traumas. "Teeth

135

marks?" I attempted.

"Absolutely. There are more on the femurs, and the pelvis, and the ribs. Pretty big ones."

"Okay, so ..." I still couldn't understand what she was so concerned about. "Once the corpse was dumped, some dogs, even some wild hyenas, fed on the remains before the ants finished it off."

"I thought so too. But here we have something a little different." Her attention drifted to the stripped right arm. "Do you know what these are?"

There were three narrower and shallower indentations, running parallel. I shrugged.

"They're claw marks. Dogs, even hyenas, don't have claws like these."

She frowned.

"I thought at first, buzzards. I had to check back through the records quite a way before I found something that really matched. And when it did ..."

Her voice faltered. Her entire manner became stiff, embarrassed.

"The only marks that match this, Abel? They came from a cat."

"A *big* cat?"

And I almost laughed out loud.

Alice looked perfectly serious, however. Serious enough to make me want to check it out.

I called Police Plaza. Had any big cats escaped from a zoo in, say, the last couple of years? I asked them. Or from the wildlife reserves, although the latter was highly unlikely. Every large animal in the reserves has a tracer implanted. Besides which, the nearest park with big cats is Hwange, more than three hundred klicks away.

I was shaking my head when I put my phone away. Alice's embarrassment deepened, her eyes going damp.

"You got it wrong, Dr. Sususa," I told her, trying to do it gently.

Just as wrong as anyone could ever get. The habitat which sustained big game is now completely gone. No elephants out there, nor rhinos. No buffalo, zebras, wildebeest anymore. Industrialization wiped the crocodiles and hippos from our rivers. And there are *certainly* no big cats.

"I'll have to think again," Alice conceded after a while, her head lowered and her voice a whisper.

"Yes, I think that's best."

I should have been annoyed at her, for dragging me out of my home on such a far-fetched premise. But she looked so forlorn, I didn't have the heart.

There was more about Nkomo on the eight a.m. bulletin, the next day. Followed by even worse news. Earlier this morning, a colleague of Alice's had gone through her sat-com records of last night, found the stuff about the big cats, and reported it to their superior. Who had suspended Alice on the spot. The story had leaked out.

The newscasters were practically in fits about it, calling her 'Dr. Alice in Wonderland.'

"If Simon Nkomo were still alive, Dr. Sususa, there'd be one question he'd ask. What's eating *you*?"

"What's the connection between Dr. Alice Sususa and Tweetie Pie?" Steve Petrie asked me, when I picked him up from his house around nine. "They both tawt they taw a puddy-tat!"

I didn't laugh.

Things in Binaville had pretty much returned to normal. There was police tape all over the place, of course. And a few kids hanging around there. But the whole circus that had surrounded the corpse's first discovery? Those things vanish just as suddenly as they appear. The tides of time were closing over poor Mr. Nkomo, without leaving any ripples.

There was one small thing that was different. Over near the scrubland where the body had been found, a group of about a dozen homeless men had gathered. Ragged, bearded, old beyond their years. Most of New Harare's derelicts wind up out on the edge of town. They're less hassled by cops and hoodlums, and there are plenty of easy pickings on the farms.

A stretched black limo with reflective windows suddenly came rolling up the street. It pulled right off the pavement, went across the grass toward the little band.

I immediately recognized the tall, middle-aged guy who got out from the back. You could hardly not do, dressed the way he was.

America has its militias, Europe its neo-fascists. Africa has butt-holes like this so-called 'Chief Manuza,' leader of the tiny but vociferous Tribal Party. Excuse the language, but these people make me terribly annoyed.

He was wearing old-style tribal robes. There were open sandals on his feet, and balanced on his round head was the kind of pillbox hat Kissi used to wear to the Federation Day races. He was carrying a flywhisk, and he twitched it in his hand as he walked over to the hobos.

Then he did something that left me amazed, coming from a man so arrogant. He actually squatted down before the filthy derelicts. And started up a conversation with them.

Steve started across toward them, but I grabbed his arm, holding him back. All I wanted to do was watch.

After a while, Manuza started nodding. Then he handed them some objects—it was too far away to make out what. And, next moment, he did something even more peculiar.

Got up to his feet, and threw himself into a hopping dance, twirling around on the spot. The hobos watched him intently, following his every movement.

Once done, he bade them farewell, then got back into his limo. All the ragged men stood up, began to melt away into the landscape.

Steve turned to me. "What the hell was that about, Abe? Why didn't you go talk to him?"

I shook my head softly. "We'd have found out nothing. You know what Manuza's like around authority. And with *you* here? Even worse. Imagine how that racist pig would act, confronted by a white policeman."

Then I clapped him on the shoulder. "Let's see if we can turn up any of those hobos he was talking to."

We searched through the brush for twenty minutes, but they were gone. I called to Petrie, and we went back to my car.

"I'm going back into town," I told him. "Go from house to

house, perhaps? Try to pick up anything the local cops have missed?"

He nodded. There was a bus that he could take back home.

I won't say my blood was actually boiling as I went back along the highway, but it certainly was on the simmer. I knew quite a lot about this 'Chief Manuza.' His real name was Saul Agusi, and he came from a normal blue-collar family in Sherwood Park. The fake name he'd adopted from the history books, an old-time supreme headsman.

And the policies that he and his small handful of fanatics advocate? The reclaiming of the old ways. The return to villages, and tribes, and superstition. 'Identity,' they call it.

The Tribal Party had just two cramped rooms in an office block in a seedier part of town. I was kept waiting for practically ten minutes, before the 'Great Chief' would have me in his sanctum. There were posters on the walls around me, all with slogans such as *Tribe is Pride* and *Not Europe, Not America, This Is Africa!* At a desk opposite me, a secretary sat. A perfectly lovely woman in her early twenties, made to look ridiculous by the get-up she was wearing, some kind of sarong thing, and a tall white turban on her pretty head.

Manuza insisted on seeing my badge, actually taking it out of my hand. And while he studied it, I looked at the artifacts he'd decorated his office with. Shields and spears, clubs and hatchets, and even bangles made up of what appeared to be lions' claws. I eyed those carefully ... they gave me pause.

Satisfied at last, the man handed me back my badge, a sarcastic grin crossing his pockmarked face.

"So, Lieutenant *Enetame*?" His voice was a croaky drawl. "An African name that approximates an English word. 'Entamed.' How appropriate."

He was looking me up and down with apparent disdain. It was a struggle to keep calm, under such scrutiny. Did he seriously expect me to dress like him? Did he seriously expect all of us to embrace the awful days of yesteryear? Go back to poverty and hunger, corruption and conflict, massacre and the belief in bad spirits? Was that the kind of prospect he was offering my son?

I asked him straight out, "What were you doing at Binaville, with those homeless men?"

"I went there as soon as I heard about the lions." He said it perfectly seriously.

"There are no lions."

Manuza snorted, and then rocked his head from side to side.

"Those men. Those derelicts. By force of circumstance, admittedly, they live closer to the old ways than anyone else in this great prison of a city. Closer than me, and a thousand times closer than you. They live off the land, under the open sky. And at night, they gather around and tell stories, thus exchanging knowledge. They have seen the lions."

Was I dealing with a complete madman here?

"Two of their number, in fact, have been killed by them, not that the authorities would care. That is why I gave them the protective amulets, and showed them the dance which might appease the mighty lion chief."

Something could be learned, I decided, by going along with this nonsense for a little while.

"You think hopping around will stop a big cat?"

But the man grinned hugely, his manner superior. "No, you do not understand. The real free lions are gone. These are Ghost Lions. Spirit Lions."

"Really?" It was hard keeping a straight face.

"Born out of the heart and soul of Ancient Africa Herself," he went on, "and come to avenge Her. And they are just the first, you see. More spirits will join them. And they will rip to shreds your false gods, and will smash and tear your chained society, till the people see the truth and reclaim what they once were."

I was wasting my time here, I could see. I'd come all this way for nothing.

"You can change the way a people dress, and feed, and live, and even dream," he was still ranting as I started getting up, "but you can never change that which is deepest in their hearts!"

I thanked him for the speech, and let myself out, with relief.

One thing nagged at me, however, as I drove back to the office.

And was still bothering me when I arrived back home. Those artifacts on the walls, those lions' claws? Could it be that some of Manuza's people ...?

No. It was a perfectly insane idea. But ... could someone be faking lion attacks, to try and revive some of the ancient superstitions? It was as lunatic a theory as I'd ever come up with. But Manuza *was* a lunatic, I had no doubt of that.

I arranged for Josh to spend a second night next door, then prepared myself. I got my gun out of my bedside drawer and checked it carefully. Then I drove back to the outer edge of town, for what seemed like the hundredth time.

Binaville was as quiet once again. I cruised silently into the lee of the Nkomo farmhouse, and switched off my engine and lights. Wound up my window to keep out the insects, settled back. And ... waited for something to happen.

After a while, I began noticing something odd. There were a few tiny monkeys in a nearby tree, although they seemed rather quiet and nervous. Where were all the other little creatures? The fields were completely empty, and I couldn't understand how that could be.

At about ten o'clock, a distant shriek brought me jerking up. It was coming from the sparsely wooded slopes. But I calmed down quickly enough to recognize it had to be those baboons I'd heard about. The noise stopped, soon after, and I settled back.

Some time around midnight, I sat up again, believing I had noticed something through my heavy lids. I peered beyond the windshield, and then even switched my headlights on. They revealed nothing whatsoever. So I must have dreamt it.

By about two a.m., I had fallen asleep.

"Heavy night?" Steve Petrie grinned, when I stumbled into the office the next morning. "Don't tell me that you got lucky, you old dog?"

My back was killing me, and I was not in the mood for such remarks. So I'm afraid that I was rather sharp with him.

He'd had no success with the farmer's neighbors. I explained what I had been up to. And he looked incredulous at first.

141

"Yes, I know it sounds far-fetched," I nodded. "But I'm going to spend a couple more nights up there, just to make quite sure."

"So I'm not your partner any longer?"

"You ...?" I blinked at him surprisedly. "I don't expect you to do stake-out duty, man. You've got a little kid."

"And so have you. I'll take the next shift, okay? You genuinely look like you could use some rest."

"Oh, and by the way," he added. "Happy Federation Day."

I stared at him awkwardly as he walked away. The most important event in the African calendar, and I had been so busy, so engrossed, I'd completely forgotten it.

Fortunately, Josh was happy to watch the big parade on the web-vee. I slumped in my armchair, feeling a hundred years old. The crowds in Moya Plaza were enormous. They yelled and hooted, many of them waving furled umbrellas, as the marching bands and floats went by. The weather had taken one of those unexpected turns that we are used to in these parts. Come early evening, the sky had blackened, and there was the occasional rumble of thunder, although no lightning or rain as yet.

"So far, so good!" a reporter in the crowd informed the studio. "We're all praying that it holds off, and the weather doesn't spoil things!"

Then, the camera swung to a float on which stood a gigantic inflated Rockin' Rooster, the God of Good Eating in the Enetame household. Josh leapt to his feet, delighted.

The phone rang.

It was Petrie, calling from his car in Binaville. But the interference from the coming storm was so bad I could barely make him out.

"Steve! Speak louder!"

"There's something ... the fields. Halfway to ..."

I could hear enough to tell that he was genuinely frightened.

"Abe, what ... do? There's ... moving out there!"

"Stay there! Do not get out of your car, Steve! I'm coming out ..."

But the connection had gone dead.

I phoned both my neighbors, but they were not at home. When I stuck my head out onto the street, most of the windows around me were dark. The parade, I understood. I even tried calling Mathilda, but I just got her machine.

Ten minutes had passed since Petrie's call, and he'd sounded so desperate. And I hated what I was about to do, but I could see no other choice. I hurried Josh into his coat and shoes, and literally bundled him into my car. Belted him in tightly, before speeding back toward the highway.

He looked fascinated, and as pleased as Punch with the excitement.

"Where are we going?"

"Just a job I have to do."

"Are you going to shoot some bad guys?"

I hadn't even bothered putting on my jacket—he was staring at my gun.

"No!" I told him sternly, concentrating on the road. "That's just on the web-vee. You must be quiet now, okay?"

Good as gold, he did what I asked.

Steve's car was not visible when we arrived at the Nkomo place. By this time, I was sweating. Lord Almighty, was I crazy, bringing my son here? I swung the nose of the Impala out toward the wasteland again, putting my beams on full. And yes, more than halfway out toward the mountains, there was Petrie's Assegai Victor, the driver's door wide open. I could make out no sign of the man.

Inwardly, I cursed him, for not listening to me. And myself, for not getting here sooner.

We bumped out across the scrub till we were some thirty meters from the other car. There I stopped. Got out carefully, my hand on my Walther. And told Josh, as sternly as I'd ever told him anything, "Lock all the doors and stay here. Do you understand? Do not let anyone in, unless it's me."

He nodded, not the slightest bit worried. Perhaps he thought that this was simply a game?

I waited till he'd shut himself inside, then went across to Steve's car. The young Caucafrican was nowhere to be seen. But there turned

143

out to be a flashlight in his open glove compartment. I clicked it on, swung the beam around me. Then looked back at where I'd parked, with my stomach flipping slightly. Josh was peering back at me through the dark windshield, looking very small indeed. I held up a finger, indicating he should stay exactly where he was. Then I began to search the ground around me much more thoroughly.

The beam of my flashlight soon alighted on another gun, just lying there on the hard earth. Steve's. I picked it up and sniffed it. It had not been fired.

Just three meters further on, I found a pool of blood.

It was fresh. My heart was pounding, and I could hear my own breath in my nostrils. There were drag marks, leading off from here toward the silent, shadowed mountains. Thunder kept on rumbling overhead.

This was going to take me even further from Josh. And I hated that. But what if Steve was still alive? I stared back, making sure that my boy was okay. And then I drew my pistol and followed the trail at a crouch. Expecting to be confronted by what, at any moment? A crazed Tribalist with claws strapped to his fingertips? Or perhaps even a catlike ghost.

I was at the foot of the mountains before too much longer. Was in front of a huge bush. Except that the trail led inside it.

I parted the branches, shone my beam. And finally understood.

Behind it, there was an opening carved in the rock, doubtless to the old uranium mine. This entrance must have lain abandoned for the best part of fifty years. How long had it been since any light had shone in it at all?

How would Josh feel, as he watched me disappear? I was angry with myself, feeling like the most negligent of fathers. But I went inside.

Before too much longer, the main corridor started to branch off into more tunnels. I recalled the place's history. People thought they'd really struck it rich here, half a century ago, and had been grievously disappointed. There was only one medium-sized seam, which had been mined out in the first two years. That hadn't stopped them looking though, trying to find another one. This whole place had to be a warren. And … what exactly was happening down here now?

A thin trail of blood across the rock floor led me deeper, till my nose screwed up. An awful, pungent stench was growing stronger by the second.

It was mostly decayed human flesh—in my job, you become familiar with that. But there was something else as well. A heavy, choking, animal stink, like all the zoos in the world in a heatwave. A smell that churned my stomach, and made something in me want to run.

I didn't. Needed to find out what was really going on. So I went forward. To find myself in a wider section, virtually a cave.

There they all were, piled up in a corner. Only one of the cadavers wasn't decomposed. Parts of both legs and the face had been chewed away. But there was blond hair—it was Steve Petrie. A lump formed in my throat.

As for the rest, they were merely bones with mould on them. Some of them were dogs and little antelope, and a strange, fanged skull that I supposed might have belonged to a baboon. But the rest were human. Two of the skulls were child-sized, the vanished little girls. Others were of adults. There were scraps of ragged clothing mixed in. My beam alighted gently on the remains of a gingham frock.

Why wasn't Simon Nkomo here, then? Why had he been left halfway? The distance, I realized. Whatever had killed him hadn't been able to drag him the entire way from the farmhouse.

But … what kind of wild animal could have survived down here, hidden in this way? And what kind of beast had the intelligence to leave its victim on an anthill?

I turned around on the spot very slowly, waiting for a snarl, a leaping carnivorous shape. Nothing came.

And if the creature wasn't here, then where …?

I stiffened.

Josh!

Running back up the tunnels. Through the bush. Back across the wasteland, faster than I'd run in years, every fiber in my body propelling me onward. I could see the car before much longer. Could make out Josh standing up on his seat, turning around and around and staring.

There were large, dim shapes on the move, outside my vehicle.

"*Josh!* Keep the *doors* locked!" I was bellowing now.

Large heads turned toward me, in the dimness. I could make out glowing eyes. I stumbled to a halt ten meters from Petrie's car, my gun held out. And, at that moment, a bolt of lightning finally flashed over our heads. The creatures hunkered down, closing their eyes. They were obviously used to living in the dark, and didn't like this sudden brightness. But, for a moment, I could see them very clearly.

And I could have sworn, in that first instant, I was looking at Manuza's Spirit Lions. There were twelve of them. An entire pride.

I think I went very rigid at the point. Except for my heart, which slammed around my chest like a wild animal.

There was hardly any yellow in their fur, the pigment bled away until they were the selfsame color as the shadows. They seemed a touch smaller than the lions in the zoo, their legs shorter, their bodies lower-slung. And their paws seemed overly large, adapted to padding over rock perhaps?

The brilliance faded. Darkness claimed the landscape once again. And from that point on, all I could make out were blurry shapes.

Their eyelids slid back open. They were unnaturally large eyes, glowing a faint luminous green.

I could smell them. A low growling began. And … they were making the grass crackle with their tails. These were not ghosts.

My thoughts churned furiously. For how long, how many generations, had this pride lived in the old uranium mines? How in the world had they managed to escape attention?

I looked directly at the one nearest the car, the largest one and with the thickest mane, presumably their leader. And, peering deep into its gaze, I thought that I could see intelligence. Low cunning

146

at least. Caution, and a patience that seemed measureless. Had this one kept the others safe for these decades? Kept them hidden, and away from harm?

Some of the others were drifting toward me. I came back quickly to myself. Drew a bead on the nearest one, and fired. The glow of its eyes vanished again. But a moment later, I could hear soft stirrings in the brush around me. Fear was dripping off me with my sweat by now.

Petrie's car door was still hanging open, not too far away.

I swung my weapon left and right, firing a couple of blind shots to keep the cats at bay. Then I was running again. And threw myself into the Assegai, yanking the door shut behind me.

Something slammed against it, on the other side. Claws raked down the glass. Something else landed on the roof, making it buckle slightly.

Steve had left the keys in the ignition, thank the Lord. I fumbled with them till the engine turned. Switched on the lights. And, with one hand on the horn, began swinging the car around in circles, kicking up a cloud of dust.

The creatures on top of and beside me disappeared when I did that, and the others shied away.

People in Binaville began noticing the racket. Blinds were pulled up, and then doors coming open. The green eyes around me vanished again. For good, this time?

I pulled the Assegai across and skidded to a halt next to my own car. Waited a few seconds, satisfying myself that the pride had completely gone. They wouldn't dare hang around, with all this attention.

Then I sprang out, clambering back into my own driving seat. Hugged Josh tightly. And finally got us away from there.

The picture that we made as we went back along the highway? It was a re-creation of another scene, from own my past, a long time ago. The grave little boy and his silent, grim-faced father, thinking about what they'd just seen. Except now, I'd turned into Pappy. And Joshua had replaced the younger me.

147

After a long while, my mind started working properly again. And I wondered what action the authorities would take, when they heard about the lions.

Send people to study them? Round them up for some zoo? But no, I figured. They would simply take the straightest, most expedient course. Send hunters in. Or even block up the tunnels, and then fill the place with gas.

No muss, no fuss, no more dead farmers.

If I told them.

There were certainly good reasons why I ought. The two girls, and the derelicts, Nkomo, and poor Steve. Excellent reasons in each case.

And yet, I was not simply thinking about that. I was remembering things, too.

That far-gone past, when I had been a year younger than Josh was, and the Mukuvisi Woodlands were still there.

That damned giraffe on the Mutare Road. The startling look in its one good eye.

How terrified it had been. And yet, it had kept on struggling, hanging onto its existence right up to the end.

And were these lions any different?

They had nearly killed me, terrified me to the core. And yet, when I'd first seen them clearly, there had been a quality to them that can't be seen in any of their captive kind. The way they stood, and the way they moved. A strength, a spirit, that can only come with freedom. It was something wondrous I'd never encountered before. They had managed to keep going despite all the odds against them. Managed to survive, in spite of everything that modern Africa had done.

And could I, in all conscience, have a hand in ending that?

They were simply marking out their final days, I could see the more I thought about it. Lack of prey was forcing them further from the tunnels. That was why they'd gone in the Nkomo house. And, sooner rather than later, someone else would come across them. Then the men with gas would come.

But I was remembering one other thing, too. That expression on

148

my father's face … of something re-found, only to be snatched away.

Maybe even Manuza was right, and you cannot change what's deepest in the heart. Whatever, by the time I finally pulled off the road, I had pretty well made up my mind. Whoever betrayed the pride, it was not going to be me.

I held Josh by both shoulders, felt he wasn't even trembling. Peered down at him gravely, and asked, "I'm so sorry. Are you all right? You must have been scared."

"I was, a little bit." He nodded.

But then he gazed up at me with his eyes full of the kind of wonder I had once been capable of. Then lost, until tonight.

"But I'm very glad I saw the lions. Aren't you, dad? Aren't you?"

Staring at the thing, the statue, almost seemed to hypnotize him.

A Town Called Youngesville

ONE

Liberty Square

Ms. Mackenzie—her first name turned out later to be Judith—met them at the house itself, and was not dressed the way that they would normally expect a realtor to be turned out for an appointment. She was in sneakers, loose-fitting jeans, a faded blue blouse, and had her hair tied back with a red-and-white bandanna. As if she had been momentarily disturbed from working in her garden, rather than trying to sell a property. But Frank and Joannie both dressed casually themselves on most occasions, so they didn't mind that. Not at all.

P. J. O'Rourke—whatever you might think of his political opinions—tells an interesting story. How he visited Haiti once, one of the poorest countries in the world. And, wandering among the seething, refuse-strewn slums, he met a little boy who had drawn a picture of—well—his idea of heaven. It was a large, single-story house with an integral garage, a car parked on the driveway and a TV dish up on the roof.

Maybe we have gone there, to that same mundane paradise, Frank thought. *Died, but in a slightly different way.* He'd felt a part of himself—the student-ish, rebellious part that had still survived into his mid-thirties—curl up and cringe when he'd first looked at the place. Oh my God, a provincial-looking home in a small town. He couldn't quite believe that they were considering this.

"It's an extremely roomy property," Judith Mackenzie told them, and then reeled off some statistics about square-yardage of floor space, which were always lost on Frank.

"Let's take a look," she suggested once she'd finished.

On the way to the front door, she enquired politely, "Have a good drive up from L.A.?"

Joannie screwed up her nose a little, her eyes turning glassy. It was left to Frank to answer. "It was a perfectly clear run, once we'd gotten out of the city."

Judith Mackenzie released a tiny, knowing laugh at that. "Yes, I know what you mean. I used to live there, once upon a time. And I *always* hated the traffic."

All three of them stepped up onto the porch, and she produced a set of keys. As she hunted for the correct one, Frank turned away from her and looked around him, taking in his new surroundings in one clean sweep for the very first time.

They were on the outer edge of Youngesville. To either side of him stretched houses pretty much like this one, although each one of them slightly different in design. The main part of the town could not be seen, and he found himself staring at the desert instead. It was, he was forced to concede, a pretty amazing view. And, now that he admitted it to himself, he had always carried around in his head a little fantasy that involved living in a part of the world like this. All this space and freedom.

Judith Mackenzie was saying something about the tax advantages of living in Nevada, but he wasn't really listening.

The colors were amazing, swirls of ocher, streaks of brownish-red. There were three Joshua trees within several hundred yards of him. The mountains in the distance were like mirages in a heat-haze. And the sky that pressed down on them was the clearest eggshell blue he'd ever seen. A buzzard wheeled above the landscape, and he'd always had a big thing about birds of prey.

"Frank's a graphic designer, freelance," Joannie was explaining.

"So he works from home. How lovely to be able to do that."

The door clacked open and he heard Joan say his name.

His first impression as they stepped inside was that they could fit the whole of their apartment back in L.A. into just this living room, and still have space left over. Jesus. The fact that it was bare of furniture increased the sense of size, he knew that. But this great pristine expanse of gleaming pine-laminate and off-white painted walls? It was like some massive canvas all lain out for him to draw on. He could hang up every picture that he ever wanted, buy and lay out some amazing rugs. And Christ, his Bauhaus recliner would look great in here.

Joannie started walking around, and he noticed how excited her step had become.

The sliding windows overlooking the backyard were massive, filling the place with clear, crisp daylight.

"Let's take a look at the rest, shall we?" suggested Judith Mackenzie, after an appropriate pause.

*T*hey'd been woken first by sirens, then by squealing tires, and finally by pistol-shots, right below their second-story window on Van Nuys. That had yanked them out of their initial drowsiness like two submerged corks being released and rushing to the surface. A gun battle was actually taking place right outside of their own home.*

Thinking quickly, Frank pushed Joannie off of her side of the bed, so that she was safe behind it. He yelled, "Don't go near the window!"

And then promptly ignored his own advice.

He went at a low crouch to the corner of it, and lifted his head carefully—very nervously—over the rim to find out what was happening below.

The three large figures hunched behind the skewed black Chevy didn't come from this part of town. They were gang members, Polynesians by the look and bulk of them, and had obviously been pursued here before being stopped and cornered. Right now, they were fighting like trapped rats.

Four patrol cars had surrounded them, the officers crouching too. A helicopter started clattering overhead, its spotlight darting across the battle scene. As Frank watched, one of the gangstas reached into the Chevy, produced something that was probably an Uzi, and then began firing upward.

He ducked back.

"Frank?" Joannie's head had cleared the mattress. "Get away from there!"

He waved at her to keep down, then went back to watching till the sound of shattering glass, below him, told him windows on the lower floor of this same building were being hit. That knocked some sense into him. He spent the remainder of the gunfight down on the floor with his back against the wall, where he supposed he ought to have been in the first place.

When it finally was safe to lift his head again, two of the gangstas were sprawled out, apparently dead. The third was being led away in handcuffs. And some paramedics were attending to one of the cops.

Frank got up slowly and went to find Joannie. She was actually lying face down on the floor behind the bed by this time, crying fiercely, mumbling the same thing over and over to herself.

"No. I won't do it. I cannot bring up children in this place."

After the whole house had been inspected—both of them suitably impressed—Judith offered to take them on a tour of Youngesville itself. All three of them climbed into her big silver Mercedes. Judith pressed a button and the whole roof folded back. The hot afternoon sunlight struck at Frank, making him squint.

And in that moment, he saw something move in the front window of the house next door to their prospective one. A figure passing by it. And—he noticed straight away—quite a figure too. A woman, at least six foot tall, Amazonish in her height and build, with wavy, coppery hair rolling down her back. Was this his potential new neighbor?

Except that—in that same half-blinded moment—he imagined there was something slightly wrong about the way she looked. He couldn't put his finger on it, but ...

She was gone from the pane before he could take the notion any further. Maybe it had just been his imagination.

Judith put the big car into drive, then started heading toward the center of the town.

Goddamn, he thought as front yard after front yard drifted by them. He really did like the house, and could not deny it. But the town itself was suburbia personified. Legoland, all the houses near identical, with only small details changed to differentiate them. He had never lived like this, in a place like this, not even when he'd been a child.

Always a slight fan of science fiction, he remembered something Brian Aldiss had once written. 'There is nothing so bourgeois as children.' And was this what their desire for kids was now dragging them down to? It felt like they were at very least considering giving up the whole way they had lived up until this point. Joannie might have a fairly mundane job—although one that she was good at, handsomely rewarded for—but half of their friends in L.A. were creative people of some kind or other, with a scattering of Goths, hippies and harmless outright freaks among them.

"A good number of arty types have moved here in the past couple of years," Judith told them, as though she had read his thoughts. "Writers, painters, book critics, even musicians. One of them lives next to me, a flautist. He practices early in the morning, and I have to say it's real nice to wake up to."

Joannie, who was already beaming, beamed a little wider. Frank wriggled slightly uncomfortably on the back seat, getting the strong feeling that a noose was tightening gradually around him. Cutting off, not his supply of air, but his reasonable arguments.

Another block of largely similar houses went by, and then they were on the main street, Younge.

It was middlingly busy, very neat. Seemed to have more than its fair share of coffee shops with outdoor tables. There were small, trendy boutiques, and medium-sized, European-looking restaurants. Then he spotted an arts supply store, which immediately knocked down yet another of his slight objections. There was a cinema, an independent one, currently showing the new Almodovar. And even a little theatre. The posters outside it made reference to Eugene O'Neill.

"There!" said Joannie, pointing out the logo of her bank above a wide glass door. It needed a new manager, and she could be transferred here any time she liked.

They followed the broad avenue the whole way to what he presumed was the dead center of the town, a large, flagstone-covered square. 'Liberty Square,' he noticed from the signs up on the lampposts. A contradiction in terms, he immediately thought, since how could you be square and still have liberty?

Still thinking like a teenager, a more mature part of his brain told him, *and possibly an out-of-date teenager too. Do kids still even use expressions like 'square' any longer?*

He realized that he didn't know. God, was he getting old?

The broad area that lay before him was bathed in hot sunlight, like everything else around here. Women walked across it pushing strollers. Moms and dads of about his and Joannie's age were leading toddlers by the hand, or simply watching as their offspring wandered. This appeared to be a place where families came. Without even touching her, he could feel Joannie stiffen, her neck craning up slightly.

And if this place was called Liberty, then it had its own statue too. No Frenchwoman with a torch raised in one hand, however.

It looked, in fact, so incongruous in a place like this that Frank felt his jaw dropping. Joannie's gaze was being drawn to the thing just as much as his was. He heard her murmuring under her breath, "What's that?"

The statue—if that was exactly how you should describe it—was about twelve feet tall, and seemed to be made of colored glass, or some similar material. It was as abstract as any structure he'd ever seen. There were tube shapes in it, most of them in spirals. There were globes. There were pyramids. No squares at all, he noticed straight away. No ninety-degree angles.

There were discs; there were ovoid-shapes; all of them in different colors, deep reds and rich greens and even traces of bright gold and silver, all of them translucent. The sunlight beating down and passing through the statue made the ground directly beneath it look like some huge, bottomless pit filled up with impossible hues.

Judith Mackenzie had stopped the Mercedes. She twisted around in her seat, grinning, understanding their reaction. She presumably took all her clients on this tour and so presumably was used to it.

"It's a little unusual in a town like this, I know. But the man who commissioned it ..." she paused for emphasis, "is pretty unusual too. You must have heard of him—Lyle Tamborough?"

Yes, of course. When Frank had Googled this town, a week back, that name had immediately come up. Youngesville's single claim to fame, so he imagined. A great man lived here.

Lyle Tamborough, winner—only two years ago—of the Nobel Prize for Physics. After Stephen Hawking, the most famous quantum physicist in the world.

"It's called 'New Hope,'" Judith was continuing. "It was constructed, to Lyle Tamborough's exact design, by a fine local artist called Bob Meaks."

And Frank had run across that name as well. Maybe this town wasn't so mundane as he had first expected.

"And Meaks keeps adding on to it, to Tamborough's instructions, almost every month," the woman told him, noticing how interested he was, "so that it's a work constantly in progress, like the Sagrada Familia in Barcelona. Although on a far smaller scale, of course."

Comparing this bland-looking town to Barcelona, which they'd been to, almost made Frank want to chuckle, except that his throat had become a little tight. His mouth had gone dry. Staring at the thing, the statue, almost seemed to hypnotize him. He had no idea what it was intended to represent, but ingenious thought had obviously gone into its making.

You just ... couldn't get a grasp on its entire shape. It appeared to alter from one second to the next. Colors seemed to slide into each other and then re-arrange themselves again. And the way that it reflected the sunlight was ... the very definition of unusual, perhaps?

He wet his lips.

Joannie said, "I think it's beautiful in an unworldly way."

And he supposed that she was right.

"We can go see Tamborough's house, if you'd like?" Judith suggested. "He often gets gawkers, so I'm sure that it won't bother him. There's a park on the way with a lake at the center, stocked with perch and small-mouth bass. Do either of you like to fish?"

"Haven't since I was a kid," Frank answered. Although, recently, he had been thinking of taking it up again.

My God, *was* he getting old?

Joannie took the wheel of their big Lexus SUV as they headed back toward the city. They argued gently the whole way, trying hard not to get too frustrated with each other.

"Our friends can come and visit us. God knows, we'll have the space to put them up, which we currently do not have."

Frank closed his eyes and remembered the Tamborough residence. Set behind a security fence, it was built of red brick, long and low, standing like a marooned ship in grounds that looked almost like a cardboard cut-out of a landscape. What had struck him most was the massive sense of isolation that had hung about the place. And was that what he wanted for himself, working alone in a big house, with only the desert for company?

"And I'm sure we'll easily make new friends too," Joannie was insisting. "You heard what Judith said. They sound like our kind of people."

Later on in the journey:

"When do we ever go to the theatre anyway, Frank? We haven't been for almost a year, and that was fringe, and not very good if I recall. Besides, they have a theatre, so we'd probably go *more* often, if anything."

Later still:

"If small-town life gets too much for us, well, it's—what?—only four hours' drive at most to San Fran. We can stop over the weekend, take in a Giants game, see Jack."

His younger brother.

"We'll have the best of both worlds. Can't you see that?"

The city came in sight at last, merely a shifting, blurry pewter-colored strip on the horizon at first. As they got closer, though, the scent of smog became apparent. And, as soon as they were onto the ingoing freeway, they ran straight into a tailback that stretched off ahead of them as far as they could see. Thousands of red taillights kept on blinking at them. They had to turn the air-conditioning to inner-circulation, or else breathe exhaust fumes.

Joannie hunched forward till she almost banged her head against the steering wheel.

"I can't take this any longer, Frank. I've hated this place more and more the past couple of years, and no one can live like that forever."

By the time they finally got home, they'd both agreed that they would sleep on the idea of moving. Joannie, rather glumly, dropped the subject altogether. Frank cooked supper for them, conchiglie pasta with a simple tomato, basil, and garlic sauce. He imagined himself doing the same thing in that big house back in Youngesville, and wasn't at all sure how he felt about the image that created in his head.

They ate mostly in silence. Later, they sprawled on the couch, the constant stir of traffic from the street outside making their windowpanes shake slightly. Frank slipped into the machine a DVD they'd rented, one that they had missed at the movies and were only just now catching up with. It was the recent re-make of 'The Stepford Wives.' He loved the book. They both did. So they stared at the new film attentively, but only ended up watching it halfway through, comparing it unfavorably with the original.

Their attention, both of them, was focused elsewhere. Inwardly, in truth.

Joannie decided to turn in early, claiming that the whole trip had exhausted her. Which was a slight lie, Frank knew. It was the uncertainty that was tiring her out, her waiting for him to come to a decision. *Was he being at all fair?* he wondered. *Did he have any right to do this to her?* Her mind already seemed to be made up.

He switched off most of the lights and sat in the semi-dark, pouring himself one small shot of Seagrams, then another. What to do? He didn't even like this place they currently lived in, that was for sure. But …

He thought about the town's main street, how pristine it had been. He thought about the desert, and the way that it had seemed to stare back at him when he'd looked out at it.

By the time he finally got to bed, he was slightly drunk, and bumped against his nightstand several times before finally climbing in. Joannie was flat out, and didn't even notice. In spite of all of which … he couldn't seem to get to sleep. He tossed and turned for over an hour.

When he finally tried lying flat out on his back and staying very still, all that he could smell was her. Her hair. Her skin. A soft, natural perfume like scented talcum powder. Between one moment and the next, he became aroused.

And when he looked across at her, her eyes were wide open and she was staring at him hugely.

He reached across and pulled her nightshirt off in one smooth motion—she helped him by raising both her arms. He rolled on top of her and started kissing her face.

Normally, when they did this, there was a good deal of foreplay. But this time, Joannie pushed his boxers quickly down around his thighs, then guided him into her.

She was very much ready for him, and he began sliding backward and forward evenly, trying to take his time. He was usually quite good at that, but this time the brakes that controlled him appeared to have failed. His strokes became faster and harder, his head filling with a clear white light that usually didn't arrive until much later.

It struck him in the next instant. *Is this the moment we conceive a child?*

He usually felt a very slight ambivalence at the prospect of that, but biology was driving him on by now. The muscles in his arms and shoulders bunched, and he pounded harder.

Joannie's eyes were firmly shut, her entire face screwed up, and she was making little noises he had never heard before. Like an infant being tickled very softly with a feather. Was that the potential child inside her, making itself known?

He kept on thrusting. Was something inside her changing? Something inside both of them?

Their lips locked as they moved, and they began kissing the way they'd done on their very first date. Fiercely, their mouths trying to find different ways to meld against each other. Joannie was making squealing noises, pushing them down his throat like solid objects, her body tightening and squeezing against his. The white light in his head was brightening to gold, and he was lost in the sheer energy of all of this.

Nothing mattered except this moment. Nothing existed in the entire world except this sensation and this rhythmic motion. The golden light was trying to break his head apart. Frank clenched his teeth, and ...

A fire-truck went by on the street outside, its siren blaring. Mr. Mojencu's German shepherd, in the apartment above theirs, woke up and began barking furiously. Then its owner came awake and started shouting at the dog.

Frank and Joannie both stopped moving. The moment—so intense a few seconds ago—was lost completely. It had vanished.

He could feel himself deflating quickly. They stared at each other. *Damn, will she be angry?* he thought. *Was that the right moment for her to conceive a child?*

He got his answer when Joannie began to laugh. It started as a gentle chuckle, and then became stronger and more infectious, till he finally joined in.

They lay there, him on top of her and their bodies still locked, gasping and sputtering and guffawing until their ribs began to hurt. *The hell with it,* Frank decided between furious snorts. *What's the point of living in a place that won't even let you finish making love? Coitus Interruptus Mansions—who in their right mind wanted to live here?*

"Okay!" he managed to get out at last. "Okay, we'll take the house!"

Joannie's laughter died away. Her eyes, in the dark, became very huge and damp. And then she wrapped her arms around his neck, and began kissing him all over again, even more intensely than before.

TWO

Visitors

When the doorbell rang, Frank looked up from his drawing board, surprised. He'd moved from his study at the back into the living room, to make the best of the afternoon light. The sliding windows were all closed, the air-conditioning humming softly in the background. He'd been immersed in his work, and expecting no one. Joannie wouldn't be home from the bank until at least six-thirty—they had a routine inspection going on down there.

Since moving in, they'd had a good few visitors. Several old friends from the city, bearing unusual potted plants and shinily chromed parmesan-graters. Joannie's folks had flown down from Illinois, and had genuinely approved of their new house. "Didn't like to say so at the time," Joan's father had informed them, "but I never did think much of that apartment that you had before."

And they had, of course, gotten to know most of the neighbors, all of who turned out to be of the same general age and in the same general income bracket as themselves. Youngesville was a pretty new community, as it turned out. Most of the people who lived here now had only moved here in the past couple of years.

There was a Japanese couple, Sam and Jasmine Yakamura, who tried to outdo everybody in their sheer homespun Americanism—they wore baseball caps the whole time, and they hosted a big barbeque the first weekend that Frank and Joan arrived. There was a pair of African-Americans six doors down, Paul and Iris Goodhew, who were both lawyers and already had an eleven-month old daughter. Otherwise? White thirtysomethings, all along this street and all throughout the entire town, like ears of corn in a whole field of it.

The only people that they *hadn't* met were their immediate neighbors to the left—Mike and Leonora Strang, they were informed. That house had stood dark and empty since they had arrived. The Strangs, they'd found out, spent one month every year in Cancun, and their moving-in had coincided.

As he set his pencil down and headed for the front door, Frank could see, glancing in through the spare bedroom's window, an open-topped Porsche sitting on the next-door driveway. Their final set of neighbors were finally making their presence known, he presumed. Maybe he ought to be carrying a cup of sugar with him.

Frank opened the door, and was immediately struck with a huge waft of rather musky-smelling perfume.

Leonora Strang stood, in her leopard-print high heels, almost exactly his height. Her smile was broad and very white, her pale blue eyes were as wide as opened flowers. She was standing with her hands on her hips, one knee tucked softly across the other.

Wavy, coppery hair flowed down across her shoulders. This was the same woman that he'd caught a brief glimpse of when they had first been looking around this place.

She bit her lower lip gently before speaking out in a mild Southern accent.

"So you're our new neighbor? Well, I can't say that I'm disappointed."

And, before he even had the chance to respond to that—if he'd even known how—she had walked in past him, without so much as being invited. She brushed against him as she did so. He could feel how warm her skin was.

Frank turned on the spot, watching her surprisedly as she stared around. She was dressed in denim cut-offs—cut-off barely within the limits of decency, he noticed—and a tight blouse, knotted high above her midriff, the same pattern as her shoes. Her skin was tanned to the color of light chocolate, with plenty of dark freckles in it, especially at the tops of her arms and—he saw when she turned back around to face him—in the cleavage of her very ample breasts.

She'd been twirling a pair of pink-tinted shades in her left hand, and now chewed gently on one of the arms as she looked him up

163

and down.

"Am I disturbing you? You working?"

Frank shrugged. She was starting to, but in a rather different manner to the one she meant.

"No. It's okay."

"I'm Leonora, by the way."

"I guessed that, yes."

"And you're Frank. I already know that too." She pulled a slim, pink cell phone out of her back pocket. "Global village these days, see. Just can't stop the gossip flowin'."

"Sorry Mike can't be here," she continued without waiting for him to reply, "but I had to drop him straight off at his office. Always working, that's our Mikey. Import-export, mostly from—guess where—Mexico. So he's always busy, always doing deals, even on supposed 'vacation.' He's one of those people who's not comfortable relaxing. Whereas, me? I'm entirely the opposite. Hey, you've done a nice job with this place."

Did she speak entirely in non-sequiturs? Frank wanted to lean back on something, look more casual, but there was only thin air to lean back against unless he moved.

"It's not exactly finished yet. There's so much space to fill."

"I meant, I was expecting packing crates and, you know, disarray. Mike and me were living out of boxes the whole first three months we got here."

Frank felt himself shrug again. "We decided to get all that out of the way as quickly as we could."

"How wise of you." Leonora turned her rapt attention to his leather-clad recliner. "Hey, I just *love* these. It's some kind of German design, ain't it? Kraftwerk?"

"Bauhaus," Frank corrected her, keeping his tone polite.

"Yeah?" And when she looked back across at him, an excited gleam had flourished in her eyes. "Do you mind if I …? I'd love to."

Before anything more could be said, she had straddled the recliner and was sprawling out across it, albeit she was being careful to avoid the leather with her heels. She tucked both hands behind her head and wriggled slightly, like a cat.

Staring down at her, Frank was reminded of the word that had come into his thoughts the first time that he'd glimpsed her. *Amazon.*

Stretched out like that, her shorts rode even higher up her long thighs, tightening at the zipper. And her bust and cleavage became even more prominent. She closed her eyelids and tipped her head back, letting out a dreamy sigh.

"My God, this is so sublimely comfortable. I could spend most of my life on this thing. Would you consider letting me stay here, almost forever?"

"I … don't think that my wife would be too delighted."

His neighbor's eyes came wide open again, and she stared at him boldly. "She works at the bank, right?"

"She's the manager."

"But you're more the creative type, I hear? A draftsman?"

"Graphic designer."

She got quickly up at that, and walked across to his drawing board. Studied what he'd been doing, and then beckoned him urgently across.

"Show me what you do."

Frank walked slowly over, being careful not to stand too close to her, and began to explain the designs on the sheet.

"It's for a global finance company. They need a different logo for each of their six international branches, but all sharing similarities, all based on the same theme, so there's an overall identity. I chose—"

"No," Leonora interrupted him.

Somehow, he'd got this wrong.

She indicated the stool he'd been sitting on. "Please, show me what you do."

Oh, okay. Carefully, he sat down. Cleared his throat. Picked up his pencil. Began adding to the logo he'd been working on, feeling rather awkward.

Leonora moved in right behind him and, bending over, brought her head down next to his, peering across his shoulder.

"I thought so. You've got a fine, delicate touch."

She edged a little further forward, and one of her breasts settled against his shoulder. Frank felt his pulse quicken.

165

"Um …" He was desperately trying to think of something that would allow him to stand up. "Would you like to see the rest of the house?"

Leonora straightened, and said "Sure" so eagerly he realized he'd made the wrong suggestion.

He deliberately took his time showing her the kitchen and the bathroom. And she appeared to notice that, appeared to be amused, her bright eyes twinkling like she was laughing silently, inside. She was watching him wriggle like a fish on a hook—that was how it felt. He showed her the guest bedroom and the room that they used, currently, for storage.

"Are you going to show me the garage next, Frank?" she asked. "I don't need to see the garage."

He gave her what he hoped was a baffled look.

"You've left out the master bedroom. I'm not sure: is that a PC term these days?"

And when he still didn't respond, she smirked and asked him, "What, are you guys kinky? You have leather sheets and chains in there, stuff you don't want other folks to see?"

She was only kidding, toying with him. People from the South had an unsubtle sense of humor, didn't they? And so he laughed.

"No, we haven't got that bored yet."

Which was supposed to be a joke as well. But was, again, the wrong thing to have said under the circumstances. Frank felt trapped now, and could not see any way of backing down.

And so he led her through. She walked right up to the foot of the bed, then turned around slowly.

"This is lovely, yet again. Kind of sexy in a romantic way. You guys must both head in here as soon as your wife gets home."

Frank pulled a face and, without thinking, told her, "Joannie'll be late this evening."

Third wrong thing to say, he knew, the moment it had fallen from his lips. *Three strikes and you're out.* He felt his face grow slightly hotter.

Leonora seemed to notice that as well, walked languidly back over to him. Stood within a foot of him, so that her perfume almost

166

overwhelmed him.

"Ain't that a bitch? All this space, all this comfort, and it's largely wasted 'cause the person that you're with—like mine—is working the whole time. Shame to waste a bedroom like this, don't you think, Frank?"

And she did something that startled him. She pushed her chest forward until her nipples, poking through her thin blouse, brushed against his shirt. She fixed her gaze on his in the same instant. And she waited.

She was extremely attractive in a very obvious way, and he couldn't deny that. He felt drawn to her, and his pulse was tripping. But …

It didn't happen on a regular basis. But, once every so often since he'd gotten married, an attractive woman had come on to him. He'd always felt flattered—who dislikes, after all, being looked upon as sexual and attractive? And he'd often felt a strong twinge of temptation.

But to betray Joannie in that way? Worse, to have to lie to her about it afterward? The silent guilt that he would always carry around with him, even if she never found out. For a pointless fuck? It wasn't worth it, not then and not now.

So he stepped back from the woman, saying, as firmly as he could, "Sorry, but I really do need to get back to work."

Leonora gazed at him quietly for a few seconds, her expression unreadable.

"Back to the drawing board?"

"Yeah, 'fraid so."

And then a change came over her eyes. Not one he'd anticipated, either. He'd expected her to appear disappointed at the very least. Hurt even. Offended.

Instead of which, she was coolly appraising him all over again. And seeming to approve of what she saw. She gave a tiny nod.

Her whole manner had altered, when he showed her back to the front door. She was less chattery, less demonstrative in the way she moved. Her body was exactly the same, obviously, but she wasn't flaunting it any longer. She'd transformed—in a bare handful of seconds—from a strident sex-bomb into somebody far more passive, calm, and thoughtful.

"Tell you what," she told him, stopping in the doorway. "What are you and Joannie doing this Saturday?"

"My brother's coming to visit. But after that, we are completely free."

"Okay, then. Mike and me were thinking of throwing a dinner party. We'd be just delighted if you guys could come along."

She waited, with the gentlest of smiles caught in her gaze.

"We'd ... be delighted to," Frank answered slowly.

"It's a date, then. Well, bye-bye for now."

She raised one hand, gave him a little, flapping wave, then strode away to her own house.

For a full minute after she had gone, Frank stood with his back against the doorframe, breathing deep and sweating slightly. What the hell had all that been about?

The weirdest thing was, he got the strange feeling it had been some kind of test.

And—if so—had he passed it?

"You know what this place is?" Jack told them over filet mignon at Claude's Brasserie on Saturday evening. "This place ain't Youngesville at all, dude. This place is 'Yuppieville.'"

He forked another portion of the expensive meat that they were paying for into his mouth, and grinned at them sardonically.

Eight years Frank's junior, Jack was nonetheless approaching his late twenties, and a little old to still be part of Generation X, a fact he never seemed to cotton onto. He worked at some indie record store down in the Mission District, rented a studio apartment in the Haight, commuted between the two on the same old motorcycle that he'd owned for years. He wore his hair, always slightly greasy, in a ponytail and sported a thick crop of stubble on his chin and jowls. Jack additionally had two tattoos—a unicorn and a dragon—that were visible, and doubtless several others that were not. Pierced ears ... they didn't even *want* to know pierced-what-else. And he didn't have a regular girlfriend, but was no slouch in that direction. Certain kinds of women warmed quite easily to his directness.

He was talking in his usual loud voice, and other patrons of the crowded restaurant kept glancing around at him. Which would have been quite irritating, Frank reflected, if they were not fully used to it. They indulged him, if anything. Joannie was looking slightly pained, but they both understood that, underneath the rebellious façade and the brashness, Jack had a good heart.

The lighting in here was dim and amber, the table's cutlery glittering softly in it. Jack took a swig of wine and pulled a face, since he was more of a beer person.

"I mean, I don't believe you guys," he told them. "You had such a cool scene going in L.A.. Now what? You getting soft? You getting old?"

"We want a family, Jack," Joannie told him quietly.

"Okay, so do your kids a favor and bring them up somewhere real. This ain't real. I mean, just look around you. Smug, comfortable white-bread everywhere you look."

"There's a black family on our street. And a Japanese couple."

"Oh congratulations, you've got your token darkies and your nips—how all-fired friggin' liberal of you!"

Which genuinely annoyed her. "Jack, you're being very rude!"

"I speak my mind and always have done, Jo-Jo," he came back at her, uncowed.

For this evening's meal out, Jack had chosen to wear old sneakers, a pair of khaki shorts, and an X-Box T-shirt. He was hugely into video games, and a big-time techno-buff. Which didn't mean that he was ignorant in other terms.

"You know how George Orwell defined freedom?" he went on. "'Being able to tell people things they don't want to hear.' Think I ought to try it?"

Without even waiting for a response, he tipped his head back a few inches.

"You're not living *here, any of you … you're just waiting to die!"* he said, so that the entire room could hear him.

The soft murmur of conversation around them trailed off to

a halt. The clatter of a fork on china was abrupt and startling. Faces gawped in their direction. Several waiters craned their necks, wondering what the problem was. Joannie colored deeply, and Frank quietly fumed. This was partly his own fault, he knew. His brother was not used to wine.

"One of these days, maybe you'll get it," he said firmly, quietly.

"Get what?" Jack shot back at him. "You make it sound like catching a disease, and perhaps you're right."

Joannie tried to change the subject, but her brother-in-law was so fired up that he was having nothing of it.

"I mean—apart from you guys, obviously—is there *anybody* interesting in this place?"

"There's plenty of artists and musicians," Joannie told him, recalling what Judith Mackenzie had told them. Although in truth, since moving here, they had met precious few.

"Anyone I've ever *heard* of?" Jack quizzed her.

"Lyle Tamborough," was Frank's triumphant retort.

And he finally was rewarded with the sight of his kid brother stopping in his tracks.

"The quantum-physics dude?" Jack leant back in his chair, his manner softening. "Okay, that is impressive."

Tamborough had, among other things in the past couple of years, defined two separate types of dark matter and given science a much better understanding of the dimensional nature of black holes, and Jack was interested in such stuff.

His gaze became pensive, musing, his crusading spirit of a few seconds ago evaporating, as though it had never been. Dropping brand-new information on him sometimes had this kind of strange effect on Jack, as if he was being forced to readjust the train of his insistent thoughts.

"Do you know that, until about four years back, he was a total nobody. Just an unknown professor at a nowhere Southern college, publishing the occasional paper that simply got ignored. And then suddenly, *boom!* Mental explosions on a cosmic scale! He's everywhere, he's the most influential scientist since Newton, he's winning the Nobel Prize!"

"Late developer?" Frank suggested, resisting the temptation to add 'like you.'

"He's supposed to have some pretty weird beliefs as well. Something of a hard right-winger, so I've heard."

"Aren't many of those Braniac guys like that?"

"Einstein wasn't," Joannie put in. "He was something of a humane-minded philosopher when he wasn't explaining how the universe worked."

Frank glanced across at her—he'd never even realized that she knew such things—then back at Jack, getting ready to play his trump card.

"Tell you what. Soon as we're finished here, there's something that we haven't even shown you yet."

"It's called 'New Hope'," he was telling his brother half an hour later.

Liberty Square was almost empty, very quiet, all the parents and kids long departed. From here—because there were no high roofs in Youngesville—you could make out the shape of the distant mountains. They still looked like a mirage, if that was even possible in darkness. The stars were out, the moon was full. A satellite winked as it made its swift passage overhead. The sculpture took the astral light and did very peculiar things to it, its shape harder than ever to pin down now that night had fallen.

"It's still in progress," Joannie explained quietly. "Keeps on being added to."

Jack looked suitably impressed. A little awed, in fact. His tone was rather hushed when he spoke.

"It looks like a machine," he murmured, "perhaps for taking you through a black hole."

Now that he mentioned it, the sculpture *did* look a touch mechanical. But, given the person who had thought it up, what else might you expect?

Frank walked carefully around the thing. "Think this place is boring now?"

171

"Well, frankly, yes, I still do," Jack said. "Except for this. This is pretty damned cool."

On the way back to the car, he told them, "Look, if you guys are genuinely happy here … I know I've ragged on you most of the evening, but it's your lives after all. When you start getting tired of this place, though, you're welcome in San Fran any time you like."

Frank grinned quietly to himself. Because, the way his brother had said that … as though he could put them both up in the tiny studio he lived in? He certainly couldn't.

He was sleeping under their roof tonight. They had paid for all his food and drink. And Jack still saw nothing wrong with holding forth and criticizing, and then acting like he owned the place, and the whole Bay Area into the bargain.

But he was still Frank's baby brother. So all Frank did was reach out, put an arm around Jack's shoulders, squeeze, and murmur, "That's nice of you. Thank you, bro."

"Think nothing of it, dude."

THREE

Polite Conversation

Leonora Strang opened her door when they rang the bell and said, "You city folk! There's no such thing as 'fashionable lateness' around these parts. Everyone's already here."

But she was beaming, joking, as she said it. Wasn't cross at all.

She was dressed, this time, in a tight pink trouser suit that, despite the fact that it showed less bare flesh, was as indicative of her figure as her last outfit had been. Frank had told Joannie about her dropping around, obviously—how else were they here?—but had left out many of the genuine details of that first visit. The word 'obviously' reared its head again.

She greeted Joannie warmly, giving her a firm peck on the cheek. But as she did the same to Frank, he tried to catch her eye, wondering 'was that a test, that first time?'

Exactly what had Leonora thought that she was doing?

But her face remained cheerfully blank, and he got no indication of her real motives at all. They were taken through into the living room, introduced to the other guests, some of whom they'd already encountered in their first couple of weeks here. There were Lionel and Judy Elfman, both dark and noticeably intense. There were Alexis and Gabe Beddows, she stern-looking and heavy-boned, he slightly built and short, and apparently happy to live in her shadow. Sam and Aimee Stock they already knew perfectly well—they were their next-door neighbors on the other side.

"They're great to live next to!" Aimee announced to the rest. "Never hear a peep from them at all!"

Neither the Yakamuras nor the Goodhews appeared to have been invited. That put Frank in mind of his brother's remark about

173

'tokenism' just last Saturday.

Mike, Leonora's husband, came on through. He'd been helping in the kitchen, and was wearing one of those novelty aprons that imposed the body of a Chippendale across his own. His own was five foot five and rather tubby.

They all settled back down and Leonora fetched them drinks— she quickly turned out to be a hostess of the tireless, somewhat flappy kind. The conversation, at first, moved along its usual paths. Work. The day's news. Property.

"I see the Harris place hasn't been sold yet," Lionel Elfman ventured.

And Frank knew exactly which house the man was referring to. Five doors down in the Stocks' direction, it had been standing darkened since they had arrived, a 'For Sale' placard out on the front lawn. They got the history of it now. It had belonged to a couple in their fifties who had lived there for a year, but they'd separated after that and moved out of Nevada.

Joannie asked where everybody hailed from. Mike and Leonora, it turned out, were both out of Georgia; Gainesville and Atlanta respectively. The Elfmans were from Oakland. The Beddows, like them, were from L.A. Sam and Aimee Stock had moved the whole way down here from upstate New York, but Frank and Joan already knew that. No one had lived here for more than a couple of years. Apart from a few older houses down by Younge, the entire community was shiny, spanking new.

They were ushered to the dining table, where a tapas starter was served—Leonora pronounced it 'tappers.' And then Mike carried through the main course, which they'd spent most of the afternoon preparing. It was a huge vegetable couscous—both of the Elfmans and Alexis Beddows were vegetarians, as it turned out. Leonora spooned the grains out onto white, broad plates.

"There's supposed to be seven different kinds of vegetable in this," she announced apologetically as she served. "But I could only find six. It's a deficient couscous, I'm afraid."

"It's delicious," Gabe Beddows piped up, over a mouthful of the stuff. "Another vegetable would spoil it, really."

Here was one odd thing though, as the meal progressed. There was more wine than you usually got these days. Leonora—as Frank had already noted—was a rather bustling hostess. She'd come wobbling across to help if you so much as dropped a napkin. That applied to keeping glasses full as well … she never seemed to stop. Who drank this much these days, in polite society at least? They'd been to dinners back in L.A. where the only bottle on the table had been Perrier. Everyone was too polite to refuse the woman, though. And, in consequence of that, their talk became more casual, looser, as the evening progressed into night. They all agreed what a great place Youngesville was, how lucky they were to have moved here.

"But you know what worries me?" Aimee Stock put in, her voice thick but a little anxious. "It's the way things can change these days, even in a place like this. Sam and I've had first-hand experience of it."

They had lived, back in New York state, in a town not unlike this one. It had always been a pleasant, quiet community, and had remained so for the first couple of years they'd been there.

"And then the drug dealers started moving in," she told the table, "like gremlins out of thin air. Graffiti appeared, men in hoods began hanging around corners. Before you even knew it, Main Street's not a place you want to be around after dark any longer." Her face rumpled up. "The older kids got sucked into that culture, then the younger ones. Next thing, there are gangs being formed, your next-door neighbor's boy is carrying a gun. It sounds incredible, but we've experienced it. And it genuinely worries me that the same thing could happen here."

Frank ventured something along the lines of, "You can't keep the world out." But he was largely ignored.

The conversation moved to crimes of general, mindless violence and their victims, how prevalent it was in the world beyond Youngesville. Out of habit as much as anything else, Frank interjected a few remarks about the causes of it, social injustice and the like. And back in L.A., his comments would have mostly been greeted with thoughtful nods. But here, they got him a pretty stiff and cool reception, especially from large-boned Alexis Beddows.

The woman fixed him with a steely gaze and asked him, "Can I tell you something that you might not like to hear?"

Which reminded him of something else that Jack had said last week. And so he nodded and then listened, his head swimming slightly from the wine.

"Back in L.A., I had this very close friend, the same age as me." Alexis Beddows drew herself up straight-backed in her chair. "She worked at one of the women's glossies, was this beautiful, warm, charming, giving person. One evening a week, she even taught yoga in one of the poorer neighborhoods—for free, you understand, out of the goodness of her heart.

"But this one evening—about three years back—she was the last one out of the community center, everybody else was gone. She'd been practicing some advanced moves after the class was over, and lost track of time. She was alone.

"Her car was the last one in the parking lot. She was halfway to it when six—boys, I suppose you'd call them—from one of the local gangs surrounded her. They beat up on her so badly it left scars. And they raped her of course, for over an hour."

The women at the table were all tight-lipped in their silence by this time. But there was no tremor in Alexis' voice. No dampness in her eyes. Just deeply- restrained, stringent anger. She looked to Frank like a block of ice with a hot flame burning deep inside it.

"The police caught them all," she continued. "When they showed up in court, they pled guilty—what else could they do? And then it came to sentencing and mitigation, and all their lawyers could talk about was how poor they were, how deprived they were, such bad backgrounds, on and on interminably.

"My friend? Her marriage, which had been a happy one, disintegrated. She had to quit her job. She can never have children, but that hardly matters, because she moved back in with her folks and she doesn't so much as come out of her room some days."

Her gaze was boring into Frank's.

"So you're poor? So you're deprived? I can understand—I'm not an imbecile—how that might lead you to steal. But to do that to another human being, hurt them that way, wreck their life that way?

How does that help you? Does it make you any less poor?

"All these ugly little brutes in our society, who walk around feeling sorry for themselves and take it out on other people? We shouldn't be excusing them, which seems to be your attitude."

"Then what should we be doing?" Frank asked carefully, his voice rather tight. He found it hard to swallow, just thinking about what had happened to Alexis' friend.

"Maybe we should put a bullet through each of their heads. Put them out of their misery, before they go spreading it to someone else."

Ten-thirty, the same evening:

"I used to do drugs myself," Aimee Stock confessed a little slurredly. "Cocaine, and then crack later on. I used to buy them from those same dealers who ruined our town in the first place. There's me—respectable, a schoolteacher—and every few evenings I'm heading down to Main Street, hanging out with criminals and getting high."

"It was my fault," Sam tried to insist. "I was working eighteen hours a day at that point in our marriage. Aimee felt neglected, lonely—"

"But that's hardly an excuse for what I did. The really scary thing is that it can happen to anyone. You don't have to be a scumbag from the wrong side of the tracks. It's like this … disease, this plague, that indiscriminately strikes people down."

"It's everywhere, and it's entirely our fault," Judy Elfman put in. "We may not be the generation who started this whole narcotics thing, but we're the ones who made it more acceptable."

"So what's the answer?"

"If it's our fault in the first place, then it's our responsibility to stop it."

Nearly midnight:

"*Big* confession," Leonora Strang announced. "Not one that I'm proud of, but I'm gonna say it anyway. Mike already knows this, so he ain't gonna be shocked. Back in Atlanta, in my first marriage, I—me and my ex—we used to swing."

She rolled her eyes and knocked the remaining wine in her glass down.

"I was like … this freak, out of my head on booze and Exes the whole time. Barely knew what I was doing. Two whole years of partying goes by like a weird and distant dream. And then one evening, at another of these parties—I didn't sober up exactly—but I had this moment of revelation. Of startling clarity. There was this unfamiliar guy, like—you know—on top of me. There were other people all around us. I wasn't even attracted to him, or *any* of them, come to that. And suddenly this question appears in my head in big block letters. So I asked it out loud.

"'Why am I doing this?'"

She spread her hands out as she said it, like she was holding the big, heavy question in between her palms.

"The guy stares down at me, does this kind of shrug thing with his face and says, 'because it's fun.'

"And I realize, no, no, fun's not why I'm doing this. I'm not even enjoying it too much. I'm doing this … because nothing in my life has any meaning anymore, not even making love. I'm all filled up with pointlessness, so much of it that it's become addictive and I actually seek it out. And so I put my clothes back on and I got out of there. Started running. Never went back."

"Luckily for me," Mike grinned affectionately.

"Yeah." She bent across to him and kissed his earlobe. "Count your blessings, honey."

Later still:
"We went to London for our vacation last year. Visited Notting Hill because of, you know, the movie. And you know what? It was full of black guys—not decent ones like the Goodhews, but the type you get over here in the projects. Baseball caps, hoodies, baggy pants—dozens of the suckers, everywhere you looked. And the movie made it seem like such a nice place."

"**F**or God's sake, Frank! Everyone was a little drunk!"

Including them, and they still were. Frank swung on his wife, indignant.

"Shoot the poor?"

They had waited till they'd got inside before beginning to discuss this.

"Everyone thinks stuff like that from time to time!"

"Shoot the fucking poor?"

"You heard what happened to her friend. She was upset, that's all. If something like that happened to me, would you be so liberal?"

"Don't be ridiculous."

"I don't understand what you're so riled up about."

"Riled up? Try offended. Bored. All that, 'ooh, I used to do drugs, but now I don't.' 'Ooh, I used to fool around, but that's behind me.' It's like they've all moved here in an effort to go neat and tidy and conventional."

"They've cleaned up their act—what's wrong with *that,* exactly?"

"It's … the *smugness* of it." Which was another of the words that Jack had used. "Everything secure and buttoned down and … white-bread."

Joannie put her hands on her hips, starting to look truly cross. "So what are you trying to tell me? That you'd like to try a few more drugs? You'd like to go in for a bit of swinging?"

He was opening his mouth to tell her she was being absurd, when she froze him with a glare.

"Who knows? If you're persistent enough, maybe you can persuade Leonora to go back to her old habits?"

He could see where this was headed. They had both drunk far too much. Joannie in particular handled alcohol badly—it made her sharp-tempered and argumentative. Give it another minute or two, and this would boil over into a full-blown, screaming row, which was the last thing that he wanted.

"I'm going out," he announced.

"Now?"

"I need to clear my head."

"Okay, then. Don't expect me to stay up, that's all."

"That's okay. I won't."

He didn't intend to do it, not at all. But on the way out, he slammed the door behind him.

FOUR
'New Hope'

He was headed in toward the center, Younge, without even properly noticing it, his chin tucked down, hands in his pockets. His whole body was bent over, and a dreadful feeling of tiredness was trying to rear up and engulf him. The question came to him once again. *Was he getting old?*

He gazed up through his eyebrows at the ranked houses around him. All of them pitch dark by this hour, not a single light on anywhere. All of them built along the same general theme, as if they'd come off a production line.

It wasn't—he tried to analyze it—it wasn't what had been said this evening that had really gotten underneath his skin. He'd heard far worse in his time, let's face it. It was ... the lack of disagreement. Of argument, debate. Everybody had routinely nodded over everything that had been said. A herd mentality. A bland consensus. The well-heeled inhabitants of a well-heeled little town agreeing that they'd gotten life right in a way that no one else had managed.

And—Joannie didn't seem to get this at all—it wasn't that he was actually *for* either cocaine or swinging. And he did feel *deeply* for Alexis Beddows' friend. But there had to be more to life than housekeeping and dinner parties, didn't there? They might as well be living in the early Fifties.

His head was swimming rather badly. Jesus, why'd he allowed Leonora to pour him so much booze? And—he kept on wondering—how did her little speech this evening tally with the way she had behaved when she had walked into his living room?

Had she been testing him somehow? But for what? He still wasn't at all sure.

He crossed an intersection. Started passing by more of the same houses. Peered bleakly around him, remembering the movie they had watched the same evening they had agreed to come and live here.

Stepford.

He also recalled the term that Jack had used a week ago.

'Yuppieville.'

When exactly had security become the number one priority in everybody's life? That had been the question that he really should have asked.

That was what he ought to do! Knock on the door of everyone who'd been there, reconvene the dinner party, pose that question to them!

Jesus, he was even drunker than he'd thought.

He was almost the whole way to Younge. Glancing along past that street, he thought he saw an unexpected flash of green light.

When it came again, he realized that it was emanating from Liberty Square. Well, at least *something* was happening.

But, he wondered, what was going on?

Younge was entirely empty, 'closed' signs turned around in the doors of all the stores and cafes. Not a single security grille anywhere—there was absolutely no need for them. Mannequins gazed out at him from a few darkened windows, slightly nonplussed, wondering why he was there.

As he got closer to the square, Frank could see that he was not quite as alone out here as he had thought. A small figure was hunched below the curious statue. Was down on its knees, in fact, and tinkering with something.

It was a man, who got up after a while, giving Frank a better view. This guy seemed to be in his mid-forties, and was rather short, completely bald save for a cowlick at the front. He was dressed in a plain white shirt and rather scruffy jeans, and had a long nose and a dull, lugubrious expression.

But he was so caught up in what he was doing that he didn't even notice Frank approach. And Frank started to figure out who this might be.

"Bob Meaks?" he called out, when he was close enough.

The man looked around startled, his thin eyebrows coming up. Then, "Sure." His shoulders relaxed. "Do I know you?"

Frank walked slowly across the square, both his hands lifting from his pockets.

"Frank Lansbury. I moved here—me and my wife—a few weeks back."

Bob Meaks produced a handkerchief and dabbed at his fingers with it.

"Ah, yes; heard something about that."

"You working on the statue? At this time of night?"

"A constantly on-going project," the man told him proudly. "Surely you've already heard?"

Frank stared at it all over again, trying to figure out what new thing had been added. But he couldn't spot it.

"I'm just fine-tuning," Meaks informed him, figuring out what he was looking for.

Which made the thing sound even more like a machine, as Jack had pointed out.

"Did I see it actually light up a short while back?" Frank asked.

"You did."

"I didn't even realize it was connected to a power source."

"Sure it is." Meaks looked awfully pleased with himself. "Mr. Tamborough can light it up remotely, or there's a hidden switch right here."

"So how come it's not lit up the whole time?" Frank asked.

Meaks glanced down at the ground briefly. "That's not the idea. Mr. Tamborough intends that function only for special occasions."

Frank began to circle around the statue slowly, trying to make out where the source of the green brilliance had been. He could not see any actual bulbs. "New Year's Eve, that kind of thing?"

"That kind of thing," Bob Meaks agreed. "If you don't mind, I'm not quite finished."

"Mind if I watch?"

"Sure, be my guest."

The man seemed to forget that he was there from that point on, and went down on his knees again. He reached toward a rectangular projection near the base, and pressed his thumb down on one part of it. The whole section sprang gently open—it served, apparently, as a lid. Below it was a row of switches. Meaks selected two of them, then put his index finger to a third.

"I'd turn your face away," he warned. "This is going to be a pretty bright one."

Frank did as he'd been asked. And the next moment …

The entire square was flooded with a dazzling green glow, so bright that he was forced to squeeze his eyelids shut, even though he was no longer facing it. The emerald brilliance seeped through anyway, and started playing strange tricks in the darkness there. God, for something ornamental, this was horribly intense. What was the point of that?

"Optical fireworks, he calls it," he could hear Bob Meaks explaining. "You'll see, when you re-open your eyes."

The glare faded and then finally vanished, although its residue stayed in Frank's head.

He … re-opened his eyes, blinking, glancing around him. For a scant few seconds, things around him appeared to be different. Not inside the town itself, but beyond it. In the desert, and above.

The mountains looked far closer, higher, looming above Youngesville like a tidal wave. The sky seemed to be lower, darker, and devoid of stars or moon. He even thought he saw a bolt of lightning flash across it—that *had* to be his retinas short-circuiting. And then the whole thing vanished and his normal sight returned.

He rubbed his eyes.

"You see?"

And, for the first time since they'd met, Meaks was actually grinning.

"He can do anything, can Mr. Tamborough. A brilliant man. A genius indeed."

"But what's …?" The question came oozing out of Frank like thick and viscous fluid. "… what's the point of this?"

Meaks shrugged, his smile fading the same way the light had done. "It's not quite finished yet. When it is, I promise you you'll get it."

184

This had all been one strange evening, although not in any good way. Frank still felt pretty weary as he came back in through the front door. He'd sobered up a lot by now. The house was dark and silent. Joannie, good as her word, hadn't even waited up for him.

Probably just as well, he thought. They'd only begin arguing again, going in ever-tightening circles. He slipped off his shoes and, in his stockinged feet, went up the stairs. *No point in waking her,* he thought.

But, when he pushed the bedroom door wide open, Joannie was lying there in the darkness with her eyes shining again. She smiled at him inquisitively.

"Hi," he muttered.

"Hi yourself. Is it all right now? Is it good, between us?"

"Sure. Of course it is."

"I was being stupid, back before. We both were."

"We're allowed to do that, sometimes, being human beings."

"So let's just forget it. Come to bed."

And that was good to hear.

When he snuggled down next to her, it was not like back in L.A.. They took ages, and were very gentle with each other. When he came, it was like silk slipping down his entire body. Joannie released a soft, protracted moan at the same instant.

She kissed him on the cheek, and fell asleep shortly after she had done that. He could hear her steady breathing. Then Frank turned away from her, letting his own eyes slip shut.

Soon, we will have children, he thought.

He still felt a touch ambivalent about that. But he was slightly ambivalent about so many things, these days.

FIVE

The Beazleys

One evening a couple of weeks later, coming home from work, Joannie told him, "Guess who's applied for a job at the bank?"

Judith Mackenzie, as it turned out. The realty business in Youngesville had dried up altogether.

"She's sold her very last house, the Harris place."

Frank went through into their bedroom and looked out through the window. Sure enough, the 'for sale' placard on the front lawn five doors down had gone.

"Surely people move, though? Even here."

"Why? What reason would they have to? Most people are pretty recent here, remember?"

That was true.

Word about the new arrivals got around quickly enough. They were called the Beazleys, as it turned out, Joe and Margaret. They were both in their late thirties. He was some kind of accountant, and she was apparently planning to open a bookstore.

"Sounds to me as if they'll fit right in," said Aimee Stock approvingly.

The day arrived. A massive moving truck rolled up, accompanied by the Beazleys in their matching cars. They were Mazda sports models, red for him, canary yellow for her.

One thing struck Frank as a touch unusual, when he strolled across to say hello. Loud music was blaring from Joe Beazley's stereo—he had not switched it off when he had parked the car. It was ... thrash metal of some kind. An odd choice for an accountant.

Joe himself was of medium height and rather stout, with deep brown eyes and curly dark hair that, frankly, would have looked far

186

better on a young Elliot Gould. He was dressed in what Frank was sure was an Armani suit, the white shirt open at the neck. But he was friendly, beaming, busy-looking, shook hands like a pro.

Margaret Beazley was a little taller than her husband, which seemed endemic around here. Willowy, with short-cut red hair. She wore Prada and, although charming enough, came across as being slightly aloof. But her husband's temperament let you ignore that.

"I'm sure we're gonna be great neighbors," Joe was chortling. "Come on over, any time you like. We're moving two refrigerators in, and the biggest one is for the beer."

Frank left them to settle in after a while. The whole street did the same. The moving truck was gone by the time Joannie got back home.

"Is that thrash metal I can hear?" she asked, rather suspiciously.

Had Joe left his car stereo on? Frank went back to the bedroom window, opening it slightly.

No, the Mazda was silent, its hood pulled firmly up. The music was coming from an open side door of what was now the Beazley's house.

It went on, loud enough to be heard clearly from a distance, until well after eleven.

So perhaps Aimee Stock was wrong, and they'd not fit in quite so easily after all.

The street's jungle drums resounded constantly to their name, the next few days. They played that music all the time. They sunbathed in their backyard in the skimpiest of outfits, and one time Margaret removed her top. Joe Beazley was usually to be seen chewing on a fat cigar, but Judy Elfman was *certain* she had glimpsed him at a window, one fine evening, with a joint.

"You think the music's bad?" asked Iris Goodhew, bumping into Joannie at the grocery store.

The Goodhews lived right next door to these new arrivals.

"You should hear the sounds that they make later on." She feigned a blushing look. "If high-pitched moaning were an Olympic event, that girl would have a *shelf* full of medals. And the *language* that they use."

Come Friday, Frank was standing in the living room, his drawing board abandoned, lost in thought, when he saw Leonora Strang going past on the sidewalk. She was stepping briskly, purposefully, her shoulders thrown back and her chest thrust out. And was dressed almost the same way she had been on her first visit here. Except, this time, she was wearing a black leather mini-skirt, instead of the denim cut-offs.

Puzzledly, Frank went back to the bedroom window to follow her progress. Sure enough, once she had reached the Beazley house, she turned and headed for the porch. There was only the red Mazda sports car out in the driveway, he noticed. Margaret Beazley was obviously away somewhere.

The door came open and Leonora disappeared inside. Frank waited a few seconds longer before turning away, although he was deeply puzzled. Did she apply her 'test' to everyone who moved onto this street? And if so, what exactly was she trying to prove?

He returned a short while later, but the Strang woman had not emerged.

Several minutes after that, though, something unexpected happened. The yellow Mazda reappeared and rolled up on the driveway. Margaret Beazley climbed out and then went indoors.

He was ashamed to admit it to himself, but he felt the slightest twinge of *schadenfreude* when he saw that. If Joe was up to something with his neighbor, sparks would fly for sure.

But the Beazley house remained entirely silent. He watched it for a good long while, his puzzlement growing. What was going on in there? Maybe Leonora had already left, and he'd simply not seen it?

It was none of his business really, he supposed. His work beckoned, and he became absorbed in it. He only lifted his head past an hour later, when a sound like a front door being banged shut issued loudly from the same direction he'd been watching.

Going back to the same window, he could see Leonora Strang marching very quickly down the street, in the opposite direction to the one she should be headed. God, had something happened to her? Her long hair looked all mussed. Her whole body seemed rigid.

He *had* to know what was going on. So he slipped on a pair of canvas shoes and grabbed his keys, then went out on the sidewalk. Followed her at a cautious distance. She seemed terribly agitated, and didn't even notice him there.

The woman was heading down toward Younge. She had fished her slim cell phone out of her purse and was talking on it, with her free hand lashing at the air. She was upset or angry about something, but Frank was much too far away to make out what it was.

Reaching Younge, she made her way along it till she reached the Italia coffee house. Judith Mackenzie, Frank realized, was sitting at a table by the window, presumably on her break, since she was working at the bank by this time.

He watched as Leonora went inside and sat down hurriedly at Judith's table. The two women's heads instantly locked, so it was pretty easy for him to slip in unnoticed. He sat down in the booth behind theirs. There was a plywood divider between them, but he could hear them both quite clearly.

That honeyed quality to Leonora's tone of voice had vanished, and been replaced by an icy hissing.

"He *failed*!" she was telling Judith. "I barely had to shake my titties at him and he had me up on the kitchen table with my panties down around one ankle! And it gets worse! He was halfway through fucking me when his wife walked in!"

"And?" Judith Mackenzie asked.

"She didn't even blink! She reached into her purse, took out this vial of coke, snorted some, and then just stood there watching us with this big dirty grin on her face. And then, when he was done with me, she asked if I was into women too."

"And did you?"

"Well of *course* I did—a girl's gotta have *some* fun in this dump!"

Frank was listening to this stunned and partially in shock. There went that whole impassioned dinner-table speech, now didn't it? Jesus, what a liar and a hypocrite!

"We even watched a porno later on—they've got this huge

189

stash of them. But the point, my dear, is this, in case you missed it. You have totally, but one-hundred percent, dropped the ball at the eleventh hour."

Judith tried to protest, but the Southern belle was having none of it.

"You're supposed to do all the initial screening. I'm just here to double-check. So tell me, how on earth did you manage to sell that house to a pair of dedicated players?"

Judith's voice had become noticeably small and apologetic when she came back with an attempted excuse. "They appeared ... so respectable when I first met them."

"Aw, the worst ones always do!"

Frank's head was reeling slightly by this stage. He simply couldn't understand what they were going on about. Screening? Double-checks? For what? What precisely did this have to do with Youngesville?

"It comes down to this," Leonora was saying. "They are simply not acceptable. Which means the—"

Someone called out for a waitress and he missed the next couple of words.

"—be filled. They simply have to go, and be replaced, and quick. You get it? Do you understand?"

Their conversation dropped to a low murmur after that, and he could not make out another word of it. They were conspiring, he supposed, trying to work out a solution to the 'problem' that the Beazleys posed.

But what exactly was that?

His head continued spinning as he made his way back home. He couldn't even get a solid grasp on what he'd heard. The way that Leonora had been talking, it was almost as if she believed she was trying to seduce her neighbors in some kind of *official capacity*. And what on earth sense did that make?

Back safely in his own living room, he picked up the phone and dialed for San Francisco. Jack was alone at the store as it turned out, not particularly busy, and so willing to converse at length. And so Frank started to explain what he had seen and heard. To his frustration, his kid brother's first reaction was astonished ribaldry.

"*What?* She lets you poke her if she disapproves of you? Man, how much do you suppose she'd disapprove of me, a week's worth?"

And he burst out laughing.

"Jack!"

"Oh dude, what you suburbanites get up to behind your chintz curtains!" Jack spluttered.

"Cut it out!"

"Hey!" His baby brother gave another snort. "I thought you were open-minded? So how come you're so upset?"

"I genuinely think there's something happening here. I get the feeling this is organized."

"Or maybe she just likes to fool around and tell her friend about it … you might consider that possibility?"

Frank went through it in his head again, for what seemed like the thousandth time. Those words they'd used. 'Screening.' 'Double-check.' 'Acceptable.' They hammered at him like they had the first time that he'd heard them. And that final verdict, that the Beazleys had to go quickly and be replaced. For what?

"It's some kind of test. As if … for some kind of secret society or something."

"Like a cult?"

"Maybe something along those lines. They appear to be looking for couples who are well-behaved and fit in nicely."

"An extreme way of going about it, wouldn't you say?" Jack pointed out.

"Well exactly. That's what's really bothering me, kiddo."

There was a troubled pause out on the far end of the line

"But the way you described it, this Leonora seems to like the bad-behavior stuff."

"That's right. It's all so frigging contradictory. I can't figure for the life of me exactly what they're doing."

"You tell Joannie yet?"

He hadn't, and wasn't looking forward to doing so, because it would entail describing Leonora Strang's first visit here. Even though he'd firmly turned her down, his wife would not be pleased to hear about it.

"I could do some checking around," his brother offered. "That only means one thing, these days. I'm taking it you're still a total doofus with the Internet?"

"'Fraid so."

"Yeah, suspected as much. I can do it though, no sweat. Give me those names again?"

The rest of the afternoon passed in a dull blur, during which he got no work done. He simply kept on turning the whole matter over in his brain until it lost all form or slightest focus.

One thing, however, became certain. Jack had been right—he had to tell Joannie. She'd be angry at first, most likely accusatory. But she had the right to know about this, whatever it was.

Her key turned in the lock, at last. Joan came in through the front door. Frank was surprised to see that she was beaming hugely, her whole manner far lighter than usual. And her eyes were sparkling. She looked younger and fresher than she had in years.

She'd apparently had a very good day. Which made him hate what he was now about to tell her. Seeing her so happy like this? It was heartbreaking to bring her down.

But he had to do it all the same. Frank knew it, and began clearing his throat.

"I've got great news, honey!" Joannie told him, hurrying across the room. "I'm pregnant!"

SIX

The Lecture

So—of course—he never got around to telling her. What was the real point in upsetting her, worrying her badly, when he didn't even have anything remotely solid to go on?

The lecture happened two days later. They'd bought tickets for it a month back, and had no reason at all not to attend, despite the recent news. Their lives were going to become rather more limited after a few trimesters, let's face it, and so they'd better make the most of the few months of freedom they had left.

A BETTER REALITY, a conversation with Lyle Tamborough, the posters outside the theatre on Younge had been promising all week. One of the alarms had malfunctioned on Joannie, closing up the bank this evening, and so they got there slightly late.

The place was already full as they edged in, almost every last seat taken. The Yakamuras and Goodhews were there, as was everybody from the dinner party. Judith Mackenzie was in attendance as well.

Leonora Strang noticed them coming in, and flashed them both a big white smile.

The Beazleys weren't here, Frank took note. They apparently had so much other stuff to do, they didn't have the time or patience for this.

He mumbled a soft apology to each person he disturbed and, reaching his seat, quickly settled down.

"—setting up the basis for the facts that we now know about our universe and other ones."

He'd seen photographs of Tamborough before, but the man was far more frail looking than he'd imagined. He had to be in his late sixties, and stood at the podium on stage with a noticeable stoop.

His silver hair was thinning, but he had a dense moustache of the same color. He wore tortoiseshell-rimmed spectacles, which was something Frank had not seen in a good long while. His spindly fingers, nicotine-stained, fidgeted against the microphone stand as he spoke. His voice was high and slightly grating.

He had drawn a succession of overlapping discs on the blackboard next to him, and was pointing at the top and bottom ones. Frank listened carefully, trying to catch up on what he'd missed.

"The alternate universes at the far ends of the scale will, obviously, be entirely different from our own. So different, in fact, that four-dimensionality—the fourth dimension being time—might not exist as we understand it. But closer to our own reality –"

He indicated the more central discs.

"—what we might very well find are universes like our own, but with slight variations. And who knows what those could be? A world where Yellow Cabs are red, perhaps? Or where politicians are honest?"

The audience laughed dutifully.

"My central point is that science and the human psyche dovetail very neatly in this proposition, as they often prove to. Because I ask you, what has been the central dream of mankind down the millennia, encapsulated in nearly every major religion on this planet? Why, the concept of Heaven! Paradise! A better world, a happier and trouble-free form of existence! Even to this very day, even in this age of science, mankind yearns for that. Fundamentalist Christians in the heartland of this very country eagerly await the end of this tainted and imperfect world, the coming of the Rapture. Fundamentalists of *other* creeds actually kill themselves, and take others with them, to escape this life and thus enter a better one."

Frank blinked slowly. What was this about? The man seemed to be describing what he, personally, had always regarded as dumb notions, lunatic behavior. And if he was trying to lend validation to it …?

"My point is, you don't have to die. A better universe *is* out there, free of spite and violence and crime and war. The only thing we have to do is find it."

"Could we actually go there?" someone in the audience asked.

"The truthful answer is, not yet. But I'm working on it."

Which got him another, bigger laugh.

It went on in this manner for another forty minutes that, to Frank, seemed considerably longer. Most of this, so far as he was concerned, was pointless mumbo-jumbo. But the audience was listening attentively, almost raptly. And that included Joannie. He was surprised at first ... he'd always thought her far more levelheaded. But considering her new condition ...

The more he turned that one thing over, then the more that it made sense. How tempting all this had to sound to a woman newly pregnant. To bring up your first child in a world far calmer, safer, happier than the one that they were in—how massively appealing did that concept have to be?

A very pleasant fantasy, yes, he had to admit. But he'd been expecting something rather more substantial from the winner of a Nobel Prize.

The lecture finally petered to a close, to a massive round of applause. Judith Mackenzie actually climbed up and helped the old man off the stage—Frank hadn't even realized they knew each other.

When they emerged into the lobby, a tight cluster of women were chattering away excitedly. He knew them all. Leonora, Aimee, Alexis, Judy Elfman. Judith Mackenzie joined them having, presumably, relinquished her charge.

"I suppose I'd better tell them the good news," Joannie announced brightly.

But he was in no mood for it himself. The flatness of the lecture had left him edgy and a little tired. And besides, of the gathered women, there were two he didn't feel inclined to hang around with all that much.

"You go ahead. I need some fresh air," he answered quickly. "See you outside."

And it turned out Joannie was okay with that.

Standing on Younge, his hands in his pockets, everything looked vaguely unreal around him, like a studio set. He remembered, once again, what Jack had said.

The gleaming, darkened windows, and the ocher streetlights rearing up against a calm, purple-black sky. Tamborough's statue, which was visible from here, looked like it had been transplanted from the set of an old science-fiction movie.

Couples were going by him, talking, all of them casually, but not cheaply, dressed. Climbing into good models of cars, Mercs, Beamers, and luxury SUVs. Everything the same around here, and everyone quite similar. God, but it still grated at him sometimes.

He recalled Aimee Stock talking about her old hometown in New York State, the way it had declined. *"You know what worries me? It's the way things can change these days."* Everybody, these days, seemed so anxious about that.

He didn't personally care for this equation where 'change' equaled 'bad.' Keeping things the way that they were might make other people feel comfortable, but it left him with a sense of being trapped.

A tall blonde woman, getting into a sports-model Lexus, lit a cigarette. And, on a sudden impulse, he went across and bummed one off her. Christ, he hadn't done this in years.

The first lungful of smoke made his head reel, but it sparked off all of the familiar nerve endings. And he wondered for a moment why he'd even given this thing up. The small matter of strokes, emphysema, and cancer, he reminded. It had been the right thing—the sensible thing—to do.

And how had his life gotten so fucking sensible?

The last time he'd used any harmful substance, before this one? It had been getting slightly tipsy at the Strangs, not long after they had first arrived here. And that was the sum total of it. Getting mildly drunk, just one time.

He remembered, back in college …

Well, those days were properly behind him now.

The second drag made him start to cough, and he threw the remainder of the cigarette down a storm drain. *That's your idea of kicks these days, Frankie boy,* he told himself. *There's your wild side. One-and-a-half draws on a Virginia Slim.*

And then he wondered whether all of this was merely just a

panicky reaction to the massive new responsibilities that were about to descend on him. *Am I being chicken-shit?* That notion slowed him down.

Joannie was taking her time, wasn't she? He went back to the theatre door. The women were all still there, and in the same positions. But, instead of the delighted and congratulatory bustle he'd expected, they looked lost in earnest conversation. Joannie seemed to be listening fixedly, squinting slightly puzzledly, but then nodding when she was asked things. Whatever those things might be.

And … he wasn't really sure he liked the look of this. Two of these women, at least, were conspirators of some kind, although he wasn't certain what their game involved. Was Joannie being drawn into whatever might be going on?

Or it was possible that he was making a fuss about nothing, and Jack was right. Maybe Leonora simply messed around and then told her friend about it for additional and mutual kicks. Could it be as smuttily mundane as that?

He had to wait practically another five minutes, before Joannie remembered he was there. She made her excuses, walked toward him. She was smiling gently, thoughtfully, like something had occurred to her that hadn't been obvious before.

The film they'd watched before they'd moved here came to mind again. *Okay,* he thought, *you gonna replace me with a robot?*

"Pretty involved conversation, by the look of it," he remarked instead, as they made their way back to their car.

"They were giving me some good advice."

"But none of them even have kids yet."

"They all know people who do," Joannie pointed out, a little crossly. "And besides, did you know Alexis and Leonora both used to be nurses?"

Or at least wore the uniform in one case, Frank supposed.

He'd been planning to go a little deeper into the whole subject. Find some way—preferably a subtle one—of conveying to her his growing unease. But as they got into the car and closed the doors, Joannie sniffed the air and asked, "Have you been smoking?"

"A few puffs."

She looked astonished, and quite affronted.

"Jeez, you've chosen quite a time to take *that* up again."

"I told you, I took a couple of draws and then threw it away."

"Why pick it up in the first place?"

Which was a good question. So they pulled off from the curb and rode in silence for a while.

"Were you girls talking about anything else?"

"Why would we be?" Joannie asked, glancing at him rather oddly. "Frank, have you got something on your mind?"

They were almost at the corner of their street, by this stage. And he was trying to think how to phrase this. When a siren, rushing up behind them, made them both look back.

A patrol car was hurtling up in their direction, with its beacons flashing. But he wasn't even doing the speed limit, so Frank doubted it was after him.

He pulled over to let it pass. The whole SUV shuddered as the cop car thundered by. They watched as it went speeding out into the desert, leaving a thick trail of dust. It was rare for the police to even use their sirens here.

Frank was ready to pull out again, when more flashing lights became apparent. Another cop car, an ambulance, and then a fire truck, went heading off in the same direction that the first vehicle had disappeared.

He and Joannie exchanged troubled glances.

"What do you suppose is wrong?"

They came to a slow halt about three miles out into the desert. The whole scene in front of them was washed in flickering red and blue. All four of the emergency vehicles had stopped. Figures were moving around, mere silhouettes. Frank could see that there had been some kind of accident.

"Wait here," he told Joannie, thinking about her condition. "Let me go and see what's up first."

The air smelled very dry and sharp as he got out. But it was overlain with several odors. Was that burning rubber that he got a hint of? Was that gasoline?

He went around the fire truck. And stopped. Just stood there, not even blinking.

It was hard to be certain in this oscillating light, but that seemed to be Joe Beazley's Mazda lying overturned on the parched desert dirt. Its whole frame was crumpled. By the look of it—the distance it was lying from the blacktop—it had flipped over several times after leaving the road. Its shattered windshield had only triangular splinters remaining, like a maw of jagged teeth.

Behind those, and suspended upside down, part of Joe's face could be made out. The eyes were wide open and glassy. There was blood in one of them. And there was something wrong, as well, with the shape of his head.

His wife was not with him. It looked like Margaret had come out on the first flip, was lying near a roadside ditch. Her Prada-clad torso was practically split in two, and her limbs were lying at peculiar angles, all her dignified aloofness taken from her.

As he watched, a couple of paramedics walked toward her with a body bag. The fire crew started at the Mazda with a cutting tool, and sparks filled the night air.

Frank's gaze wandered over numbly to a pair of elongated, curving skid-marks on the road. Then a cop he knew, Don Hendershall, came ambling across.

"You know these people?"

"Just a little. They lived on my street."

"New here, I understand?" Don asked.

"Relatively new. What happened?"

"They were going way over the hundred mark, I'd say from the length of the skids." Another cop had started photographing them. "My guess is a blow-out. Can't be any other reason—this is a completely empty road."

"That can happen?"

He was rather numb, and Don peered at him with a tight, quirky, enquiring smile. "Sure it can. A car ain't a toy. Happens all the time, in fact."

... her limbs were lying at peculiar angles, all her dignified aloofness taken from her.

Margaret was halfway in her body bag by this time. Joe Beazley continued staring outward through the broken glass, oblivious to the racket going on around him.

Frank remembered what he had overheard Leonora say, *"They simply have to go."*

Well, then, this was an extremely lucky break, in her case.

SEVEN

The Date

About four o'clock the next afternoon, Joannie phoned home and asked him, "Do you mind if I'm about an hour late this evening?"

"Of course not," he told her. "What's up?"

"It's just, me and Judith have been getting on well recently. We thought we might go out for coffee."

"Judith Mackenzie?"

"Right. Any problem with that?"

He couldn't think of any objection he could sensibly make without explaining to her the entire conversation that he'd overheard. So he found himself murmuring, "No, none. See you later, then."

Which was not to say he liked the whole idea. He thumbed his eyeballs gently as soon as he put down the phone. That discussion Judith Mackenzie had been engaged in with Leonora Strang washed back into his mind like a flood of dirty water. The sharp urgency of it, the tense, conspiratorial tone. Whatever they might be up to, he hated the idea of a pregnant Joannie getting even remotely involved.

But what to do about it, without telling her everything? And why was he slightly afraid to do so?

She was home at a quarter before seven, the light fading at the window at this time of year. Frank watched her as she came along the driveway. She was smiling to herself, her step was light and easy.

When she came in, she beamed at him. Asked, "Have a good day?"

"Yeah, just fine. Yourself?"

"I'm getting on so well with Judith these days, Frank. I've never really talked to her before, and it turns out we've a lot in common."

Not everything, I hope, he thought, feeling his insides flip-flop slightly.

"It was only you two girls, then?"

"No. Oddly enough, Leonora Strang joined us. She just happened to be passing by."

And, her movements still calm and casual, Joan went through into the bedroom to change back out of her working clothes.

Frank paused a moment before following her in. Blinked at the empty doorway where she had been standing.

Simply … happened by? So his wife had taken coffee with the pair of them. He didn't like the sound of that one little bit.

When he went on through, she had stripped down to her underwear. She had on sheer, flesh-colored hold-ups, and was bent over a chest of drawers, searching for a T-shirt. Her skin had an almost luminous glow to it. He couldn't remember when she'd looked so sexy, and it softened his mood up a little. Perhaps he was simply being paranoid.

"What did you girls find to talk about?" he asked, as casually as he could.

"Oh, you know. My pregnancy again, a lot. The town in general. And the lecture last night."

"No mention of the *accident* last night?"

Joannie shrugged. "We didn't want to dwell on it. Bad things happen, and you simply have to move on."

And no one had liked the Beazleys anyway. That was something that you oughtn't mention, so she didn't.

Her manner was so relaxed, so self-contained and happy. It was almost like she'd taken some kind of mild drug. The glow he'd noticed to her skin was coming from deep inside her. But Frank still wasn't too happy with the company that she'd been keeping.

"Leonora mention anything about them?"

"Who, the Beazleys? How d'you mean?"

"I thought she was friendly with them? Saw her dropping around there, once."

When Joannie glanced at him across her shoulder, her face was entirely blank.

"If she did, she didn't mention it. And we had so much else to talk about."

She found a T-shirt that she liked, turned around and slipped it on.

Beamed at him again.

"I'm so glad we're going to have our baby here in Youngesville, Frank. The best decision that we ever made."

So far as *he* was concerned, though, the jury was still out on that.

"T here's absolutely zip on Judith Mackenzie, or on Leonora Strang," Jack told him over the phone.

There was punk rock playing in the background, and somebody was shouting something about a Killers album.

"The Beazleys show up on a few of the swingers' sites, although they call themselves 'Alex' and 'Dierdra' on all but one. *They* look like a fun couple."

Frank bit his lip. He hadn't told his brother what had happened to them, and he wasn't sure he wanted to, since it would only make Jack anxious.

"Let me have a couple more names, though," Jack was saying. "I'm kind of enjoying this, dude. 'Jack Lansbury, Cyber-Sleuth.'"

So Frank gave him Mike Strang's, and a couple more besides. How else was he going to get to the bottom of all this?

"A few more weeks, and I'll have search-engined the entire town," Jack chortled rather gleefully.

He really was enjoying this, then. Who'd have even guessed?

T he calendar stuck to the fridge had a red cross inked upon it when he wandered down to breakfast the next morning. It was centered on October 24th, which was less than three weeks away. Joannie was already up.

"What's the occasion?" he asked her mildly.

She looked up from bisecting a grapefruit. "Lamaze Class."

Which boggled Frank slightly.

"Isn't it a little *early* for Lamaze?"

He'd thought couples only went to that when the woman was heavily pregnant.

"They teach a preliminary class here," Joannie told him, "and then refresh it in the third trimester. It's supposed to make the whole thing more instinctive. Simply the way they do things in this town."

All that he could do was shrug. Okay then.

"Make sure you keep that date free," Joannie insisted. "This is really something that we should do as a couple."

So he promised that he would.

She started dropping around to see the neighbors far more than she'd previously done. Started hanging out in the kitchens of Aimee Stock, Alexis Beddows, and—yes—Leonora Strang. Talking to them on the phone as well, and fairly frequently.

"—he won't buy it, there's no point," he heard her saying quietly, one time.

Then she looked around surprisedly, noticing he'd come into the room.

"Who won't buy what?" he asked, once that she'd put the receiver down.

"Oh, that was Judith. We were talking about some client at the bank."

"You're spending an awful lot of time around those guys."

"I've started to fit in. You ought to try it."

But she didn't say it in any kind of admonishing way. In fact, she hardly ever so much as raised her voice to him, these days. Every time that he glanced at her, she was smiling. Everywhere that she went, it was with a happy, tripping step.

He was forced to admit it, in the end. There was only one explanation for this new, contented mood of hers.

She'd turned out to be one of those lucky women pregnancy suited very well.

A new couple was living in the Beazley house within two weeks of the fatal accident.

"They're renters," Joannie explained. Judith Mackenzie, apparently, knew all about it.

"They got here pretty quickly, all the same," Frank murmured, recalling another detail of that conversation which he'd overheard.

The new people—the Landaus—were an attractive pair in their late twenties, who both turned out to be Mormons. They were friendly enough when you bumped into them on the street, but kept largely to themselves.

The first Saturday after their arrival, as soon as Mrs. Landau went out shopping, Leonora Strang came striding across to their porch, all skimpily dolled up for her 'test.'

She never even got in past the front door, and went away from there looking quietly, coldly satisfied.

Joannie kept reminding him about the date, the 24th.

"You're nagging," he scolded her, after the eighth time.

But she only looked hurt at that. "I'm just so looking forward to it."

"Okay. Sorry." And he hugged her.

He was waiting for the slightest cloud to move across her sunny disposition. But none arrived—Joannie was blissful the whole time. She would sit cross-legged on the couch sometimes, staring at the far wall, her whole face suffused with joy.

If he'd known that being pregnant would make her this happy, he'd have considered the whole thing sooner. If it wasn't for his worries, maybe he'd feel the same way himself.

One time, when he walked into the kitchen, she was chopping up bell peppers on the pine laminate worktop. And was humming gently to herself.

He stopped, listening, trying to recognize the tune. And when, at last, it came to him, he considered how long it had been since he'd last heard it. Not since grade school, in fact.

It was 'There is a Happy Land, Far, Far Away.'

J ack sounded rattled when he phoned next time, which, given his brash personality, was pretty unusual.

It was late on the evening of the 22ⁿᵈ. Frank sat up stiffly in his chair and listened.

"I think—just think—I might have something. I'm not going to say what right now."

"Why the hell not?"

"I really, *really* need to be sure, bro. There's so much gossip, rumor, not to mention stuff that's made-up, on the Web. Ever hear of 'The Blair Witch Project'?"

Yes, of course he had.

"So I want to be absolutely certain."

"Can't you—?"

"No, dude. Really. Just a couple more days. Let me do some serious digging. You can wait a couple more days, can't you?"

B ut that clinched it for him. Something—who knew what?— *was* badly wrong. He'd known it ever since the coffee house, and had been hiding it for Joannie's sake.

The next day, when she came home, he sat her down at the dining table.

"Why so serious?" she asked. "What's this about?"

"I'm … really not sure I want to stay here."

"What, in this house?"

"No, in this town. In Youngesville."

Her face tightened and she began standing up. But then, she appeared to have second thoughts. Sat right back down, and heard him out.

"I've given it a damn good try—you can't say that I haven't," Frank went on. "But I find life here pretty stultifying. I feel isolated too."

"You've always worked from home."

"But in the city it was different. Stranded in suburbia like this? It's honestly driving me nuts."

She nodded patiently. "Anything else?"

"I've got to thinking—maybe Jack was right, that time he visited us. Are we really doing our child any favors, bringing it up in an enclosed environment like this one?"

Joannie took it all without the slightest show of disagreement or annoyance. Which, considering how much she liked it here, astonished him. Once that he was done, she looked down at her knees for a few seconds, and then smiled up at him.

"If you're not happy, well, I have to accept that."

Frank felt a wash of relief, his insides unclenching.

"But you're surely not suggesting we move house while I'm still pregnant, are you? And environment won't matter to the baby for the first couple of years."

Which was reasonable enough, but it was not going in the direction he'd been hoping.

She reached across and took one of his hands in both of hers.

"Look, I'm your wife. Your happiness is my first concern. But let's get ourselves settled as a family first, and then we can worry about other matters. You can wait awhile, can't you?"

He was forced to nod at her, conceding that he could.

"Besides," she added brightly, "you might even change your mind when the baby comes along."

The next morning, a bright and sunny one, was Lamaze Day, the 24th.

"Make sure you're here when I get home," Joannie advised him briskly. And then she kissed him on the cheek.

He watched her almost skipping out through the front door.

Time, after that, passed at an incredibly slow crawl. Wouldn't seem to speed up, whatever he did. When was Jack going to call again?

He was sitting back down at his drawing board for perhaps the dozenth time, when the phone began ringing, very loudly in the empty room, making him jump badly. *Well, at last!* He hurried over to it and snatched the receiver up.

"Mr. Francis Lansbury?" asked a dry and unfamiliar voice.

"Yes."

"Mr. Lansbury, I'm sorry to bother you this way, but my name is Alden Greaves. I'm a lieutenant with the P.D. here in San Francisco. And I'm afraid I need to talk to you about your brother."

EIGHT

Message Board

His heart crashed against his ribs. Was Jack in trouble somehow? It wasn't that he couldn't get the words out, after that. It was that he simply couldn't get them in the right order, however hard he attempted it. Lieutenant Greaves seemed used to this, and tried to calm him down. But there was something about the man's dry, collected manner that only served to make this all the more frustrating.

Greaves went carefully through what had happened.

Jack had gone to bed last night quite normally, without incident or any sign of something being wrong. And, at about three in the morning, someone had gained entry to his studio apartment through the window in the bathroom. Snuck into the living area, loomed over Jack as he lay sleeping.

And had tried to stab him through the heart.

"It …" Frank was still trying to take all this in, "… wasn't a burglary, then?"

"Apparently not. Attempted murder."

"Why?"

"I was hoping you could tell me that."

His mind was utterly blank at first. He could not make even the slightest hazard of a guess why somebody should do that to his brother.

Then it came to him. Those searches on the Internet? But no … that was perfectly ridiculous. He held his tongue.

Jack was in San Francisco General, by this hour. He was in a bad way, but his condition was stable—he was expected to make a full recovery. Frank found himself thanking whatever gods there were for that important piece of information.

"How soon can you get here?" Alden Greaves asked him.

Frank glanced at his watch, all other considerations entirely forgotten. "I'd guess … about mid-afternoon."

"That's fine, then. Phone ahead, and I'll be waiting for you."

"You're sure he's going to be okay?"

"I promise you. Your brother's very lucky."

To be knifed in his sleep? Precisely what kind of luck was that?

Frank pulled on his shoes and a light baseball jacket. Then he remembered that he ought to let Joannie know what had happened. He phoned her bank. She was in a meeting, and had left instructions not to be disturbed. And so he left a message she should call him back.

He had already joined US-50 by the time his cell phone rang.

"Where are you?" Joannie almost screamed.

"On my way to San Fran," Frank replied.

The Sierras were looming up in front of him.

"In the car?"

"Of *course* in the car!"

Joannie sounded very badly shaken up. And was it simply for his brother's sake, or was there something else she was concerned about? There was a long pause, as though she were trying to think exactly what to say.

"Are you sure you should be driving right after a shock like this?"

"I can manage."

"Are you sure? You sound so anxious—I don't blame you. But I'm worried for you, honey. Just turn back, okay?"

"Not going to happen."

"I can come home early. We can go see Jack tomorrow."

"*What?*"

"I'm so scared you're going to have an accident. Turn back, please?"

And was this anything to do with the somewhat premature Lamaze class?

"Isn't one of you in the hospital enough?" Joannie tried.

Her entire tone was so reasonable it almost sounded wheedling.

211

Which simply made him angry.

"Joannie, what is going on here?"

"I just … when do you think you're getting back?"

"When I get back!" he yelled.

And he hung up.

The Lexus started climbing before too much longer. He'd been speeding heavily until this point. But now, the opportunity even for that was swiftly disappearing. Some traffic slowed him down, although it was all moving smoothly. And the road became far twistier the higher up he got.

The air around him cooled, although in the state that he was in it didn't even occur to him to switch on the heater. Another while, and Lake Tahoe was gleaming before him. Snowy peaks reared all around. He barely even looked at them.

His brain was churning like a tumble-drier, had been all this while. And it wasn't simply what had happened to Jack that was troubling him. Other thoughts came boiling up as well.

Lieutenant Greaves had hinted at no motive for this crazed assault. And could it possibly be … Jack had hinted, just a couple of days back, that he had come across something on the Internet. Something forbidden?

That was ludicrous and paranoid. But why else would anyone attack him?

Then there was Joannie's reaction to all of this. She hadn't actually come out and said it, but the subtext had certainly been there. What was it about this evening?

He was heading down the far side of the range by now, the lush greenness of Northern California spreading out before him. Like the mountaintops, it barely even registered. He felt like a small fly caught in a spiderweb. And there were far too many narrow strands.

The Bay Area finally came in sight. The sprawl of Oakland, then the bridges and the high towers of downtown San Fran, tiny in the distance. The water gleaming like a blue-gray diamond. The first time in months he'd been anywhere near a big city.

It took him another while—the traffic got far heavier—to make his way downtown. But finally, he was driving down Portero, and then finding a space in the parking zone. He followed the signs toward the Trauma Center.

Alden Greaves was waiting for him in the lobby. He turned out to be a very tall, thin man, with touches of distinguished silver at his otherwise-dark temples. Had a rather pensive manner, and a habit of clucking his tongue vigorously whenever he was thinking.

"Mr. Lansbury? What can I say, under such circumstances?"

They began heading down the corridor.

"How badly exactly is my brother hurt?"

"The first, most serious stab wound missed his heart by barely an inch. Fortunately, at that point, your brother woke up. Pushed the assailant off him, and then starting screaming loudly. That woke all his neighbors up, which is probably what saved his life. The perp tried a second time, but your brother managed to fend him off. His remaining wounds are purely defensive ones, on his hands and arms."

"But why?"

"I'm still kind of hoping you can point the way to that. Did your brother have any enemies?"

Jack had such a big mouth that he'd doubtless made a few. But anyone who'd try to kill him? Frank genuinely doubted that.

Those searches on the Internet, though? He had already decided to remain quiet on that subject, at least until he'd talked with his brother.

"Has the guy who did this been identified?"

"Not yet. Forensics are still there, and they're hoping to come up with something. In the course of a knife attack, there's a very high chance of leaving DNA behind."

The lieutenant slowed down a little, rounding the next corner. A uniformed policeman, Frank could see, was sitting on a folding chair outside a private door.

"Is my brother still in danger? From knife-men, I mean."

"Probably not, but until we know what the motive was, we

thought it better to err on the side of caution."

Frank could see the sense of that. He took a good, deep breath, then went inside.

Jack was asleep or unconscious. He was naked from the waist on up. There was a large, square, medicated patch taped right across his chest, his hands and arms were swathed in bandages, and there were several IV drips attached to him and an oxygen tube in his nose.

His face was very pale, his lips entirely colorless, and there were dark rings around both his eyes.

But when Frank approached the bed, they came open a glimmer, just enough for Frank to see that they were badly bloodshot.

He attempted a forced smile, but it didn't really work. Jack tried to push himself up on his pillow till Frank stopped him.

"Don't do that. How are you, bro?" he asked in a strained whisper.

"Never better," Jack husked out. "Man, if someone had told me, I would've gotten stabbed and tried this morphine stuff much sooner."

So whatever else had been injured, his personality was still intact.

"What the hell happened?"

"Didn't the cops tell you?"

"I spoke with them but, Jesus … did you recognize the guy?"

"It was dark, dude. He was just a shape. All happened in a blur, you know?"

"But *why*?"

"Well, I think I might know that."

Frank was concerned that his brother didn't tire himself out too much. But Jack seemed determined to tell the entire story. There was a sharp and anxious urgency to the way he conveyed it.

"You remember me talking about finding something on the Net?"

Of course he did. Frank nodded coldly. *Was it really that?*

"Well, man, I dug like I've never dug before. And ended up

214

finding something I definitely wasn't supposed to. Not even a full-blown site. More like some kind of coded message board."

Frank wasn't even sure what such a thing was, but he kept on listening.

"Took me a while, but I finally cracked it. Turns out that, for years now, your Nobel Prize-winning science honcho has been into the occult."

"Lyle Tamborough?"

"The same. And not the candles and crystals type of occult either. Really heavy, nasty stuff. He was part of a cabal who call themselves the Chevaliers of Satan. That means 'knights.'"

"I know," Frank murmured.

"Several of them are in jail by now, for pedophilia and murder. It's a seriously dangerous crew, into all kinds of bizarre profanity."

"And Tamborough's still a member?"

"No. He split from them a few years back and then went off along his own route. And they don't seem too delighted, but there's nothing they can do. They're actually afraid of him, so far as I can tell."

And why was that? Frank wondered, his own heart thudding.

"You know when it was that he struck out on his own?" Jack asked him. "A month before his paper on dark matter. Pretty well a year before he got his Nobel Prize. It coincided with his getting famous, in other words. How suspicious does that sound?"

Except Frank didn't get it. What exactly was his brother suggesting?

His voice was getting weaker, but Jack kept pushing on.

"I keep remembering what we mentioned when this whole thing first came up. The possibility of a cult in Youngesville. If there is one, and if Tamborough's involved, it can't be anything that you'd call good."

All the incidents of the past few weeks came rushing back, and Frank rose to his feet. That coffee evening with Judith and Leonora. All those trips his wife had made around to the neighbors' houses.

"Bro, what is it?" Jack was asking.

"Oh God! I think Joannie's gotten in with them."

215

Her lighter mood? The blissful state that she was always in these days? Almost … a religious one?

When he explained it, a determined glint filled up his brother's gaze.

"And she's pregnant as well," Jack pointed out. "That could be a part of it too. You get back there, right away."

"Go home!" he insisted when Frank looked uncertain. "Throw her over your shoulder and carry her out of there if you have to!"

"But—"

"I love you, man, and Jo-Jo too. And I'll be fine without your help. Now go!"

Lieutenant Greaves was caught up in a conversation with the uniformed cop when Frank went back outside. The tall detective looked up sharply, but Frank simply walked right past him.

"Mr. Lansbury?"

A few steps, then a clawing urgency leapt up in him. He started running down the corridor. Could still hear the lieutenant calling after him, but from a rapidly increasing distance.

"Mr. Lansbury!"

Frank simply ignored the man.

NINE

Youngesville

He was headed back toward the bridge, except that the rush hour had already started. It took him a while to hit I-80.

When he reached the tollbooths at the bridge, long queues had already formed. That left him seething with impatience, but at least it gave him the chance to re-use his phone.

Joannie was not at the bank, despite the fact she should have been. He called the house.

"Hello?"

"Joan? What are you doing home?"

"I came back early. I was so worried that I couldn't concentrate on anything since we last spoke. Where are you?"

Not 'how's Jack.' No mention of that at all. Frank wasn't sure what was going through her head, but he gave her his location.

"You're on your way back? Oh, thank God!"

"I'll still be a few hours. Joannie?"

"Yes?"

"I'll explain it when I get there, but stay put till I arrive, okay? Don't go out. Don't answer the door to anyone, not even your friends. In fact, *especially* not your friends."

He'd fully been expecting to be quizzed on that, but all she did was respond with a pensive-sounding "Well, all right then."

So did she know far more than she was letting on?

He stayed in the left lane until he rejoined US-50. Started climbing back through the Sierras at long last. There was plenty of traffic up ahead of him, and—he glanced at his dashboard—it was barely doing twenty. Why was that?

They went around a bend, the road straightened out for a good

217

distance, and he got his answer. There was a massive tanker right up front, too far too large and heavy for the gradient, maybe fifty, sixty smaller vehicles following behind it like a string of worry beads. The frustration he'd been feeling at the booths boiled over. He clenched his teeth and felt like leaning on the horn, but what good would that do?

Kept on thinking about Joannie, alone in the house with their first child inside her.

The peaks went by him, barely noticed, all over again. Except the sun was getting far closer to setting, with the shadows growing longer. He imagined them stretching out across Youngesville, across his street, his home. And that whole notion made him desperate to get there.

Progress became a little faster as the gradient relaxed, except the tanker kept on braking every time it neared a bend, until Frank felt like he was trapped inside some kind of giant yo-yo. He was cursing underneath his breath.

"Jesus Christ! Come on! *Come on!*"

All the cars in front of him had put their taillights on, the view ahead becoming definitely gloomy. The casino illuminations outside Tahoe were winking like gaudy jewels in the gathering murk.

"Fuck it! Move!"

But plenty of the cars up ahead of him had exited. And finally, heading down, the road straightened out completely, and he found himself waiting his turn to overtake the truck.

As soon as he was past it, he floored the gas. The speedometer needle climbed until it brushed one hundred. The moment it did that, his cell phone went off.

"Where *are* you?" Joannie yelled at him.

"I'm coming! I got snagged up in the mountains, but I'm getting there!"

"Jesus, Frank, there's not much time left!"

"Time for what?

"For *everything!* Get *back* here!"

He wasn't even sure what she was talking about. But he couldn't go any faster, and she had to understand that.

The last remaining sunlight, it was fading very quickly. He barely remembered to switch his own lights on. The desert kept on sweeping past him, and then more of it, all of it looking exactly the same. God, why'd they even *moved* to such a place?

Finally—and it was almost pitch dark by this juncture—the exit for Youngesville loomed up in his headlamp beams. Frank didn't even slow down, simply swerved onto the ramp.

The chassis bucked a little, then recovered. And from that point on, Frank was hammering the Lexus furiously across the last few miles remaining to his home.

I t wasn't too much longer before the lights of the town were looming up like some big swarm of static fireflies. Oh, thank God!

His phone went off for a second time.

"Frank?"

"I'm nearly there! Only about a mile away!"

"Please hurry! I—"

Joannie stopped abruptly, then breathed, "Oh my God, it's started."

"What's started? Joan, what's happening?"

When she spoke again, though, it was not into the phone. It was like she was addressing someone else, or perhaps the empty air around her.

"Please, not yet! Not like this! Please, we're not r*eady!*"

And then words seemed to fail her, and she let out a heart-rending sob.

The line went dead.

Ahead of him, at the direct center of the town, a bright green glow had become apparent. Liberty Square, he knew without question. That statue of Lyle Tamborough's. This was the same emerald brilliance he had seen the night he'd met Bob Meaks.

Except that this time, it did not confine itself to the town's center.

It spread out in a massive pool, the edges of which expanded swiftly, until everything in Youngesville was engulfed by it.

That wasn't the end, however. Because the light grew steadily, intensely brighter. Was so violently bright, in the end, that Frank was forced to pull over and cover up his eyes. Even through his fingers, he was still aware of it. It finally died away, and he let his hands drop.

A dense afterimage had been burned against his retinas, and he couldn't see properly at first. But he kept on blinking, rubbing at them, with a sense of dread now filling him.

And at long last, his vision cleared.

Frank almost wished it hadn't.

He could only sit there frozenly, staring through the dust-smeared windshield.

The entire town—out beyond it—was gone.

TEN

Far, Far Away

Ice filled him. His hands. His throat, his heart, his chest, his brain. The only sound that he could hear was the creaking silence of the desert.

And he thought of picking up his cell phone. Trying to call Joannie again. But would she, now, reply?

After a while, almost robotically, he put the Lexus into drive again and trundled slowly forward, his mind working furiously. That lecture Tamborough had given, about better worlds, superior universes. And the possibility of reaching them? The way his wife had been so busy with the others afterward. How happy she had been.

At the idea of bringing up her child in a world far more pleasant than this one? Was that possible, or even sane?

But he could see it with his own two eyes. Exactly where had Youngesville gone?

He reached what had once been the outskirts of the town. Not a single hint remained of what had been there. Not a post. A cable. Not even a manhole cover. Desert, like the sections he'd just passed through, stretched unbrokenly ahead of him. *My God!*

But there was still, he could make out, a faint glow of green, where Liberty Square had been located. He headed over to it as if in a trance.

He had to find some way to get to Joannie. Find some way of following her, wherever she had gone. He recalled that final pained sob that she had let out. She hadn't wanted to reach Heaven on her own.

Crazy—crazy—crazy! his mind kept on telling him. But Lyle

Tamborough had done it, hadn't he? Spirited the town elsewhere.

The statue—'New Hope'—was still there, but only just. It seemed to be trying, itself, to head off along the same route that the town had gone. It had become slightly translucent, and was getting thinner as he watched, faint green light still pulsing all around it.

As he clambered out, he noticed it was making a faint, high-pitched screeching noise. Which meant it was definitely some kind of machine.

Time was running out, so he approached it quickly. How to make it work?

He remembered Bob Meaks at that concealed panel. Flipped it open. The switches were revealed. But which of them …?

Frank knelt down in the dirt and flicked them all. They felt malleable underneath his touch, not quite there, and were hard to work because of that. But, pushing frantically, he managed it.

The green glow steadied and then brightened once again. Spread across him and the car. Became so fierce that he was forced to close his eyes a second time.

All he felt was a tiny jolt.

But as soon as he was capable of looking around at his new surroundings, a silent bolt of lightning flashed above him, making him crane his neck sharply. The sky was darker than he'd ever seen it, a quite pure and depthless black. And he could not make out a single star. Why was that?

He was back inside the town. It was all around him, all lit up by streetlamps. Liberty Square was as it had always been, apart from the fact the statue was not there. And his SUV was where he'd left it.

Lights glowed through the windows of the restaurants on Younge, but he could see no people.

A second flash of lightning brought the landscape out beyond the town's boundaries into sharp relief. Frank gasped, his spine becoming very straight.

The mountains were not distant any longer. They were looming right over the outer edges of Youngesville. Vast and bare and black and craggy, nothing like the white-capped, cool Sierras.

What were they? What was this place? It didn't look like any kind of 'happy land' at all.

He returned his attention to his more immediate surroundings. And he noticed that the whole place was entirely silent. Which raised the question … what were all the people who had come here doing?

His whole body quivering, he began walking along Younge. Something was glittering on the sidewalk outside Claude's Brasserie, and his pace quickened when he saw that it was broken glass.

He came to a halt in front of the place, his heart in his mouth and his eyes as wide as they could go. The whole front plate-glass window had been smashed. And inside … devastation, everywhere he looked.

Furniture was overturned. Food and wine were scattered on the floor. There was broken crockery, and glassware too. So what on earth had happened here?

That was when he took in the appalling fact … some of the red liquid on the floor? It was not wine. Frank took a careful step inside. It was blood, and plenty of it, pooling on the tiles, staining the ripped tablecloths.

Oh Jesus!

Something even more troubling came to his dazed attention a moment later. There were drag marks in the gore, a load of them. The kinds of marks left when a pair of heels got hauled across the floor. There were no signs of any bodies. And the marks extended a few yards, and then gave out completely.

He checked several more cafes and bars, only to find precisely the same. Frank was trembling furiously by this time, and breathing hard.

Oh my dear God.

Joannie!

S peeding to his house, he could see the same pattern everywhere. A lot of lights were on, but there were no signs of life beyond them whatsoever. A good few doors had been smashed open. Many windowpanes were broken. Who had done this? He was scanning around anxiously for any possible culprit.

223

His own home still looked intact as he pulled up on the drive. As pristine as it had been, and filled up with a bright electric glow. He fumbled with the keychain and let himself in.

Saw almost immediately that the kitchen door, out back, had been pulled halfway off its hinges. He went quickly through.

Joannie had obviously put up a fight. There were saucepans lying where she'd thrown them, broken vases, even the meat tenderizer. All, apparently, to no effect. There was even a carving knife lying on the tiling by the fridge, but no sign that she'd been able to use it.

And there was another pool of drying blood, with drag marks running from it. Which stretched almost to the back door. And then, like all the others, disappeared.

Had she and her assailant simply … vanished into thin air?

Frank felt his nose begin to clog, his eyes filling with salty moisture. Only one thing was stopping him from breaking down completely.

He *still* didn't have the first clue what was going on.

There had to be someone still here who could tell him.

The Tamborough house looked very dark when he pulled up outside of it. But, when he entered the front hallway, he could see the faintest chink of ocher light emerging from an open door at the far end. Moving as quietly as he could, he went in that direction.

It turned out to be a study, almost the whole of it swallowed up in thick, heavy gloom. But at the center of it was a desk, a small, weak lamp glowing on the leather top, casting just the faintest circle of illumination.

Lyle Tamborough was very much alive, and seated calmly behind it, looking much the same as he'd done at the theatre. The thinning silver hair and dense moustache. The tortoiseshell spectacles. He'd lit a cigarette and was blowing streams of smoke at the lamp, the heated air making them rise and swirl.

When he noticed Frank was there, his gaze flickered upward and he gave a brittle smile.

"Glad you could make it," he said quietly, in that creaky voice of his. "We were wondering where you'd gone. So now the quota's been fulfilled."

Quota? Frank had taken several more steps in before something made him stop.

He couldn't be quite certain, but ... he thought that there might be a couple more people standing behind Tamborough. Frank couldn't see them properly, but sensed that they were there.

"What is this place?" he barked out, horrified.

Tamborough stubbed his cigarette out and then peered back at him silently.

"Is this your idea of a 'better world'?"

The gaze behind the lenses sharpened.

"Of course not," the old man snorted. "Why, this is a realm of demons."

All the anger left Frank in that moment, drained away by total shock.

"I discovered the existence of this place a few years back," the old man was explaining, "by, let's say, not entirely scientific means. Its inhabitants and I learned to communicate, and then we made a deal. They'd give me what I wanted. Success. Recognition, obviously. And then I'd reciprocate."

Frank's mouth came open, but no sound came out. So Tamborough asked the question for him.

"And what was my side of the bargain? What exactly did they want? What do demons always want? Fresh meat, fresh blood, and plenty of it. Brand-new souls to feed on. Innocents."

He let out a small, dry laugh.

"Not pure of heart, exactly. Human beings are never that. But at least trying to be, as you all were, or why else would you come to Youngesville?"

And Frank was not merely shaking, by now. It was a much, much stronger thing than that. His whole body was tremoring internally, like it was caught up in an earthquake.

He heard himself croak out, "You ... planned this whole thing, on your own?"

225

"Oh no," Tamborough replied, with a mild shake of his graying head. "Meaks helped, although he never really understood what he was doing. And I believe that you've already met Judith and Leonora?"

In the darkness behind his chair, two pairs of eyes suddenly came open. Except that they were almost perfectly round, with no pupil at all. And they were glowing a bright carmine. Frank lurched sharply back.

The pair of them stepped into the weak light. They were covered entirely in dense, unreflective scales. Their heads were bald and huge. Their ears were pointed, and their mouths were fanged.

The taller one—Leonora?—was holding something in her clawed right hand that was still dripping. Could it be … a human heart?

Terror filled Frank like a blinding white light. *Run,* was all that he could think. He swung toward the doorway.

But it had been filled, and the corridor beyond it, with dozens more red gazes. Even more were crowding up against the window.

Run, his brain kept telling him.

But there was nowhere left to run.

Tamborough let out another small, dry, creaky laugh.

EPILOGUE

One Year Later

The countryside of Maryland swept by them. God, it was good to get out of Washington for a while, the top of the Volvo folded down. A mild and sunny day too. What a treat.

Carol had the map and was giving him directions. Sam Wooding eased the car on at a gentle pace, savoring the entire journey.

They turned left at the next intersection. Came, at last, to the top of a hill. And there it was, spread out below them. Newboro, MD.

Reaching it, they looked for Bramford Street, then cruised down it till they found the house. It looked exactly the same as in the brochure, except rather bigger, Sam thought happily.

The realtor was waiting for them on the porch. She walked over to them as they both got out.

"Judith Mackenzie?" Sam enquired.

"Pleased to meet you," she said, smiling, offering her hand. "Did you have a good drive out from D.C.?"

"*Always* glad to get out of the city."

"Then you'll like it here, I'm sure."

She seemed extremely professional, despite the fact that she was casually dressed.

"Been in this business long?" Sam asked.

"Longer than seems possible, sometimes," she told him, turning back around and leading them to the front door.

About the Author

TONY RICHARD's novels have been published by HarperCollins, Tor, Headline, Dark Regions Press, and Pan Macmillan, with his latest book—*Tropic of Darkness*—due out in 2013 from Simon and Schuster. His debut work—*The Harvest Bride*—made the shortlist for the HWA Award for Best First Novel, and in 2008 his collection *Going Back* was shortlisted for the British Fantasy Award. He has seen into print more than a hundred short stories, with his tales appearing in *Asimov's, Hitchcock's, F&SF, Weird Tales, Cemetery Dance,* and many top anthologies including *Best New Horror*. Widely traveled, he often uses places he has visited as settings for his work. His fiction includes the Raine's Landing dark fantasy adventures, a group of stories set in the imaginary town of Birchiam-on-Sea on the south coast of England, and his Future Africa mysteries in *Hitchcock's*. Amongst his previous collections are *Shadows and Other Tales* and *Our Lady of the Shadows*, from Dark Regions Press.

About the Artist

M. WAYNE MILLER made his mark in the 90's as a consummate b/w illustrator for numerous book and magazine publishers as well as several role-playing game publishers. While the b/w market was a fine place to cut one's freelance illustrator's teeth, and he did well, it was a stepping-stone to the more competitive and lucrative color illustration market. After an artistic conversion to color work, Wayne re-emerged as a cover illustrator for specialty press and mass-market book publishers, as well as for role-playing games, online publications, and private commissions. In 2009, he made the conversion to all-digital workflow, and traded physical brushes for virtual ones. His list of clients includes Dark Regions Press, Tor/ Forge, Marietta Publishing, LORE Publishing, Thunderstorm Books, Dark Renaissance Press, Genius Publishing, Journalstone Publishing, Gamewick Games, Dias Ex Machina, Chaosium, and Orson Scott Card's *Intergalactic Medicine Show*. Wayne intends to add many more pleased clients to this list this year, and continuing his quest to learn and grow as an artist and illustrator. He lives in Greensboro NC with his wife, Carmen, and a very large cat.

Colophon

The text was set in **Adobe Garamond**. **Champers** was used for titling and drop caps.